Common Ground

By the same author

Words

Helen Stancey

Common Ground

ROBIN CLARK LTD
LONDON

First published in 1986 by Robin Clark Ltd
A member of the Namara Group
27/29 Goodge Street, London W1P 1FD

British Library Cataloguing in Publication Data
Stancey, Helen
Common ground.
I. Title
823'.914[F] PR6069.T24/
ISBN 0 86072 100 0

Typeset by MC Typeset, Chatham, Kent
Printed and Bound in Great Britain
by Nene Litho and Woolnough Bookbinding
both of Wellingborough, Northants.

1

'So you see,' said Duncan, folding his arms and leaning his shoulder against the edge of the blackboard, 'our knowledge is tentative. We can never prove that under certain circumstances something will always occur. What many people think of as the scientific laws under which the physical world operates – these are really just theories which have not yet been disproved.'

Fifteen assorted adult faces gazed at him with varying degrees of doubt. A sixteenth tilted back and nodded gravely, puckering his brow. The seventeenth reared up from a notebook. 'I'm sorry, Mr Drummond. What did you say after "scientific laws"?'

Duncan relinquished the blackboard and took a step towards him. 'I was pointing out that we can't accurately use the word "prove" about the acquisition of scientific knowledge because we can never test all the possibilities. All we can hope to do is to find supporting evidence. But that still isn't proof.'

'Oh yes indeed. Thank you. But what exactly came after "scientific laws"?'

'Well, for example, we all assume that the sun will rise tomorrow morning. However, we can't prove that it will. Still less can we prove that it will next week or on the same day next year. And still less that it always will. We have a lot of evidence that it always has in the past, but that doesn't mean that it always does and will as an immutable law.'

One of the fifteen faces broke cover. 'Though if something

has happened regularly in the past under certain circumstances, it must make it more likely that it would happen again under the same circumstances.'

'But only likely. We're always dealing with probability and it could be wrong. There's the tale of the inductivist turkey who thought that the farmer always came to feed him in the morning. And he was quite right – until Christmas Eve.'

The sixteenth face laughed appreciatively.

'I'm sorry to go back again, Mr Drummond,' said the seventeenth, 'but I lost myself after "scientific laws". What was it that came next?'

'Don't worry about it too much at this stage,' reassured Duncan. 'It's a concept that can be quite hard to grasp. But we'll keep coming back to it as the course progresses, and gradually, as we deal with more examples, I think it will become clearer.

'Oh, I understand the idea, thank you. It's just that I didn't write down what you actually said. It was a bit too fast for me. You said "What many people think of as the scientific laws . . . " and that's as far as I've got. What came next?'

'I think you'd find it easier,' Duncan said, stepping closer again, 'if you didn't try to write down every word. Just jot down the main words to keep the general sense.'

'That's what Dr Danzack used to say in Political Structure last year. She was a terrible fast talker. A bit fiery too, to be sure, but she knew her stuff right enough.'

'Dr Danzack knew about notetaking as well. You'll always be behind if you try to write down everything. Just put down the main points.'

'Ah yes, but then it goes dry on me after. If I write it all, your voice stays in it and it's much more entertaining to read later on.'

Duncan stepped backwards.

'Mr Drummond, you didn't tell me what it was that came after "scientific laws".'

'I can't remember,' said Duncan shortly. 'I don't learn a script off by heart. Now, shall we move on?'

'You said: "What many people think of as the scientific laws under which the physical world operates – these are really just theories which have not yet been disproved,"' said a pleased voice. A brightly smiling woman in the front row held up a few back pages in her spiral-bound notepad. 'Shorthand,' she explained. 'I can get down everything with no trouble.'

' . . . are really . . . just . . . theories . . . ?' wrote the seventeenth face.

' . . . which . . . have . . . not . . . yet . . .,' dictated the shorthand woman.

'Could you sort it out between yourselves afterwards?' interrupted Duncan. 'I'd like to move on a bit further with this evening.'

'Mr Drummond,' said one of the other faces meaningfully and jerked her head and eyes towards the door. The blue figure of the caretaker lurked outside. He bent down and glared through the glass porthole in the door, then dangled a bunch of keys in front of his face.

'We've another quarter of an hour yet,' said Duncan, looking at the clock above the door.

'That clock's slow,' said the young woman who had noticed the caretaker. Duncan checked with his watch. It was.

'It caused Dr Danzack a whole lot of aggravation last year too,' said the seventeenth. 'She'd have me climbing up on chairs putting it right but as soon as you looked away it would slip back into its own time again.'

'Well, I suppose we'd better finish for this evening,' said Duncan.

'Have we any news yet of the book box?' enquired the shorthand writer.

'News of the book box?' Duncan had forgotten about the list of recommended reading he had concocted some months earlier.

'The box of books that the University sends out. I was wondering if it had arrived yet but I suppose you'd have known about it if it had.'

'That's another thing that causes trouble,' said the seventeenth. His flat pink face and blue eyes looked sorrowfully at Duncan. 'It's always late arriving. Mind you, I'd have thought they'd have made a bit more of an effort this time after Dr Danzack put the fear of God into them last year.'

'Though we couldn't issue books for a couple of weeks anyway,' said the young woman.

'Couldn't we? Why?'

'University regulations,' said the shorthand writer. 'Then one of us acts as librarian and takes charge.'

'I see,' said Duncan, relieved. 'Would you like to do it when the time comes?'

'Actually, I'm usually class secretary,' she confided. 'I look after the register and any admin that crops up. Shall I carry on with that?'

'And I'll do the library if you like,' offered the young woman.

There was a jangling noise. A large hand had appeared round the door and was shaking its bunch of keys violently in the air.

'We'd better show our heels,' said the seventeenth, joining the others who were beginning to leave the room. 'Good night to you, Mr Drummond.'

'Good night.'

'Good night, Mr Cussins.'

'Night, Mr O'Connell,' said the caretaker. 'I see we've got another keen one this year.'

'It's the true love of learning.'

'Like the sound of their own voice too much if you ask me.'

'No, no, Mr Cussins, it's the impartation of knowledge. A noble occupation.'

'If they did a proper hand's turn they'd be glad to pack up on time. I started at seven this morning.'

'Good night, Mr Drummond.'

'Good night, Mr Drummond.'

'Good night Mrs – er – ladies.' Duncan rubbed the chalk off his hands and gathered his notes in his briefcase. He put on his jacket, picked up the case, let out a long breath and approached the door.

'Good night,' said Duncan.

'I started at seven this morning, you know.' The hand reached into the classroom and flicked off the lights.

'A very long day,' agreed Duncan.

'Mr Drummond, may I have a word?' The sixteenth face and its body leapt out of the wall. 'Arthur Pontiff,' he went on immediately. 'I found your lecture enthralling, Mr Drummond. The Philosophy of Science – it's a subject I'm becoming increasingly interested in.'

'Ah good,' said Duncan warily. He had only the flimsiest understanding of the area and had almost exhausted his knowledge already.

'Will we be going deeper into these matters, Mr Drummond, as the course progresses?'

'Not much deeper,' said Duncan. 'Greater depth wouldn't really be relevant to our needs. They are, after all, lectures on Psychology, not Philosophy. I just introduce a few ideas that might be useful later on.'

'Yes, I see. I wonder then if you could recommend some texts to me so that I can follow it up on my own.'

Duncan patted the air reassuringly. 'When the book box comes,' he said, 'I think you'll find several works of interest to you. But I shouldn't devote too much time to it if I were you. There won't be a question on it in the exam.'

'No, I do realize that,' said Mr Pontiff. 'My interest is for its own sake.'

'Very commendable,' said Duncan, beginning to go down the stairs.

'I find that on these courses it's terribly easy to acquire just isolated pieces of knowledge without the background to set them against and give them coherence – as you yourself were saying when you introduced tonight's topic. I don't want to flatter, Mr Drummond, but I must say how much these introductory words gave me confidence in you. At last, I thought, a lecturer who isn't content with the piecemeal, a lecturer who wishes to convey a sense of the fundamental, of the totality. I'm very much looking forward to the rest of the course.'

'Thank you,' said Duncan. They were in the entrance hall. Corridors led away into gloom as lights were switched off throughout the building. A few tardy students, clutching the paraphernalia of various other evening classes, hastened through the swing door. Mr Pontiff held it open for Duncan.

'I should very much like to continue our conversation, Mr Drummond,' he said, following him out. 'I have one or two ideas of my own that I'd be grateful for the chance of airing with you. Would you care to join me in a drink?'

'Not tonight, I'm afraid,' said Duncan. 'My wife is

expecting me.'

'Ah, of course.' Mr Pontiff swung his arms around his body. 'We mustn't inconvenience your good lady. Some other time perhaps?'

'You could go up to the University Library,' suggested Duncan. 'The librarians there are most helpful. They would direct you to the central and latest publications.'

'Would I be allowed in?'

'I'm sure. Show your registration card and you should get a ticket with no trouble. Good night, Mr Pontiff.'

'Oh yes, I will. Thank you, thank you. Can I give you a lift anywhere?'

'It's all right – I have transport.' Duncan was halfway across the yard. 'Good night.'

'Good night, Mr Drummond. Many thanks. I'll take your tip about the library. Until next week then. I'll be looking forward to it. Good night.'

Duncan's footsteps clomped on the lino of the staircase outside their flat. At the kitchen table, Roz quickly ran her eye over the page of exercise book, corrected a spelling (the sarfternoon), gave it a red tick and VG at the end. She closed the book, wrote a mark by a name in a register, placed the book on a small pile of others, laid these crosswise underneath a larger pile, balanced the register on top and held it all together as she pushed back her chair.

'Supper not ready yet?' said Duncan arriving, briefcase to the fore.

'Almost,' said Roz. 'I was doing some marking.' She looked round for somewhere to put the books. The kitchen and the other living area were part of the same room, arranged round a corner at right angles to each other. Roz stood up and carried the books round the corner. As usual, the bureau was covered with Duncan's work. 'How did it go?' she asked. She put her pile on top of Duncan's papers on the bureau.

'Not there,' said Duncan. 'I've organized everything so I can go straight back to it. You'll get it all muddled. Take them somewhere else, can't you?'

'Sorry,' said Roz. She put them on the television set and

returned to the cooking part of the room. Duncan's briefcase and jacket were on the table. She hung his jacket round the back of a chair and carried his case round the corner to the side of the bureau. Duncan was sitting on the sofa, his head back, supported by a cushion.

'Were they difficult?' asked Roz sympathetically.

'Difficult?' Duncan raised one lid and brow. He lowered them again and sighed. 'They find it almost impossible to grasp the notion of falsifiability.'

'Falsifiability? Is that a word?'

'And the provisional nature of our knowledge.'

'What do you mean "provisional"? That it will do for the time being until further research alters it?'

'It was rather advanced for most of them. I've whetted a few appetites, though, and one fellow made a point of thanking me for the clarity of my exposition.'

'That was nice.'

'I suspect there are psychological barriers against understanding here. I suspect that's the root of the problem. It's a concept that makes them feel insecure. It's safer to think of things as fixed and reliable. It takes a more mature intellect to enjoy the challenge of the impermanent and not to feel threatened by the constant possibility of your familiar conceptions being tossed away.'

'Well, yes,' said Roz. 'You do need some routine. It would be very hard to face situations from a completely new standpoint each time.'

'Which is why most people don't contribute to the progress of ideas. They're locked into those routines, held together by preconceptions. You need flexibility and the capacity to welcome risks in order to add to our knowledge and understanding.'

'It sounds very exhausting,' said Roz. 'I'm not surprised the class has tired you out.'

'Tired me out?' Duncan sat up sharply. 'I'm hungry, that's all. Are we ever going to eat?'

'Yes – now,' said Roz. She went round the corner again. 'Sorry. I was thinking about what you said.'

'You've no need to worry about it, Roz. Your world's nicely stable. You've got the security of always knowing more than the children so your job's not too demanding and you've got the familiarity of our domestic life. You stick with these comforts, Roz. Leave the push forwards to me.'

'But I'm still interested,' objected Roz, laying out cutlery and taking the casserole from the oven. 'I know my teaching doesn't stretch much beyond the twelve-times table, but that doesn't mean my mind can't stretch beyond it either.'

'Of course not,' said Duncan soothingly. 'You've quite a good mind when you want to use it. What I mean is that you're content with things as they are, with the intellectual limits of the twelve-times table. I never was. I was always restless, always after something more, always querying the assumptions. Which is why I got out of schools and moved on in life. You didn't. You didn't feel like that and you stayed. Very good too – somebody has to.'

'I thought just now you were criticizing the people in your class for not wanting to query these assumptions.'

'Not criticizing them. Merely trying to explain their reluctance. I don't think that everybody has to want to take these risks. We're all different. For example, I do – you don't. That's perfectly acceptable. What's for pudding?'

'There isn't one. I had so much marking.'

'I'd better have a bigger helping of meat then. Did you get some more cake or biscuits at least?'

'Biscuits in the tin.'

'They'll have to do.' Duncan started on his stew. 'Can you give me a hand after supper?'

'Will it take long?' asked Roz. 'I haven't finished my marking yet and I must get it done tonight.'

'Now, Roz, what will a crowd of eight-year-olds care if their marking's late back? They probably never look at it anyway.'

'They do. I make them look.'

'Don't worry. I won't take up much of your precious time. I need to tabulate some experimental results to give Professor Reece tomorrow. Preparing for this evening's class has put me behind. If you read the scores out to me subject by subject as I write them in, it'll be much quicker.'

'I'll tell you what,' said Roz. 'You make a start while I race through the rest of those exercise books, then I'll join you.'

'Oh come on, Roz. You want me to get my PhD don't you?

The kids can have their marking back any old time. I've got to have the results ready for tomorrow.'

'All right,' sighed Roz. 'You're sure it won't take very long? How many scores are there?'

'Only two hundred and forty.'

'Two hundred and forty!'

'Roz, it's only a matter of reading them out. I'm the one that's got to analyse them. That's where the real work lies.'

'I suppose so. Shall we start straight away, then, and eat the biscuits as we do it?'

'As long as you don't drop crumbs in my papers. Oh – and leave the washing up, Roz. That can be done tomorrow.'

2

Roz got off the bus by the side of six lanes of urban traffic and went into the pedestrian tunnel under the road. It stank of urinals and was spattered with the red paint of misspelled graffiti. At night most people thought they stood a better chance with the hurtling cars above ground than with what might be waiting for them beneath.

Roz emerged in a smaller road past the railway bridge and opposite the pub. She turned right through an iron gate in a high wall and walked across to the tall grey building. The yard was almost empty for it was some time before school started, but if Roz were to leave home any later the rush-hour jams would delay her for too long.

'Hello Miss.' A small pale girl was huddled by the door. She wore a thin cotton dress and a shrunken cardigan. Her shoes were peep-toed, the ends cut open by her mother to make them still wearable after they had been outgrown. It was chilly in the early autumn morning.

'Hello Lotty. You're in good time today. Aren't you cold?'

Lotty shook her head. She would never admit to being cold or hungry or tired or ill or unhappy. Her father had disappeared and her mother found it hard to cope. There were three other children, all under school age. Lotty was often absent, helping to look after them.

Roz smiled at her and went in. The school was old, built on three cramped storeys. Dark, narrow staircases linked the floors at each end, and in the middle layer, the classrooms led off from each other with no corridor to separate them. A strict schedule operated to maintain order under these conditions and the children were not allowed inside the building before the morning whistle. Then the classes were lined up and chaperoned indoors by their teachers, one at a time, to avoid chaos and accidents on the stairs. There was at least three-quarters of an hour before this was due to take place.

Roz turned and put her head back through the door. 'Lotty,' she said. 'I've got one or two jobs that need to be done in the classroom before school starts. Could you help me?'

'Yes Miss.'

'Come on then.'

They climbed up the stairs and into the classroom, one of those on the middle floor. Roz gave Lotty the marked exercise books and asked her to give them out. She took off her coat and put it to one side while she wrote the date on the blackboard and underlined it. Then she gave Lotty a new box of pencils to sharpen.

Mr Hill, the Deputy Head, came from his classroom on the far side. 'Good morning, Mrs Drummond. At it already, I see. Still time for a cup of sweet Rosie Lee I think, don't you?'

He continued on his way to the staff room. Roz checked that Lotty was content and followed him, taking her coat with her. Personal possessions were never left in classrooms.

The staff room was minute. At breaks the teachers sat squashed against the walls on upright chairs round an old tresle dinner table. There wasn't room for anything more comfortable. There were a few coat pegs, a pot sink and an old cooker. The cleaner always put the kettle on a low light before she left. Roz made the tea while Mr Hill looked over his *Telegraph* and castigated the wild ways of the unions and local government. In came Paula, the only probationary teacher they had that year although there had been several when Roz began. Duncan had been one.

Paula smiled nervously and hung up her coat.

'Cup of tea?' asked Roz.'

'No, thanks very much,' said Paula. 'I've got to get some things ready.' She went off to her classroom – the one situated between those of Mr Hill and Roz.

'Struggling, you know, Roz,' commented Mr Hill.

'Pleasant enough girl, but struggling.'

'It can be very hard at first,' said Roz.

'She's trying to be too nice,' said Mr Hill. 'She'll learn. We aren't here to be liked.'

Roz drank her tea and wished her eyes didn't feel so scratchy. Duncan's tabulation had taken ages, and she'd sat up long after that to finish her marking. Duncan had found his evening tiring too. He'd been asleep by the time she'd got to bed and hadn't woken up by the time she'd left that morning. And poor Paula looked exhausted. That first year of teaching really was purgatory.

'Good morning, Roz, Len.' Miss Elyce, the Headmistress, hurtled in. 'Len will you take over this morning? I'd forgotten I'm supposed to be in County Hall for the Assessment meeting. There's nothing special to do – just Assembly and the usual.'

'Very good,' said Mr Hill, half-raised from his seat – his usual posture when talking to Miss Elyce in the staff room. It indicated simultaneously his respect for her sex and status as well as his own proximity in the hierarchy.

'What's the programme, Roz? India, isn't it? Everything under control?'

'I think so,' said Roz. 'They've rehearsed a lot.'

'Explain it to Len, will you, before Assembly starts, so he knows what to expect. I'm sorry I'll miss it, but I'll have to hurry. Should be back at lunchtime.'

She hurtled out again.

'Do I gather there's another multi-ethnic religious experience today?' enquired Mr Hill.

'That's right.'

'And where does it fit in? In the moral-story stroke pep-talk slot?'

'That's what they're expecting so it'll probably run much more smoothly if we keep it like that.'

'India, did you say? What are they doing?'

'A story from the *Ramayana*.'

'Tripped off her tongue like a veritable memsahib. *Ramayana*, eh? Well, Roz, nearly over-the-top time and only three of us here. Not much of an example, I'd say. Let's hope the others make it at least to the playground. Morning, Tod.

That makes four of us. You're just in time to go back downstairs again.'

'Traffic jams,' growled Tod hanging up his jacket. 'Best part of an hour in traffic jams. They're digging up the roundabout and it's tailing back as far as the baths. I feel as if I've done a day's whack already.'

'But instead we're only just starting,' said Mr Hill. 'Heigh ho, heigh ho, it's off to work we go. Come on Tod.'

Tod raised his eyes heavenwards as Mr Hill strode out.

'I'll see you downstairs,' said Roz and went to tell Lotty to join her class in the hall.

Lotty was sitting at a desk, staring at her hands as she wound a curl of sharpened pencil wood round and round her finger. She jumped as Roz came over.

'There's still these to do, Miss.'

'Never mind, Lotty. You can finish them off tomorrow morning before school again. Go and line up with everyone else now for Assembly.'

Roz collected her line of children from the yard, looking suitably severe at Carl who had been pulled out to the front by Mr Hill for kicking a classmate behind the knees so that his legs suddenly collapsed. She led them and another, teacher-less, group into the hall, where Tod was finding the correct page of the vast hymn sheet which was suspended against the wall on pulleys like those of an old-fashioned clothes rack. Martin had arrived by now, and Caroline Harris dashed in, breathless, to take over her class.

'Bloody traffic,' she hissed to Roz. 'Tail-back beyond the baths. Thanks for taking over.' She folded her arms and frowned at her wriggling charges.

Roz placed her *Ramayana* quartet – Sunita, Gopal, Leroy and June – at the end of their row and made sure that they had remembered to bring their props. Then she sat down at the piano. Somehow, a couple of years ago, she had drifted into becoming the school accompanist. When the previous, really musical, teacher retired, there had been an urgent need which Roz had temporarily and reluctantly filled on the basis of her own childhood piano lessons. And thus she had remained. She was horror-stricken at first by knowledge of her limitations, and dreaded the snickerings she imagined would result, yet it seemed that neither staff nor children noticed the wrong notes particularly, and with time they grew fewer anyway. Occasionally parents even asked if she would give piano lessons. Sometimes they referred to her as 'the music teacher', although she wasn't that at all.

Mr Hill announced the hymn and Roz played the first line as introduction.

The children sang, prayed, then sat down cross-legged with much shuffling while the story of Sita and the silver deer was acted out to the school. It was Roz who first started this with her own class. So many different cultural backgrounds were represented that when some unfamiliar festival was being celebrated she began to ask the children concerned to tell everyone else about it. Miss Elyce came into the room while such an explanation was in progress, and adopted the idea for the morning Assembly. It expanded from festivals to religious stories and so became established as a regular comparative religion feature. Parental reactions were mixed. Most didn't comment; many were delighted that their traditions were being acknowledged; some showed interest themselves in learning about other cultures; a few were enraged and complained to Miss Elyce about their young being taught heathen practices. Miss Elyce said that they were at liberty to withdraw their children from that part of the Assembly if they wished, and some children did arrive at school with a pointedly well-timed lateness, but the fuss gradually died down and the cross-cultural slot continued unassailed except that it was becoming a bit routine by now.

The story-telling over, Gopal smoothed down his *kurta* and put his hands together in *namaste*. Sunita followed suit. Leroy and June hesitated, then bowed. The rest of the school clapped, after which everybody scrambled up to go to their classrooms.

Once there Roz called her register and tried to ignore the hullaballoo coming from next door – Paula's room. It was particularly bad today. Chairs scraped and banged; there were shouts, whines, whoops of laughter and continual demands of 'Miss, Miss'. Paula's voice could sometimes be heard rising shrilly above them only to be drowned again in a fresh surge of noise as if the children had renewed their energy during the brief moments of being vanquished.

It was hard to teach against such a background, but Roz tried to behave as if nothing untoward were happening. She was sure that was the only way to help. Her own class had got past the stage of being titillated and enjoyably shocked by it and now found the noise rather wearing. 'Can't you stop them Miss?' pleaded a distracted child. Roz turned their attention back to their work.

Suddenly a sharp silence cut off the uproar. A few timid shuffles, clicks, coughs; then nothing. The silence grew more tense. Roz knew what had happened. On the other side of Paula's classroom, Mr Hill had opened the connecting door and was standing there, running his eyes menacingly over the children.

Now Mr Hill's voice. Very quiet. Very deliberate. Very threatening. Unexpectedly, it shot out in a bellow. Roz's own class jumped and quelled their giggles behind their hands. 'Do you understand me?' came in deceptively pleasant tones from next door. 'Yes Sir,' – a muted chorus. 'Good,' said Mr Hill. 'Thank you, Miss Tate. I think you'll have no further trouble.'

The connecting door rattled shut. Breath was audibly let out. A few giggles, a growing hum. 'Now children,' Paula's voice, tremulous. 'You heard what Mr Hill said.' Roz knew she had been humiliated.

Before long the roar was rising again, sprinkled with an occasional 'ssh', or 'shut up you' from among the children and equally ineffective attempts by Paula. The connecting door rattled open again.

'Twice,' came Mr Hill's voice in the rapid silence. 'Not once but twice, *twice*, have I had to leave my own class to speak to you about your behaviour. And I want to know why. What kind of disorder do you call this – eh? Simmonds? What's your excuse? Eh? Speak up. You weren't bashful a moment ago. I could hear you clearly enough then – through a wall.'

Muttered responses. More from Mr Hill. The rattle as he left. The hum gradually growing again. Turbulence contained, but barely.

At break, Paula opened the door to Roz's room.

'Mrs Drummond,' she said, in an unnaturally bright tone, 'Would you mind if my class came out this way?'

They were supposed to go via Mr Hill's. Roz agreed and let her own children follow on to the playground. A few moments later Mr Hill strode through.

'Chaos,' he informed Roz, in a loud whisper. 'Absolute chaos. You wouldn't believe it. Couldn't hear myself think – don't know how you managed. Coming for tea?'

'I'll come in a minute,' said Roz. She could believe it only too easily. Mr Hill marched out. Roz went next door and found Paula with her head in a cupboard.

'Don't worry, Paula,' said Roz. 'It can be terrible when you begin. But it really does get better.'

'*I'm* not getting better,' sobbed Paula. 'I'm hopeless. I can't stop the noise. Mr Hill can hear it, and you can too. I know he can hear them and I know he can hear me so I feel more awkward and that makes the children take even less notice of me and so it goes on.'

'You've also got the worst classroom in the school – you can't blame yourself for that.'

'They wouldn't listen to me in any case. I feel so stupid. When Mr Hill comes in they immediately pay attention.'

'He's been at it for years. And he is Deputy Head.'

'Then they know its not me controlling them. As soon as he goes out they start up again. I don't have any effect. I'm beginning to dread it. I used to like children. I thought they'd like me. But they don't seem to care. It's as if I wasn't really a human being to them. Sometimes I almost hate them. That's not right is it? To hate children? And it's my own fault. I'm no good!'

'It's not just you. Don't think it is. Nearly everyone finds it stressful at first,' reiterated Roz.

'I can't imagine Mr Hill ever having trouble.'

'Maybe not Mr Hill. Some people don't. Duncan, my husband, didn't. We both started here at the same time – and that was how we met. He got bored and left to go to university. It was too easy for him. It wasn't for me, though. I thought I'd never get through that first year.'

'But your class is so nice and well-behaved. Like Mr Hill's.'

'They weren't then.'

'Honestly?'

'Honestly.'

'So why didn't you leave? I don't think I'll stick it out for much longer.'

'We were getting married. And Duncan was a student again. We needed a steady income. And then, it really does grow easier. You find your own way of doing things. Most of it becomes second nature; you just fall into the ways.'

Paula considered. 'I can't imagine meeting a husband in this dump,' she said.

'I did.'

'I want to marry to get out of here, not to get stuck.'

The whistle blew outside.

'Break's over,' panicked Paula. 'Oh no, look at me. I must be all red and blotchy. There's no time to wash. They'll know.'

'I'll fetch your class,' said Roz. 'You go now. I'll bring your lot up last with mine.'

Break over, the noise from the next door swirled and eddied again but Paula was saved from further intervention since Mr Hill was out in the yard exhorting his shivering group to PE and gymnastic games. In the following lesson, Paula's own group had singing in the hall to a radio programme, and at lunchtime she dashed off mumbling something about shopping. It was rare for teachers to leave the premises during school hours. Roz knew that it was a desperate escape.

She took her sandwiches to the staff room where Martin was bringing his audience up to date with his personal life. Mr Hill was downstairs at dinner duty, organizing trestle tables in the hall, and the laying of knives and forks.

'We've got the house, Roz,' said Martin. 'At any rate, we have, provided it doesn't fall through. They accepted our offer last night.'

'That is good,' said Roz. 'It's just what you wanted isn't it?'

'Three bedrooms, two reception, reasonable-size garden. Only five years old so it's in good condition.'

'Patty must be pleased.'

'Very excited about it. Over the moon in fact.'

'She's a brave lady,' said Caroline. 'Moving house and having a baby at the same time. My sister did and it nearly drove her barmy. She said never again.'

'Baby or house?' asked Tod.

'Oh, house. She's had a couple more kids since then. But

she said the upheaval of a new house as well as her first was too much.'

'Patty'll manage,' assured Martin confidently. 'She can turn her hand to anything. I've nothing to worry about there. Anyway, at our age you have to be moving on in life. You ought to be thinking about it too, you know, Roz.'

'Which? Having a baby or a house?'

'Both. I mean, a flat's all right when you're first married and trying to find your feet. Then you've got to progress. And a first-time flat isn't much security either. You need to put your money into a proper house. Isn't that so, Tod? Your house is quite big, isn't it?'

'Fairly,' said Tod, filling a pipe. 'Mind you, there was a lot wrong with it when we bought it. We were doing it up gradually for years.'

'You'll get your money back,' said Martin. 'Nothing appreciates like property. It's the best form of investment. It'll pay off in the extra you'll get for the house when you move again.'

'I don't think that will be for a long time,' said Tod. 'We did it for comfort rather than to make money. We like the house; it's convenient for the girls' school and we feel quite settled in it.'

'There you are,' said Martin, as if making a point. 'Home and family. What are you waiting for, Roz?'

'It sounds as if you're propositioning her,' said Caroline. 'What about me? I'm the unattached one.'

'You've got time yet,' said Martin. 'You're that bit younger. Now Roz, you don't want to leave it too long.'

'It's not really anyone else's business,' said Tod.

'I know it isn't. But it seems such a waste and she might regret it later.'

'Just because you're having babies,' said Caroline, 'you think everyone else should.'

'Doesn't it matter, Roz?'

'Women can have other interests, you know,' said Caroline. 'There are other important things in life.'

'Is that so, Roz?'

'Well,' said Roz, 'I mean, there's Duncan's research.'

'Duncan's research? What's that got to do with it?'

'We couldn't afford to do anything else until he's finished his thesis.'

'So in the meantime he's a kept man and you can't start a family.'

'That's their business,' said Tod again, more forcibly. 'And what's this talk as if Roz were almost past it? She's got plenty of time. You don't have to be in your twenties to produce children. People have them much later.'

'My mother was forty-five when I was born,' Mr Hill's voice, fresh from dinner duty. 'In those days, you had them when you had them and that was all there was to it. I could wish our little Miss Tate would leave and have babies though. Nice girl she may be, but she hasn't a clue about how to manage a class. Where is she now?'

'She's gone out,' said Roz.

'And then back for further catastrophes this afternoon, I expect. What was it like after break? Were you finally driven to going in and sorting them out yourself?'

'It wasn't bad,' lied Roz. 'I think she'll manage if we leave her to it. She'll learn through her own experience.'

'You're more optimistic than I am.'

'I must say she always looks very anxious,' said Martin.

'Not without good reason,' said Mr Hill. 'You should be where Roz and I are all day. Then you'd know about it.'

'Is it really so terrible?' asked Tod

'Indescribable,' said Mr Hill. 'She'll never make a teacher.'

'I wasn't much better in my first year.'

'Now, Roz, there's no comparison.'

'It's true. I never felt in control and I could never get the class to be even reasonably quiet.'

'Of course you could,' said Mr Hill. 'Don't be modest. I didn't have to go and sort you out.'

'That was only because you were too far away to hear what was going on.'

'I don't believe it. And you'd be able to hear Paula Tate's lot over in the railway station.'

But Roz knew she wasn't being modest. Her first year had been a nightmare, the only consolation being that she had a classroom on the ground floor with solid walls instead of the thin partitions which formed Paula's room. Thus her own ordeal had been comparatively private, and she had been able to find her own relationship with the class without having what little credibility she possessed cut away from her by the management of more experienced teachers. She had kept her difficulties hidden, too ashamed to admit her straining panic or talk about the fragmentation of her mind as no child, it seemed, could stay put for longer than half a minute and at times even the chalk and pictures and wordgames, even the table and chairs and window frames felt only temporarily stationary – as if they might themselves whirl off round the room giggling and careless of her presence.

Duncan had been the one lumbered with the middle classroom that year, except that it hadn't mattered. It was well into the second term before Roz realized that he was, like her, only just doing his probationary year. She would never have guessed. The children were respectful, unchallenging. There was diligence in his classroom, occasional controlled laughter. Mr Hill behaved as to a proper teacher; Miss Elyce treated him like a member of the school establishment; Tod, who was already at the school then, like an accepted colleague. And Duncan was bored. Bored! Whatever else she might be, Roz was too occupied to be bored. Even when she and the class began to settle down, it took time for her to trust her initially precarious routines, to discover which methods best suited her and to get used to them so that there no longer seemed the unnerving split between her as self and her as teacher, people who might never coalesce.

Bored! Roz had been overawed. She was coping by this time, but with considerable relief. The job was just beginning to come within her capability – and Duncan was applying for university because it was too easy. He read books with words like 'ontogenesis' and 'dynamic reappraisal' in their titles and expounded at length to her the excitement of ideas, the vital importance of knowledge, as she sat with him in the pub, almost mute with admiration. He told her of his future glowing with intellectual discovery, of the strenuous mental activity that lay ahead and of his imminent financial sacrifice.

He left school and they married. They found a small flat; Duncan went to university and Roz carried on teaching. Duncan graduated – upper second (he had previously reconciled himself to the fact that the recondite iconoclasm of his final-year project would alienate his assessors and thus scupper his chances of a first, but such are the penalties of academic integrity). Roz carried on teaching.

Duncan embarked on a PhD. Now he was moving on to the real stuff. Now his rare cognitive style would come into its own. And because he had domestic responsibilities – a wife, a flat – he took on an evening class for the University Extra-mural Department. Roz carried on teaching.

'Workers' playtime over,' said Mr Hill. 'Come on, Tod. Let's round them up.'

Paula came in, wearing more make-up and closely followed by Miss Elyce.

'Afternoon,' said Mr Hill. 'Only just back?'

Paula went pink.

'Oh yes,' said Miss Elyce. 'What a meeting! Len, have you a moment? One or two points cropped up. I thought I'd just mention them to you, then we can discuss them later.'

'Very good,' said Mr Hill. 'Roz, would you go down with Tod? Keep my class till last.'

'No problems arose this morning, did they?' asked Miss Elyce.

'Nothing new,' said Mr Hill, opening the door for her.

'Are you all right?' mouthed Roz to Paula, who nodded and became very busy rummaging inside her bag.

'How is Duncan?' enquired Tod as they went down the stone stairs. 'Is his research going well?'

'I think so,' said Roz. 'In fact he's seeing his supervisor today. Of course, it's beyond me, but he seems quite happy with it.'

'And what about you, Roz? Are you happy?'

'I'm fine,' said Roz, and blew the whistle.

3

'We've got the house, Roz,' said Martin. 'At any rate, we have provided it doesn't fall through. They accepted our offer last night.'

'That is good,' said Roz. 'It's just what you wanted, isn't it?'

Three bedrooms, he was saying. Two reception. A garden. A proper house – and all your own.

'Patty must be pleased.'

There would be space. A lot of space. One bedroom could be a study. Duncan could have it to himself if he liked. She didn't mind; there would be plenty of room in the rest of the house for her. He could leave his books and papers around the study and she wouldn't have to move them to do her marking or the cooking and annoy him. The other bedroom could be a spare, for visitors, or even, maybe, a nursery.

'You ought to be thinking about it too, you know, Roz.'

'Which? Having a baby or a house?'

Would it disturb Duncan to have the baby's room next to the study? Not really. Babies sleep so much at first. If it cried she'd have it downstairs with her to play and cuddle. The television would be downstairs. When Duncan worked, she wouldn't have to give up her programmes any more. And a separate kitchen. One you could move around in. The table wouldn't be covered with marking or research papers but with wire trays of cakes from the oven. Duncan upstairs working. The baby asleep in the next room. Or in the garden playing.

'There you are,' said Martin. 'Home and family. What are you waiting for, Roz?'

She was waiting for, waiting for . . .

They only had her salary. When Duncan finished, of course, it would be different. Until then she must keep on teaching. Though she could have a baby *and* work, couldn't she? Many women did. Then who would look after the baby? Duncan? Not likely – it would interfere with his research. A child-minder? Not enough money. And a baby crammed into that minute flat. Duncan would go berserk. It didn't bear thinking about. All this demanded a larger place to live.

Martin had only one salary, too. But his wife had worked before she was pregnant. There had only ever been Roz's money. She had managed to save a small sum in case of emergency but nothing approaching the amount needed for a deposit. Martin and Patty had their flat to sell. Roz and Duncan paid rent. Nobody realized that, except perhaps Tod. They had no investment of any sort. Apart from Duncan's research. That was their investment. It meant so much to him. He worked so hard. And it would pay off later.

'Well,' said Roz, 'I mean, there's Duncan's research.'

'Duncan's research? What's that got to do with it?'

'We couldn't afford to do anything else until he's finished his thesis.'

Martin wouldn't understand. He saw life as getting on, or just getting – promotions, houses, more possessions. An acquisitive push. He would be pushing her further now, were Tod not restraining him.

Tod had a house too, and children. He looked well worn in and comfortable. He'd already seemed permanent in his life when Roz and Duncan had first started at the school. His daughters were in their mid-teens now. He and his wife must have had them before Roz's age. Was Martin right? Would she regret it? Was it being left too late, despite what Tod and even Mr Hill now were saying?

On to Paula. Babies and Paula.

'She's gone out,' said Roz.

Poor Paula. 'Further catastrophes.' Couldn't he imagine what it felt like? The noise did make teaching difficult in the neighbouring classrooms, never mind about Paula's own, but he wasn't going to help by undermining what little authority Paula had.

'It wasn't bad,' lied Roz. 'I think she'll manage if we leave her to it. She'll learn through her own experience.'

'You're more optimistic than I am.'

Because that was how it had worked for Roz herself. She was sure you learned to cope only by being allowed to do so. Tolerance and reassurance and moral support were what you needed from others. The rest you could only sort out yourself.

'I wasn't much better in my first year.'

Mr Hill wouldn't accept that. Which was a compliment, though inaccurate. It was mainly the difference in location that had allowed Roz to disguise her difficulties better than Paula could. The children had behaved towards her then not unpleasantly, but with a casual boisterousness and lack of attention that didn't occur any more. They could spot the unsure and inexperienced without fail. How fortunate were those who came to teaching with the natural ability not to produce such an effect.

Like Duncan. He always knew what he wanted and where he was going. He was always a jump ahead of his present circumstances. She continued to think about him.

End of lunchtime. Mr Hill revving up. Paula back just in time. Who was that remark intended for? Miss Elyce full of her meeting. Paula claiming that she was all right although she obviously wasn't. Roz going down with Tod to bring the children in. Since Duncan always had been ahead of the present, perhaps he was also thinking about the next step in their joint lives. He couldn't be envisaging them staying in that tiny flat, just the two of them, for much longer.

'How is Duncan?' enquired Tod. 'Is his research going well?'

'I think so,' said Roz. 'In fact he's seeing his supervisor today. Of course, it's beyond me, but he seems quite happy with it.'

Perhaps Duncan hadn't brought up the subject of their future himself because he was happy for the moment and didn't realize that she was becoming increasingly dissatisfied.

'And what about you, Roz? Are you happy?'

She would mention to to him that night. They would

discuss their future.

'I'm fine,' said Roz, and blew the whistle.

Somewhat later that afternoon, Duncan left the University Psychology building and stepped out on to the street. As usual, the visit to his supervisor had left him anti-climactic. Always, always he looked forward to the meetings and prepared for them conscientiously. Always he hoped, to the point of fantasy. Always he was disappointed. There was little from Professor Reece by way of help or encouragement or even obvious interest in the project. Hardly had Duncan arrived today, it seemed, than he was being shown the door. Courteously, of course. Those subject responses he had tabulated into the night, that meticulous statistical analysis of an earlier sample, had merely received a cursory glance and nod.

Duncan crossed the road to the University bookshop. The autumn air was crisp with anticipation of new enterprises, new academic sessions, new lifestyles. For Duncan, years in education mingled ambition, adventure, a sense of new worlds opening up with the mellow sunlight and the falling leaves. Yet: 'It appears to be progressing satisfactorily.' Duncan could have told himself that and saved the journey. He wondered to how many other postgraduates Professor Reece was rendering minimal guidance. All claimed for on his workload, no doubt. Money for old rope. It was difficult to imagine how anyone could do less within the role. Duncan knew he would never shortchange his own students in that way, even though at the moment they comprised only an extra-mural night class. He knew from his own experiences what it was like to attend evening classes after a day's work, to prepare for exams while doing a full-time job, to be writing essays and revising into the small hours and throughout the weekends. He knew what a difference the teacher's effort could make. He would do his job properly.

He looked for books relevant to himself and books to recommend to his students, then went on to the University Library in Senate House to check some references. He did and would do his job properly, as a schoolteacher, now, and later on when he himself held Professor Reece's position. He consulted his list of references.

Towards the end of the rush hour, Duncan emerged from Senate House and crammed himself into the tube for the first part of his journey home. Despite the heat of the overcrowded carriage, despite the briefcase in his back and the head under his arm as he steadied himself against the handrail, despite the insistent beat reverberating from someone's personal stereo, Duncan felt better. 'It appears to be progressing satisfactorily.' Surely Professor Reece's lack of involvement was an implicit compliment, indicating that Duncan was fully capable of pursuing his research independently. That was a realistic assessment. Certainly it was what had happened so far in his life. Each time he had attained a level of achievement and thought that was where he would stay, before long he had found that he was capable of more and could reach the next level. In this way he had moved on and on again, through his own motivation.

At eleven years old he failed the entrance examination to grammar school. This evoked no comment at home since it was the norm for members of his family and nobody had expected him to pass. Not until the results were announced did Duncan realize that he himself had not accepted failure in advance. Standing in the school hall while the list of names was read aloud, Duncan was first surprised them almost overwhelmed by his bitter disappointment. The successful children already looked more prosperous and confident, the failures quieter and slighter, or fighting back with exaggerated carelessness and bravado. He was aware that a great divide had opened up and he, with the other failures, was on the wrong side of it. They were of no account. From now until they left school were lost years, as they waited till they could join the adult world of employment and be of consequence.

Not him. He wasn't going to wait on time. He mattered. He looked across the divide. Who were they, those on the other side? They were no better than him. He'd prove it.

Resolve unabated, at thirteen Duncan passed the transfer examination to the grammar school. He felt vindicated, despite the indignity of having to wear up his old uniform, in different colours. He soon grew out of it.

'The lad's a scholar,' said his father. 'He won't have to mucky his hands.'

'He won't that,' said his mother. 'He'll get a nice job in an office.'

Which he did. A nice job in an office with optional day release. Duncan took up the option and acquired a minor business qualification. He was promoted, but that wasn't enough to make office life fulfilling. He took his A-Levels at evening class.

'The lad's going to make something of himself,' said his father.

He made a student teacher of himself and found it easy. He taught juniors and missed the academic challenge. He went back to full-time study, this time for a university degree. Then he started a PhD. Then . . . Then . . . He'd supersede some indifferent Professor Reece before so very long.

He ran up the escalator steps, confidence restored, and went to the alley by the side of the tube station where he had left his bicycle padlocked to a lamp post.

Yes, he'd moved up and up and up. There could be no stopping him now. He tucked his trouser legs into his socks and rode off towards home and Roz.

It was fortuitous that he'd met Roz when he did. Having received a financial award for his teacher training he was ineligible for a grant when he went to university, and Roz's salary, though far from munificent, meant he didn't have to fritter away mental energy on prosaic necessities like rent and food. And she certainly got a kick out of his achievements. Food. It would be time to eat when he got in. Why didn't he stop off at the fish and chip shop to save Roz the bother of cooking tonight? That would be nice for her. He cycled on home with a large warm parcel from the Neptune Fish Bar, feeling considerate.

Theirs was a Victorian semi, converted into flats. Duncan wheeled his bike up the path, pushed it through the right-hand door and left it in what they called the hall, although it was no more than a corridor to the stairs which led to their flat and the one above. Duncan climbed these stairs with briefcase and chip bag and let himself into the flat. He walked down a second corridor to the kitchen end of the living-room. Roz was setting the table.

'Perfect timing,' she said. 'How did you get on?'

'Warm up some plates,' said Duncan. 'I've bought fish and chips.'

He put them down in front of her.

'Fish and chips?' There. He knew it would be a surprise for her. She must be so pleased he'd made it an easy evening. 'Why?'

'Cook's night off. You can't work without a break. It's against regulations.'

'You didn't say you were going to buy fish and chips.'

'Surprise treat.'

More of a surprise than he'd imagined. She hadn't moved yet. Duncan smiled in contentment as he took off his coat.

'I've already cooked,' Roz said. 'It's in the oven, ready to be eaten.'

She'd already cooked. He dropped his coat on a chair and put his briefcase by the bureau. She should have waited till he got home. He hadn't said he'd be back at this time. It might have been much later. Or earlier. He couldn't predict how long he'd be. Two meals now.

'We'll have it tomorrow.' She was taking plates from the rack above the cooker, unwrapping the fish and chips. That was all right. He'd saved her from cooking tomorrow night. She'd got it to look forward to.

'I thought you'd be pleased.'

'I am, I am. Thanks.'

They sat down to eat.

'Lovely chips,' said Roz. 'How did you get on with Reece?'

Duncan sprinkled vinegar over his plate. 'Oh, he's thoroughly satisfied. He knows I know what I'm doing. Really the consultations are a formality, an official requirement.'

'So when do you see him again?'

'It's for me to decide. I only have to keep in touch.'

'You must be an ideal postgraduate, needing so little of his time.'

'I expect so.'

There was pause while they chewed

'How much longer do you think your research will take?' asked Roz

'Roz, what a question. I don't know. Not much longer, I should hope.'

'I was wondering about the future. I mean, what other plans we might have.'

'I might try for an ESRC grant for post-doctoral research. See what posts are around then. That sort of thing. They give good portions at that chippy, don't they?'

'Yes, very good. Martin and Patty have got the house they were after.'

'Have they?'

'You know who I mean. Martin works with me. They're having a baby.'

'Oh yes.'

'Martin's looking forward to fatherhood.'

'Yes?'

'He's very excited about becoming a family.'

'Is he?'

She would go on about these people at school as if they were supposed to matter to him. Still, she liked doing it and he didn't have to listen.

'He recommends us to go in for it soon too.'

'I suppose so.'

'Do you? Do you really?'

Why all the fuss? She seemed to be getting over-involved in this Martin's business. She was gazing at him as if something important had happened. Well, if you've nothing more weighty to think about . . . As for himself, he did like that thought of post-doctoral research. Could be quite near if he got a move on with the PhD. So back to it, Duncan. Finish eating, watch the news, write up some more and look at those scores again.

'What was that, Roz?'

'I can hardly believe it. I've wanted to so much but I was sure you'd be against it. To be honest, I'd begun to make quite a thing of it, working out how to bring up the topic subtly. And then you go and accept it so easily. You must have been thinking about it too, and I couldn't tell. I can't know you very well, even after all this time.'

'No, I'm a dark horse.'

What was she on about? Perhaps he'd better miss the news

and get straight down to work.

'We'll need to discuss it thoroughly, won't we? This flat's very small; could we plan moving? And then what about money? I mean, we do need my salary so we'd have to make a lot of arrangements.'

Moving? Salary? Arrangements?

'Roz, what are you talking about?'

'When we have the baby. If I'm going to carry on working, we'll have to arrange a child-minder. And we'll be very tight financially. Could you get some more extra-mural teaching?'

Oh no. She wasn't, was she? Not now, when he'd all these plans. How could she do that to him. How could she have slipped up? A baby would ruin everything. How could he work against caterwauling and no sleep and wet nappies and God knows what?

'Roz, you're not pregnant?'

That silence must be the confirmation.

'Roz?'

'No.'

'Thank God for that. What are you talking about then?'

Another silence.

'Roz?'

'We were discussing it. Or so I thought.'

'Who's we?'

'We, Duncan. You and me.'

'You and me discussing what?'

'Having a baby ourselves. Soon.'

'Come on, Roz. How could we? Be sensible.'

She got up and began to clear the table without answering. Now what? She knew their priorities. She valued his work. Where had this baby stuff come from all of a sudden? He felt as if he'd unexpectedly sat down on a crack between two chairs.

'Roz, you didn't seriously think I'd want a baby just now, did you?'

'No, I didn't seriously think so.'

What a relief. She'd had him worried. She didn't usually tease so it wasn't surprising he'd fallen for it. Unlike her. Never mind, back to normal.

'I want to look at those scores again, Roz. What are you

going to do?'

'I'll have a bath and an early night.'

Good. He wouldn't be disturbed.

'If you're tired, leave the washing up.'

'Mmm.'

'Night then.'

'Night.'

She went out to the bedroom. He picked up his briefcase.

4

'Well, I don't know,' said Beatty, relaxing her grip on her walking-stick now that she had safely sat down. 'You hear them complaining about them. But I've never had anything but kindness from you darkies.'

Pearl straightened up from arranging the cushions behind Beatty and handed her a cup of tea and a cake from the trolley. That was the dayroom patients nearly finished. She turned the trolley round to move on to the ward.

'Of course they complain,' said Ethel from the next chair. She pulled at her bushy white hair. 'They're always causing trouble, ain't they?'

'Who is?'

'Them blacks.'

'What do you mean, "trouble"? I've never had anything but kindness from darkies.'

'Noise and fighting and drinking and men going with women . . . '

'Ssh,' reproved a third old lady, fidgeting nervously with the neck of her cardigan. 'Not in front of Miss Thomas.'

'Why not?' challenged Ethel. 'I'll say what I like when I like. I've never been afraid to speak my mind.'

'You'll hurt her feelings.'

'Why should I? I don't mean her. She knows I don't mean her.'

'But you're still talking, aren't you? I mean, she probably heard you. It's not nice.'

'She knows I don't mean her. She's different. She's more like us.'

'I know she is. All the same, I don't think it's nice.'

'She's not different,' objected Beatty. 'I've never had anything but kindness from Pearl. She's just like the others.'

'Oh yes. Pearl's certainly very kind. I've no argument with you there.'

'You wouldn't find Miss Thomas causing trouble.'

'The very idea! No, she's different. She's more like us.'

And again, thought Pearl, wheeling her trolley out of the dayroom and across the landing. Even here. Always different. Different from whites, different from blacks. Singling you out so that you fitted in nowhere. Even their compliments a form of insult. Checking you off against their fixed ideas of what you ought to be like, then when you weren't, they didn't see how inadequate their list was, they didn't see the stupidity of having a list at all; they didn't adapt – they just pushed you out of the category. Different.

Still, no point in getting worked up. She ought to be used to it by now. She had her own motto; if you don't belong with anyone anywhere, then you belong entirely to yourself – make the most of it. The Children's Homes had taught her that much at least. Not that she'd made very sensible use of her new knowledge at first, she had to admit. Lucky that she hadn't got caught out more permanently. Right little terror. Wasted her school time too. Never mind, she was younger then. She hadn't got it worked out properly. She'd changed since those days. Now she knew where she wanted to go. So ignore the rest, Pearl, and get on with it.

She entered the ward where the non-ambulant patients lived. 'Afternoon, ladies.'

Non-ambulant – there was an understatement for you. Most of them were practically immobile. Once you got here, you could shrivel up gradually for years, shrink away from the edges of your body till you scarcely had any contact left with it, keeping yourself hidden somewhere deep inside. Yet they hardly ever died. Not properly, anyway; not in a medical sense. There were some old women who'd been there for thirty years or more, longer than Pearl's entire life. She felt sure that if they hadn't been woken up each morning, been washed, had porridge and rice pudding and mince spooned into their slack mouths at intervals throughout the day, they would have died quietly in their sleep years ago. But this was a hospital. You weren't allowed to die. So they were fed and changed. They were combed and turned and had their bed sores attended to. They went on, crouched further and further inside themselves.

Pearl remembered her first days on the ward. She had gone to the hospital in search of a job and, almost to her surprise, was taken on with little ceremony. The following Monday, she began. She was given her yellow overall and led out of the building on to a gravel path round a circle of grass which had an earth mound in the middle burning with carefully positioned salvias and French marigolds. She was taken into another building and up a short flight of stone steps. The walls had tiles which were brown glazed to shoulder height, then painted cream. At the top of the stairs was a landing, and the wall there was covered by a paper frieze. On a dark-blue painted background were silver stars and a moon, cut-out trees stuck on, little houses, people and animals. Oh, thought Pearl, pleased. It must be a children's ward. That should be fun. But at that moment a procession moved across in front of the frieze. Slowly, painfully, distorted shapes hobbled along the landing. Bent backs, twisted hands, rigid ankles, swollen legs, dresses that rose and dipped over the lumps and bundles of flesh. They were moving from the dayroom to the dining-room for lunch.

Pearl saw the parade in grotesque slow motion. They reminded her of a picture she had seen in a shop, of misshapen figures, gaps of ground separating them out, scattered in front of a grey sky and a factory.

Pearl was not to help in the dining-room immediately. She was to serve food from aluminium containers pushed around the ward on a trolley. The ward. White faces on white pillows. White gowns under white bedding. Blotchy white hands twisting, twitching and trembling on top of turned-back covers. A certain smell, warm and decaying. Pearl had never encountered extreme old age before, had only seen the elderly active, singly or in small groups where they were diluted by everyone else. Not like this. Pearl dished out mince and rice pudding, her own hand shaking. She spoon-fed the senile and wiped off the dribbles. She collected the plates again and pushed the trolley out. Then she was sent to tidy the linen room.

Pearl laid her head on a shelf of clean sheets and cried. What was it for? To end up an empty white shell, abandoned? Where were these women? Where were their past lives, their jokes, their hopes, their anger, love, disappointments and successes? Was all this washed away by age? They lay equalized by emptiness, their differences levelled into white. Would her own struggles and intentions amount only to this in the end? Why bother to do anything?

One of the other orderlies found her there. Sadie, plump and experienced. 'I used to be the same,' she said, fetching Pearl a cup of tea. 'At first I couldn't sleep at nights, thinking of them. You get used to it.'

Pearl did. They were terribly understaffed – just one trained nurse and the orderlies – so Pearl helped with all the jobs and soon knew everybody in both dayroom and ward. Gradually it began to seem normal. Some of the inmates of the dayroom lived in the hospital, others had their own homes and came in each day by ambulance. They brought with them news and opinion from the outside world. The ward had a quiet routine. Only rarely were the screens put round a bed which, after a brief vacancy, would be filled again by another white body.

'Hello, Mrs Haynes.'

The middle-aged woman at the bedside looked round and smiled at Pearl.

'Hello, Miss Thomas. What have you got today?'

'Sponge slices.'

'Oh good. She'll like that.'

Every afternoon for nearly five years, Mrs Haynes had come to give her mother some tea. Every afternoon for nearly five years Mrs Haynes had held her mother's hand and told her the family news. Every afternoon for nearly five years, her mother had stared back blankly and silently, moving her pursed lips round and round and round.

Pearl wondered how Mrs Haynes could keep it up. Even on Christmas Day. Did she ever have a holiday? Pearl couldn't remember her missing even one single visit. Most of the patients had no visitors. The mother was of one of those who regularly almost died – but only almost. The priest would be called, the Last Rites given and forthwith the old lady would begin to improve. Before long she would be sitting propped up by pillows again, staring blankly.

Mrs Haynes dipped a piece of sponge into the cup of tea and fed it on a spoon to her mother. Pearl moved on.

'The bloody bugger, the sodding bloody bugger. What does he know, eh? That bleeding bloody bugger. What does he know? Eh? Eh? That sodding bugger?' Louisa snatched her cake off the plate and glared at Pearl. 'Eh? Eh? What does he know? The bloody bugger.'

'He doesn't know a thing,' agreed Pearl. 'Nothing at all.'

'Bloody bugger.'

In the next bed Annie was curled up like a dormouse. She was renowned for brilliantly blue eyes and an ability to defy the laws of nature by wetting her pillow every night. Pearl would have to come back to feed her after she'd finished giving out the rest of her trolley-load.

'I'll do Agnes now,' said Sadie, coming over to collect the tea and cake which was to be spooned into another unknowing face.

They weren't all like that. Although Millie also had to be fed, because she was too crippled to do it for herself, her personality was unaffected. She had been brought up to expect next to nothing and had not been proved wrong. Now she was pathetically grateful for any care and attention she received on the ward. And Mrs McGinty. All her life in an East End slum, fighting, refusing to be absorbed passively into her own circumstances. She was still fighting, hanging on to her respect. No first names for her; she insisted on Mrs McGinty. She kept a watch on the ward, complaining to Sister if anything was not as she thought it should be. She annoyed many of the staff, but Pearl had a sneaking admiration for her denial that she had little control over her situation, for her continuing refusal to be insignificant.

Pearl went back to feed Annie, then did the rounds of the ward again collecting the dirty crockery. Mrs Haynes was just leaving. 'See you tomorrow,' she said to Pearl. Sadie was doing the dayroom. Pearl pushed the trolley into the kitchen which led off the landing and began to unload it.

Sadie staggered in with a tray piled high. 'Having a right argy-bargy about you, they was in there,' she said.

'What about?'

'Oh nothing nasty. Quite the opposite, in fact. They're trying to outdo each other saying how nice you are.'

'Not like most blacks.'

'Go on. You know Ethel. She thinks I'm a foreigner, coming from Purley.'

'Well, you are, aren't you?'

'Cheeky. Listen here. My mother and father came over from Russia to Whitechapel. It was just the same then – everything was down to the Jews. Then they did better and moved on and everybody had a go at the Irish. Now it's blacks and Asians and whatnot. It don't mean nothing really. Some people have always got to have someone easy to blame, and it's hard for the old people to adapt to changes.'

'I don't know that it's as simple as that. But you're all right, you know, Sadie.'

'I should think so – a non-believing Jew married to a lapsed Catholic. I've got to be, haven't I?'

'What did your lot think, then, when you married him?'

'Terrible, love. Both sides thought we'd burn in hell. Only in different hells, of course.'

'Did they accept it after?'

'No, no. Not really. Broke their hearts. Shame, isn't it? Damn near broke mine too. Still, we've been happy.'

'Do they accept it now?'

'Hard to tell. They've passed on. I expect they accept most things.'

Pearl grinned, though she was never quite sure whether Sadie did actually ride her life as steadily as it appeared. They were joined by one of the cleaners, a strapping pugilist named Rose, who regaled them with a description of how she'd pushed a beer glass into her escort's face the previous night when she discovered that that he was married. The three of them did the washing up to this accompaniment. Main meals came directly from the hospital's central kitchens, but tea was dealt with by the individual ward. Had the police been called? No need. He'd got out of the way as fast as he could, then she'd gone home raging. Was he badly cut? Rose shrugged.

She supposed so. His face was bleeding a lot. Wasn't Rose worried about it? Why should she be, said Rose. He was lucky she didn't have his balls off. Rose yanked the plug out of the sink, and the water ran away in terror. Despite Pearl's own background, Rose's life fascinated her, at a distance.

They put the crockery in the cupboard.

'Got your class tonight?' asked Sadie.

Pearl nodded.

'What class is this then?' demanded Rose.

'Pearl's going to night classes,' said Sadie. 'You ought to try something like that, Rose. Do you good.'

'Why? What's she doing? Keep-fit?'

'Psychology.'

'Blimey, Pearl. You going to be reading our minds?'

'Could be. You never know.'

'No – honest. What are you doing it for?'

'Well,' said Pearl, 'I think I'd like to be a social worker. Only I've got no qualifications. But if you do these classes and you pass the exam you can sometimes get on to a social-work course after.'

'Blimey,' said Rose again, pulling an impressed face. 'I didn't know you was a swot, Pearl. You never said nothing about this before.'

'I've only just started. It was the first class last week.'

'Pearl a social worker! You know, I admire that. You need social workers in this day and age. All these young kids thieving and cheeking. My dad would have flattened us if he'd caught any of us at it. But they do what they like nowadays. There's no respect any more. Know what I mean?'

'I didn't respect anybody much when I was a kid.'

'Didn't you? Coo, I did. Had to. Black eye if you didn't. Still, I'm grateful for it now.'

'Are you?' said Sadie.

'Course I am. Taught you respect, didn't it? Not like nowadays. You can't teach them anything.'

'You should go to Pearl's night class. It might teach you how to avoid married men.'

'I already know how to make them avoid me, thank you. I don't need no Psychology lessons for that.'

5

Pearl walked up the hill to the evening institute, which was more widely known as Lixbury School. This time last week she had trodden the same stretch of pavement in a state of apprehensive determination. Was she about to make an exhibition of herself? She knew why she had enrolled for the classes and she knew what she hoped they would lead to. But was she letting her ambitions blind her? From the description in the magazine article she was just the sort of person who went for adult education and the sort who might make a useful social worker later on. When she'd turned up to enrol on the course all sorts of people were there. The ones who signed her form and took her fee didn't bat an eyelid. Yet perhaps the others were different. Perhaps they'd worked harder at school, been on other courses, were more intelligent. She had almost wanted to back out last week but had made herself walk up that hill and into the school, looking for the right room. Inside, half a dozen people were sitting in silence, strung out at desks. She hesitated – 'Is this Psychology?'

'Yes, yes, to be sure it is.'

She was in, sitting in silence at her own separate desk.

Nearly everyone entered the same way – the hesitation, the question, the same reply from the same man, the choice of desk at a certain distance. Neither was she the only black person, although the other two, both women, were older. There was also an Indian man and there were various tones of Europeans. The women outnumbered the men.

'Is this Psychology?'

'Yes, yes. To be sure it is.'

This time the questioner went to the front of the class. He was tall and dark, in his thirties, serious. They watched him unpack his briefcase.

That was Mr Drummond and the class hadn't been too alarming. The content wasn't what she had expected but Mr Drummond explained it very clearly and was patient with the man who wanted everything exactly repeated. He was the one who kept saying, 'Yes, yes, to be sure it is' and he had obviously done other classes there. You'd think he'd have learnt to write more quickly by now. Pearl had managed it although she had never taken notes properly before. At school, years earlier, the teachers had dictated sentence by sentence; and anyway she'd never paid much attention in those days. So it had been satisfying that first evening to see her own written words closing in the gist of what Mr Drummond was saying. She felt efficient. Some of the faces around her looked rather daunted, but wasn't it like common sense? It was the same sort of thing that happened with a new patient. If you weren't careful you began treating her according to your expectations of old people in general. As often as not some of those expectations were wrong, which you found out when you got to know her better and then you changed what you did and said to fit in with what you'd learnt about her.

Similar, too, to the way Pearl herself had often been treated. Some people thought they knew all about you just because you were a 'darkie', except then it was often not based on what they'd actually come across, and many of them weren't willing to change their attitude once they'd been proved wrong. They were much more likely to remember things which they believed proved them right. Were scientists ever like that too? It must be important to recognize that your ideas had been disproved otherwise you'd never learn anything.

This second week, Pearl felt more at ease as she entered the classroom.

'Hello there,' cried the slow notetaker who she now knew was Mr O'Connell. 'Are you ready for battle again?'

'I hope so,' said Pearl, going to a desk which, she estimated, was sufficiently far away to be safe from him but not so far as to make her seem rude.

'Because it is a battle, don't you think so? They're such terrible fast talkers, these intellectuals. I suppose it's the enthusiasm that's the cause of it.'

'He doesn't talk so quickly,' disagreed the potential class librarian.

'No, no. I've known many worse.'

'It's *what* he's talking about that bothers me.'

'Good evening,' said the class secretary, coming through the door. 'Has our book box arrived yet?'

'Not a chance,' said the librarian. 'He probably didn't put in the order early enough. He didn't seem to know much about it last week.'

'It's often late, though, isn't it Annette? It's probably got nothing to do with him.'

'Well anyway, if it's not here by next week I'm going to tell him to complain.'

'Give it a week or two for him to settle in. I don't think he's done this before, do you, and I think he'll be quite good in the long run.'

'Don't know. Couldn't understand him,' said Annette. 'I've been looking at my notes but I can't make head nor tail of them. I don't know why we did all that last week.'

'Background,' said Mr O'Connell.

'It didn't seem to have much to do with Social Psychology.'

'I expect he has his reasons,' said Mr O'Connell. 'They usually do, these academics.'

'But if we're not going to get a question on it, what's the point? He's just wasting our time.'

'Good evening one and all.'

'Good evening to you, Arthur.'

'Has the book box arrived?'

'You must be joking,' said Annette.

'Don't worry, darling. It will, it will,' said one of the black women tolerantly.

'And in the meantime,' said Arthur Pontiff, 'there are other sources.'

'You've been looking things up already?' said Annette.

'Just following up one or two interesting points. You know, from last week. Excellent class, wasn't it? I've really been looking forward to this evening.'

'I always enjoy these classes,' agreed Mr O'Connell.

'I might if he'd get on with it,' said Annette.

'I'll take the register,' said the secretary. 'I'm afraid I'll have to call out your names till I get to know who everybody is.'

'You'll do that soon enough,' said Mr O'Connell. 'I'm – well, good evening Mr Drummond. We're all waiting here agog to know what's next.'

'Might I have a quick word?' said Arthur Pontiff.

Pearl watched him scramble out to the front after Mr Drummond. Arthur looked pleased and earnest and was brandishing a small card. He said a great deal in a quiet voice, working hard to keep eye contact with Mr Drummond while the latter continued to open his briefcase, take out notes and sort them through. Arthur's stance bent and listed; his head stuck out at right angles and his eyes bulged at the top of their sockets in the effort to maintain close facial proximity as Mr Drummond scanned the top page of his notes. Mr Drummond looked up suddenly and narrowly missed snapping Arthur's chin. Both men drew back.

'I think we'd better start,' announced Mr Drummond to the class.

There was a murmur of agreement, and Arthur Pontiff bustled back to his desk, elbows out. The class straightened their writing-pads, sat up in expectation and poised their pens.

At break, Pearl found herself leaving the room behind the secretary and Annette, the librarian.

'It's better this week,' said Annette as they walked down the stairs. 'Don't you think so Marion?'

'It's more to the point,' agreed Marion, the secretary. 'What do you make of it?' she turned to Pearl.

'Yes, it's more of what I expected.'

'This is what we'll get asked on,' said Annette, 'not last week's stuff.'

'Perhaps it will be useful later,' said Marion soothingly.

'Doubt it. There's never anything like that in the exam, thank God. It was a waste of time doing it.'

They went into the canteen and joined the queue. There were people in leotards and jazz tights, people in overalls stained with paint and clay, people in fervent discussions.

'All these activities,' murmured Marion. 'It's so interesting. Three teas please – that is right, isn't it?'

They made their way to an adjacent table and sat down. Nearby was a man in an overcoat, at his feet a large black case of strange dimensions.

'Is that a bassoon?' whispered Marion.

'Haven't the faintest,' said Annette. 'Could be. Though I can't imagine why anyone would ever want to play one. O-oh, it looks as if we're going to get a visitation.'

However, they weren't. Mr Drummond's eyes skipped over them and he moved deeper into the room.

'Good, he didn't see us,' said Annette.

'Or he didn't want to,' said Pearl.

'He probably didn't recognize us yet,' said Marion. 'They usually make a point of sitting with you when they get to know you.'

'Unfortunately,' said Annette. 'They ruin many a pleasant conversation.'

'Mind if I join you?' Arthur Pontiff loomed with cup and plate. Annette coughed and stirred her tea.

'Of course not,' said Marion and moved her bag from the spare chair.

'Many thanks,' said Arthur. He sat down and gazed around. 'Have you seen Mr Drummond?'

'He walked past a few minutes ago,' said Pearl.

'Yes, I saw him then. I tried to attract his attention but he didn't notice me. I was hoping to talk with him for a while.'

'I thought you talked with him at the beginning of class,' said Annette.

'Yes, I did. But I didn't quite finish what I wanted to say. He had to fulfil his teaching duties, of course. So I thought we might continue our discussion during the break.'

'Did you really?' said Annette.

'But I don't know where he's disappeared to.' He craned his neck round again. 'Ah! There he is. Now – will you excuse me, ladies, if I . . . ' He began to rise, picking up his cup and plate. Then he stopped halfway. 'He seems to be engaged in conversation with someone else.'

Pearl and Marion looked. Annette drank her tea. Mr

Drummond's back could be seen and the personable front of a fair-haired man in black T-shirt and bandeau, who was smiling at him.

Arthur hovered. 'Should I interrupt him? Do you think he'd mind?'

'That,' said Annette, 'you must decide for yourself.'

'Yes, you're right. No, I'd better not. Oh dear, how disappointing. Though I must say that's rather a strange-looking fellow for someone like Mr Drummond to be friendly with.'

'He'll be dancing,' said Marion.

'I beg your pardon?'

'They run all sorts of classes here, you know, not just academic ones.'

'So I see.' Arthur sat down and savaged his bun. The others had a drink of tea. Arthur stared morosely at the table top.

'Still,' he said suddenly to Pearl. 'I expect you're good at dancing too.'

'Me?' said Pearl, amazed. 'No, I'm not.'

'You're being modest,' said Arthur. 'Very charming. But I know you'll be good at movement. All you people are.'

'Gordon Bennett,' said Annette.

Duncan had deliberately avoided any members of his class during the break, having decided to maintain a professorial distance. He managed not to catch the eye of the three women who were already settled at a long table and walked with his cup in the opposite direction from the waiting queue in which Mr Pontiff was bobbing up and down trying to attract his attention. Duncan searched the canteen for a protected area. At a small table with a vacant place someone was reading a magazine. He would do.

'Is anyone sitting here?' asked Duncan, indicating the empty chair. Obviously not, but the other man took it as it was meant – a request to enter territory.

'No, no,' he said with an engaging smile. 'Do join me.'

'Thanks,' said Duncan and sat down. He poured back the tea that had slopped into his saucer then scraped the bottom of the cup on the saucer's edge to minimize drips.

The other man put his magazine on one side. 'Doing a class here?'

'I teach one,' said Duncan.

'You do? What do you teach?' His voice was rounded and effortless as if holding within it endless possibilities of range and volume and pitch.

'Psychology.'

'Really? That must be fascinating.'

'Fascinating' wasn't a weighty enough adjective to appeal to Duncan. He drew breath to embark on his continual mission of rectifying the layman's trivial concept of his subject, but before he'd properly marshalled his terminology, the conversation had moved swiftly on.

'Especially, you know, to my profession.'

'Your profession?'

'I'm an actor. You may have heard of me – Philip Hether. I was in "Tinderbox". Did you see it?'

Duncan had seen an occasional episode of the feuding family. However, he did not recognize Philip.

'I don't watch television very often,' he said. 'My thesis takes up so much time.'

'A thesis! That's impressive. Quite frightening in fact. You must have enormous insight into people's motivation. What an advantage that gives you over the rest of us!'

Duncan smiled modestly and didn't dispute the issue. This was not the serious scientific approach he usually tried to instil into people, but Philip was admiring enough in his own way so there was nothing to be gained by attempting to remould his appreciation.

'Of course, I'm particularly interested in motivation with being in the business.'

'The business?'

'Acting. You have to try to discover you characters' motives – really get to know them.'

'What are you in now?' asked Duncan.

'At the moment, I'm resting. Resting and learning. An actor must always keep on learning. The more skills at your disposal, the more you understand – the richer your work. Body and mind. I'm doing dance here.' He indicated the headband. 'But Psychology – I'd love to do some Psychology.

Do you teach on any other evening?'

'No. Only Tuesdays.'

'I suppose you wouldn't want to do too much teaching. It would rob time from your research – far more important.'

'I think so.' Duncan noticed his watch. 'Actually teaching has to rob me now too. I'll have to go back and do the second part of the class.'

'And I'd better renew my hoofing,' said Philip. They stood up and left the canteen together. 'Pity it clashes with Psychology. I should have loved to do it. Do you think you could tell me more some time and give me some professional advice in my work?'

'Well, I always have my class break at this time,' said Duncan, flattered again.

'Same time, same place then,' said Philip. 'Thanks a lot.' He turned away in the direction of the gym.

'Cheers,' said Duncan.

'Bye,' said Philip.

The canteen door swung open and out came Mr Pontiff with the three women. Duncan moved along the corridor. 'Mr Drummond,' a male voice called. Duncan pretended not to hear. He proceeded up the stairs and into the classroom, where half the group was still sitting, some with thermos flasks, not having bothered to go down for the break.

'Good. Let's continue,' said Duncan, and wrote a heading on the board. Feet scuttled in quickly. The door closed. Duncan went straight on.

At the end, Mr Pontiff lingered over his notes, packed up slowly and accompanied Duncan out of the building again.

'Hurrying back to your lady wife, no doubt?' inquired Mr Pontiff.

'Well, yes,' said Duncan. 'You know how it is.'

'Not from personal experience,' said Mr Pontiff. 'I live alone. I've never had the good fortune to meet the right person. But I have observed that commitment to his wife waiting at home often prevents a man from indulging in a little intellectual discourse over some form of refreshment.'

'I expect you're right,' said Duncan.

'Never mind. I shall have my thoughts for company. Luckily I get on well with them. I can't give you a lift either, can I? You have your own car as before in the staff car park. We lesser mortals have to make do with the street, you know.'

'Thanks all the same,' said Duncan. 'Good night.'

'No – thank *you*,' said Mr Pontiff. 'It's been another enjoyable and informative evening. I look forward to the next. Good night.'

He walked away towards the gate, raising his hand in salute as he went. Duncan nipped round the corner to where his bicycle was chained against a drainpipe. He waited a few minutes to give Mr Pontiff time to drive off, then tucked his trousers into his socks, strapped his briefcase on the back and wheeled the bike across the yard to the road. He mounted and began to pedal down the hill. A bus passed, too close, and immediately after it a figure, racing lightly along the pavement and into the road just in front of Duncan, causing him to swing wildly and curse. The figure leapt on to the bus platform.

'Sorry,' he called over his shoulder. 'My fault. Oh hello. I didn't realize it was you.' The bus picked up speed. 'Sorry – see you next week.'

He disappeared inside. It was Philip Hether.

Waiting by herself at the request stop opposite for a different bus, Pearl had drawn in her breath as the cyclist was forced to swerve. As he rode by now she saw that it was Mr Drummond. But she could not tell who it was that nearly made him have an accident.

6

It was Pearl's day off. She lay in bed and planned, her eyes wandering over her surroundings as she thought out what she had to do. The morning light was dim, not because of drawn curtains or bad weather, but because the window looked straight on to a brick wall – the side of the house next door – which kept the room in perpetual gloaming. A thickly folded piece of newspaper jammed the wardrobe door shut. Twelve inches to her right, the other bed had not been slept in: Jackie had stayed the night at her boyfriend's again. They wanted to be together permanently and for this reason Pearl had a full day ahead. Jackie's Mick lived in a single bed-sit. Jackie had been in this flat longer than Pearl. It would be so convenient for Jackie and Mick. Pearl knew what was required – she should move out.

It was just as well really, thought Pearl. Now that she was going to study. She'd need to be able to work undisturbed sometimes. She could have done a straight swap with Mick, but the journey to the hospital would be too difficult. Thus the two-pronged attack on the day. Number one – find somewhere to live. Number two – start writing an essay for Mr Drummond. Flat agencies, local paper, postcard advertisements. Then the library.

Pearl got out of bed.

'I'm looking for a place to rent,' she said to the girl in the agency. 'A small flat or something.'

'A *pied à terre*,' said the girl.

'A bed-sit would do,' said Pearl.

'I don't think we have much in that line,' said the girl, flicking through a drawer of filing cards. 'Ah. What about this? Two double bedrooms, through reception, kitchen and bathroom, separate wc.'

'Too big,' said Pearl.

'I'm afraid that's going to be the problem. They tend to be moving back towards family-style accommodation round here, and not much of that is available for letting, either. It's becoming a very popular area for the purchasing public.'

'Mmm,' said Pearl.

'Wait a minute. This might be what you're looking for. Studio flat, large airy room, shower *en suite*, galley kitchen.'

'Oh yes,' said Pearl, brightening.

The girl handed over the card. Pearl saw the price.

'Would you like to view it?' said the girl.

'It's not quite what I wanted,' said Pearl. 'Is there anything else?'

'Not at the moment,' said the girl. 'But keep calling in. There's a great demand and any accommodation is snapped up very quickly.'

'Right,' said Pearl. 'Thank you.'

'In the lower price range?' echoed the young man. He rested his hands on the desk and looked Pearl up and down, initialled gilt cuff-links protruding from the sleeves of his suit. 'No, nothing suitable, I'm afraid.'

'Not round here, my love. They're all for sale. Property's rocketed over the past year or so. Have you thought of looking further out?'

Pearl unwrapped her hamburger and read the To Let columns in the local newspapers. They were not long. Around her, shoppers and office workers ate identical meals off coardboard trays. Toddlers stuffed their faces with chips. Schoolchildren arrived in small gangs and walked out again with their takeaway orders, hands to their own mouths and each other's.

They all have somewhere to live, thought Pearl. They all have homes. How do they do it? She felt a wave of loneliness, bringing with it memories from her life before, and a snatch of her recurring nightmare at that time: sticks, old bottles, dirty bits of paper and herself, being tossed around on scummy water.

She bit into the hamburger. Shut up. How had she done it since then? Answered an advert. So get on with it. Look in the papers: 'Cheerful flatlet in much-sought-after residential area'; Highly desirable bed-sit conversion'; 'Enchanting attic room with cooking facilities'.

Where's a telephone kiosk?

'Sorry, it's already gone.'

'It's gone.'

'It's gone.'

'4th girl required for flat share. Own room'; 'Male/female for large friendly flat. Non-smoker'; 'Happy mixed flat seeks new member'; 'Girl (mid 20s) for cosy ground-floor flat. Share room'.

No reply.

Number unobtainable.

No reply.

'Hello.'

'Hello,' said Pearl. I'm ringing up about the room. Has it gone?'

'No, not yet.'

'Can I come and see it?'

'You realize it's a shared room, don't you?'

'Yes, it said so.'

'If you don't mind that, come whenever's convenient.'

'Can I come now?'

'There's nobody but me in at the moment. Everyone else is at work till this evening. But come and have a look if you like.'

Pearl took down the address. 49 Windlesham Grove. Behind Loftus Square. Behind Parker's. She'd be round in about half an hour.

Pearl walked round the block of Parker's department store and through the square of three-storeyed houses. Many were dilapidated with peeling paint and splitting wood. There were net curtains hanging from wires which sagged at arm's height below the top of the window. Dustbins jostled at the foot of the steps and buttons of several bells were lined up by the door. Other houses gleamed with white paint. In these, un-netted windows revealed sanded floorboards, bookshelves and Victorian chairs. They had brass numberplates and burglar alarms on the outside wall. A few houses in the square were unoccupied, but the bare plaster and cement mixer in the downstairs room were a clear indication of their future. This was up-and-coming family-residence land.

Windlesham Grove had moved less rapidly in either direction. They were smaller houses, some with two doorbells, but most having the appearance of permanent homes. Their nets covered the lower half of the window, the wire discreetly hidden by the wooden frame. Some had boudoir curtains, raised in scallops over a display of brass ornaments. Number 49 was neat and unassuming. Pearl's heart lifted as she rang the bell. True, she would have preferred to have her own flat, or at least her own room, which was why she'd left this advertisement till last. But it was proving much more difficult than she had anticipated and it was obvious she was going to have to compromise. The sooner she got her accommodation sorted out, the sooner she could devote herself wholly to her plans.

Did that curtain flutter? Pearl stared at the window but there was no movement. She waited, then rang the bell again. Silence. She stepped back and scrutinized the house. An elderly passer-by dragging a wheeled shopping-bag watched her curiously. Did the curtain twitch slightly again? She rang the bell. Nothing. It was the right address, wasn't it? She pulled the newspaper out of her bag to check what she had jotted down. 49 Windlesham Grove. She looked up. The sloping plastic numbers on the door said '49'. She rang the bell yet again, then knocked hard. Had she got the wrong street? Perhaps this was Windlesham Avenue, or Place. She turned and walked to the end of the road. 'Windlesham Grove' said the sign on the wall. So what was wrong? She'd told the girl she was going round immediately. She'd arrived within the time she'd said. Why did nobody answer?

There was a telephone box in Loftus Square. Pearl went back and dialled the number as she had before. No reply. She pushed down the receiver rest and dialled again. No reply.

What could have happened? Pearl left the kiosk and turned into Parker's for a cup of tea. Had the curtain really twitched, and the person hidden behind it decided then and there, on sight, that she did not want Pearl? If Pearl had been white, would she now be sitting drinking tea in a flat which would have become her home? If she had been white, would she have belonged? Her stomach tightened and her throat swelled so that she could hardly swallow. 'Shut up', she said to herself again. 'Shut up. It might not be that. Something might have happened. And anyway, even if you were white, would you want to share a flat with the kind of people who refuse someone just because they're black?' She couldn't answer.

With the local agencies and newspapers done there wasn't much left. She was down to the trek round post offices and newsagents' windows. And she couldn't face it. Did dislike and resentment lurk in everybody's heart, even if they didn't admit it? Were they all prejudiced? Jackie hadn't been. That was certainly one thing you could say for her. Nor Sadie. It wasn't everybody, and she mustn't start seeing it where it might not be.

She got up sharply and paid for her tea. Forget it. Forget it and move on. Her studies were what mattered now. She went back out into the street and walked briskly in the direction of the reference library, repeating the essay title over and over to herself like a mantra to keep out the wayward thoughts.

The reference part of the library was away from the shops up a side street that led to the Common. Inside were rows of wide tables divided lengthwise by wooden partitions and separated into individual sections, each with its own green-shaded lamp. Hush enveloped the room. Pearl felt official and efficient again as she had in the first evening class when watching her handwriting make lecture notes. She found an empty place, unpacked her workbag and aranged her books, paper, biros. She sat down, wrote out the title and underlined it. A mound of thinning hair swayed opposite at the other side of the partition. It tipped to one side. A large square hand rose up and scratched it, then disappeared, leaving some wisps floating off the scalp. Pearl drew triangles underneath her title. She wrote, 'Psychology has not been a subject in it's own right for long.' She began to fill in the triangles, moving her penpoint into the very corners. 'And not everybody thinks now that people can be studied scientifically.' She drew squares growing out of the sides of the triangles. Was it really because she was black that the girl hadn't answered the door to her? She drew zigzags round the three unattached sides of the squares. Was Psychology really a science? Was the girl really prejudiced? Was Pearl unfairly jumping to conclusions? She dragged a sharp line down from the last zigzag and stood up. She would test it out.

The telephones were in the entrance foyer, the atmosphere thinner and sharper here like water in a pale-green glass jar. Pearl dialled the number, her breath coming out jerkily as she waited. The ringing stopped.

'Hello.'

Pearl took a breath. 'Hello,' she said. 'I'd arranged to see your flat this afternoon, but when I got there, nobody answered the door. I wondered if anything had happened?'

'Oh.' There was a pause. 'Just a minute.' There was a muffled conversation. A hand had been clamped over the mouthpiece. Pearl strained to hear, but it was a jumble of intonation. The hand was removed.

'Hello.'

'Hello,' said Pearl again.

'I'm afraid it's gone.'

'What?'

'The room. It's already been taken.'

'But it wasn't when I rang up before and I came straight

away. But nobody answered the door.'

'Yes, well, there was someone else interested and they took it.'

Pearl's breath came shorter. 'But why didn't anyone answer the door when I came? It had only just been arranged.'

'I expect she'd gone out. With the room definitely being let. You were unlucky. Sorry. Bye.'

The receiver clicked. The last part had been too quick for Pearl to break in. She stepped out into the foyer. Well, was it? How could she tell? Oh, so what? Forget it. She stared towards the reference room, got as far as the door and turned again. She went back to the telephone booths, dialled the number, held her nose.

'Hello' – guardedly.

'Oh, good evening,' said Pearl. 'I'm phoning in connection with your advertisement in the *News*, about sharing a room. Is it still available?'

There was a pause, as before.

'It's you again, isn't it?' said the voice.

'I beg your pardon?'

'Don't try it on. It's you again. I can tell.'

'I don't know what you mean,' said Pearl.

'Oh yes you do. I've already told you – it's gone. Right? Gone. Goodbye.' The line went dead.

Pearl put down her receiver, then picked it up and redialled. Engaged.

Pearl put the receiver down again, walked across the mosaic tiles of the watery foyer and back into the library. She went to her place and sat down. ' . . . not everybody thinks now that people can be studied scientifically,' she read. She drew another triangle and filled it in, then went on: 'But if scientific methods are not applied it is hard to see how knowledge can progress accurately.'

Pearl built tall walls along the path in her mind which was the route to her essay. She consulted her class notes. She stood up and took books from the shelves. She filled her pages with words and triangles, and when a bitter fearfulness tried to scale the walls, she raised their height and pushed herself down the path.

At ten to nine a bell rang. The library closed at nine, and

this was the signal. The few people remaining gathered together their work. Pearl had almost finished; not quite, but she knew what was going to be in the rest of it. Her first proper essay. She hadn't been sure she could manage it. Now she felt immensely satisfied and, somehow, purged. She dismantled the evening's walls as she left the library and no longer found a threat behind them. So some people were prejudiced. So what? they were just ignorant. 'I'll study them as scientific specimens,' she thought. 'They don't affect me.' There would be other flats, there must be. She'd be less intense about it next time. There was no real rush, after all.

She walked past the larger houses along the edge of the Common towards the bus stop. Early shift at work tomorrow. A takeaway when she got off the bus at the other end, ring the two numbers which hadn't replied, just in case. Then bed. If she came straight home when she finished at the hospital, she might be able to complete the essay. Provided Jackie wasn't around. Pearl wondered who would be at the flat that night. Jackie? Nobody? Both of them? She'd soon find out. Where was that bus?

'Been waiting long?' A teenage boy, chin thrust out, arms hanging loose, began to queue beside her.

'No. Not very long.'

'It will be long though, won't it?'

'Will it? Why?' Pearl wondered if there had been a lightning strike, an accident or a bomb scare. Just as she was looking forward to being home soon.

'Buses here don't go to Africa.'

Loud cackling broke out around her. She turned to find another boy standing in a similar pose on her left, and another, hands in pockets, just behind. Two more lounged against the wall, sniggering. All white.

'Don't get too close,' shouted one of these. 'You can smell her from her.'

'Why don't you wogs wash?' said another.

'There ain't no water in trees, stupid.'

Renewed cackles.

'Rude, ain't they?' said the boy behind Pearl, moving forward until he was pressing against her back. 'But I don't mind getting close to you.'

'Shove off,' said Pearl, stiff with fear.

'Shove off!' said the boy. 'That's not polite neither. You ought to be nicer to me.' He panted in her ear.

Pearl swung back with her bag. The boy caught the handle and pulled. Pearl held on. Why was there no one else around? Cars passed and passed unheedingly in the night.

Another boy pulled at her other arm and the bag was wrenched from her. The gang gathered round, laughing. The bag was held aloft in triumph, then tipped upside down. Pearl's possessions cascaded on to the pavement – her comb, her purse, the newspapers, her books and notes.

The boy put his foot over her purse. 'Ooh look,' he said, 'writing.'

'Didn't know monkeys could write.' Her arm was tugged hard and Pearl was yanked sideways.

'Must be a clever one.' She was dragged to the other side.

'Ooh. Let's have a look at a clever one.' A leering face poked into hers.

'I've warned you about the stink.'

'Pooh yeah. Get away!' He pushed her so that she banged into one of those holding her arms.

'Listen here – "Can-not act – actually prove sci-en-tific laws".'

'Oo-er, a black swot.'

'A stinking black swot.'

'Did you bump into me, woggy?'

Then they were round her, buffeting her, pulling her hair. The bag-snatcher shouted out disconnected phrases from her notes, trod on her books and threw her bag into the gutter. Pearl's mind went dark with panic. Her arms were jerked in their sockets; hands, breath and taunts were everywhere. She tried to kick out but missed and got a knee in her stomach. Sickening pain welled up from the blow. It rose over her body, her shoulders, her head. The noise came to her as from a distance; the pushing and jerking became like a rhythmic dance. She herself receded to a tiny place in the very top of her head. Everything was happening somewhere else, muffled and regular and almost comfortable now.

A sudden blaring brought her shooting back down into her body. A harsh noise, cutting the air above the shouts and jeers of the boys. Then the movement abruptly changed. It froze. Her arms were unweighted and there was a scurrying. She opened her eyes. Lights were coming at her. Lights and blaring noise. They were getting nearer and brighter and louder and bigger. They were going to engulf her. She was caught in the light, the noise, in the looming shape, and she could not escape.

Hard and cold beneath her. Gritty.

'You're safe. You're safe now.'

Long, long grey trousers. Something around her shoulders. Papers scattered on the ground.

'My notes,' said Pearl. 'Those are my notes.' She moved on to her knees, leaning forward to reach the papers. She almost keeled over.

'Careful, careful,' said the voice. 'Don't try to get up yet.'

'My notes,' said Pearl. 'My essay. I've nearly finished it.'

'I'll pick them up,' said the voice. 'Don't worry. I'll get them. Just sit there quietly while I do it.'

He was tall, thin and angular. Pearl watched him stooping to gather her papers. Grey trousers, grey hair. No jacket. She was wearing his jacket. There was his car, lights dimmed now, half on the kerb. He took her bag out of the gutter, shook it and dusted it with his hand. He was placing things back in her bag, cleaning off the dirt and straightening the bent leaves of the books. He was going through her writing by the street lamp, smoothing the pages and rearranging them. He cast around the area of pavement, then came over and squatted down in front of her.

'I think I've got everything,' he said. 'I can't see anything else. All the pages of your essay are there, and the notes follow on from each other.'

Deep-set eyes searched hers.

'Thank you,' said Pearl. 'My essay. I'd just been writing it. I'd nearly finished.'

'Well, it's all here,' he said. 'And you. Are you hurt?'

Pearl shook her head.

'What happened? Did they set on you?'

'Just like that,' said Pearl. She started to get up. The man took her arm and supported her as she swayed then steadied herself.

'I must go home,' said Pearl. 'Thank you. I'll be all right now. My bus home will be here soon.' He was looking at her sceptically. 'I will. Honest.'

I didn't find a purse,' said the man. 'Should there have been one?'

'Yes,' said Pearl. Of course. Her purse would have gone. Of course. There hadn't been very much in it, but how could she get home now? Could she ask this man to lend her the fare?

'I can give you some money,' he was saying. 'But perhaps we should do more. Perhaps we should call the police.'

Police. The word rang in her ears and expanded inside her head. The day's events were pushed against each other, clanking. The word swelled. The events were compressed tight, tight together. Flat – prejudice – study – prejudice – attack – prejudice – police. The word exploded. Tears poured down her cheeks.

'No,' she cried. 'No police.'

'Come,' said the man, his hand on her arm. 'I live here. Come inside and rest. We won't call the police.'

He was a stranger. How could she go to his house alone? But he had been so kind . . . her thoughts petered out. She closed her eyes, exhausted. The long-awaited bus arrived and, since no one signalled it to stop, gathered speed and rattled on. Pearl opened her eyes and watched its lighted interior being taken away.

'Come,' said the man again.

Drained and weak, Pearl went.

It was one of the detached houses, set back from the road, right there by the Common. The heavy front door opened on to a hall. Pearl mistily saw an antique table, huge blue vases, a large looking-glass. The grey man hesitated as though briefly uncertain, then turned into a room on the right.

'This way,' he said. He lit a lamp and whisked something off a chair.

'Now,' he said, 'sit down. I'll make you a hot drink.'

He went out, switching on another lamp as he left.

Pearl slipped off the jacket, sank into the chair and felt as though she were melting. She was getting thinner and thinner at the edges; they were becoming transparent, they were gradually disappearing. Going, going . . . She pulled in her limbs, shook her head and looked round.

It was a long spacious room with pale walls, a high ceiling and intricate plaster moulding. A Persian rug lay over the wide floorboards, yet the marble mantle was bare of ornaments and the furniture was swathed in dust sheets, the cover from her own chair now being piled on the shrouded sofa.

They must be about to decorate, Pearl thought, though there was no sign of its being required.

'Tea,' said the man, returning with a tray. 'I'm told that alcohol isn't the appropriate treatment for shock.' He balanced the tray on the arm of the sofa and sat down on the dust covers, pushing aside the one from Pearl's chair. 'And please forgive the state of the room,' he added. 'It isn't being used at the moment.'

'I don't mind,' said Pearl, then felt rude and stupid. What right would she have to mind, anyway? And here was a room which, even in this half-hidden state, was dignified and beautiful beyond anything she had ever known before. She sipped her tea and tried to sit neatly. The tea was peculiar, scented and very sweet.

'I only have China, I'm afraid,' he said. 'I hope you don't mind it. And I had to use honey because I have no sugar. To counteract the shock, you know.' He raised his eyebrows and smiled slightly.

Pearl noticed that he kept saying 'I'. Hadn't he a wife or family? She felt shy. This was another world. She did not know about it and must leave and return to her own.

'I'd better go,' she said and drank quickly. 'I really had better go now. If, please,' she blushed, 'you could lend me some money. I'll send it back to you after.'

'It will be my pleasure,' said the man. 'But will you be able to get in? Have you still got your keys?'

'Yes, they were in my pencil case,' said Pearl. 'Silly place normally, but it turned out best as it happened. That would be all I'd need, keys gone too. Final disaster of the day.'

'Were there others as well as this?'

'Well, sort of. I did my essay. That was nice. But I couldn't find anywhere to live. I've got to move out of my flat, you see, so I was looking for another. But it's not as easy as I thought.'

'Come and live here,' said the man quietly after a moment.

Pearl gaped. What did he mean? Live with him? Could he intend . . . ? Was he a . . . ? Just like that?

'Consider it.' He was continuing as if it were the most ordinary proposition. He could have been offering her a sandwich. 'Most of the house is unused. The room at the top has its own bathroom and it's easy enough to get something to cook on. Or use the kitchen downstairs. As you wish.'

'Oh, no, no,' said Pearl, wishing she hadn't mentioned it. What was she getting herself into? 'And I must go.'

'I'll take you in the car,' he said. 'You can't go on the bus now.'

'No, no,' said Pearl again. 'I'd rather not.' She reached for her bag and stood up.

The man looked at her and grimaced slightly. 'Of course not. I'm sorry. I didn't mean to scare you. I won't drive you home, but do let me call a cab for you. It's too late to go alone by bus and you've had such a frightening experience. I'll ring the taxi rank at the station. It won't take long.'

He went into the hall. Pearl hovered, her mind whirling, unable to fathom him.

'There's a cab on the way,' he said returning. 'Do think about the offer. You might be lonely – that's the main disadvantage. There's no one else here and I'm not much in evidence. But it's absurd to have an empty house when there are people who need somewhere to live.'

It was true. It was sensible. Yet there must be a catch. She didn't know him and he didn't know her. It couldn't be so clean and uncomplicated as he made it sound. Could it?

A taxi meter ticked outside. There was a knock at the door.

'Here's my card,' he said. 'Ring me if you decide to take up the offer.'

They were outside. As in a dream, Pearl told the driver her address. The man helped her in, spoke to the driver, gave him some money. The taxi drew away, out of the gateway and on to the road. In the light of the streetlamp Pearl put her hand in her cardigan pocket to get out the card. Clovis Fordingham, it said, the address and telephone number. She stared at the card for a moment or two. How strange it was. A man she had never met before, a middle-aged, educated man with a wealthy way of life, had suggested quite as a matter of fact, that she might go to live in his house. And somehow, finally, it seemed all right. Why? Why did it seem all right? Why did he do it? Why should she trust him? She sighed and her hand dropped back down. Too much for one day. She couldn't be thinking properly after what had happened. She'd bother about it tomorrow. She pushed the card into her other pocket. Something crackled as she did so. What was that? She pulled it out to look. In the amber glow of the sodium lighting she separated them from each other – two ten-pound notes.

7

'Hello there, Duncan. How's it going this week?'

Duncan put his tea on the canteen table and sat down opposite Philip. It was the evening class break again.

'Pretty well,' he said. 'I've written up a few pages – that's the real work for the moment. This lot here ticks over. The main problem is bringing the subject matter down to the level of the course – simplifying without distorting. I suppose that's a skill in itself. How about you?'

'It was nearly a good week. It could have been a very exciting week. I just missed Iago at the Stables.'

Duncan groped for a response. He didn't know much about racing.

'Bad luck,' he said. 'Did you lose a lot?'

'I was very disappointed. Not so much financially; the pay is an insult at its best. It's what it would have done for my career. Smashing part, Iago. I love all of them – Iago, Iachimo, Bosola. All manipulators. You see, you haven't got your audience's sympathy for the role so you have to get them to look within themselves to recognize the same elements there. That's additional manipulation. Very challenging, but very exciting.'

'I am sorry,' said Duncan, catching up. 'You think it would really have made such a difference?'

'No doubt about it. Telly's lovely. They look after you so well and the money's sheer joy. But if you want to be taken seriously in the business you must do your stint with Shakespeare.'

'Perhaps,' said Duncan, 'if they liked you so much that you nearly got it, they'll offer you a part in something else later on.'

'Actually,' said Philip, looking at Duncan from under his eyebrows, confiding, 'my agent didn't even tell me they were auditioning. I heard about it on the grapevine; after it was over, of course. I was absolutely livid.'

'Why hadn't he heard about the auditions himself? Isn't that what agents do?'

'Oh, he knew about the auditions. He just hadn't bothered to tell me.'

'I thought the reason actors had agents was to help them get work.'

'This one has a fixation about what he calls "readiness". That's another term for unyielding views about how to build a career, creeping gradually upwards from fourth spearbearer. I said, "Charles, old love, I've already *been* fourth spearbearer down at Pitstop, remember?" Actually, I played Freddy Eynsford Hill, but it amounts to the same. He, the old ham, gives me a monologue on solid groundings, technique, experience, shooting stars and God knows what. It's time for me to move on. I need a new agent.'

'Hello.' A female voice, so it couldn't be Arthur Pontiff yet again. Duncan looked up. It was the class secretary squeezing by with her cup and plate, handbag dangling over her arm, accompanied by the librarian and the black girl. Luckily the table was too small to accommodate them.

'We're just passing,' she reassured him disconcertingly, as if his face had shown his thought.

'Yes, rather crowded here, I'm afraid,' he said quickly and acknowledged the other two. He didn't like sitting with students, but he didn't want to appear too standoffish, either. 'Miss Lewis. Miss Thomas.'

'Formal names,' observed Philip as the women went away. 'How unusual.'

'Is it?' Any alternative had never occurred to Duncan. 'I do think it contributes to an atmosphere of objective academic enquiry.'

'Uh,' said Philip, looking beyond Duncan. 'It must be difficult to stay objective with a sultry beauty like that one to hand.'

Who was he talking about?

'That neckline – that scoop by the throat. How do you resist it?'

Duncan was mystified. What did he resist?

'Head high. A touch of hauteur. Sshlup – it makes your toes curl.' Philip rested his chin in his palm, narrowed his eyes, blew out his lower lip and smouldered across the canteen.

Duncan shifted uncomfortably. The mood had changed to one he couldn't latch on to, like a sober person in a party of inebriates. Philip's eyes came back to Duncan. He lifted his head, sat back and laughed.

'That wonderful black girl. What did you say her name was?'

'Miss Thomas.'

'And her first name? Do you know it?'

'Pearl, I think. I'm not sure.'

'Pearl Thomas.' Philip savoured it, then abruptly changed the tone again. 'Strange, isn't it, it's people's *surnames* that I never know.'

In another part of the canteen, round another table, the class secretary and librarian were gaping at the black girl.

'But you wouldn't, would you?' said Marion urgently.

Pearl didn't answer.

'I mean, you don't know anything about him. He might be trustworthy, but you just don't know do you?'

'Mmm,' said Pearl.

'I mean – a middle-aged man offering accommodation to a young woman he's never set eyes on before! And, if you'll pardon my mentioning it, a coloured girl too. What's in his mind? What's his intention? It could be anything!'

'I suppose so,' said Pearl. 'But it didn't seem like that somehow.'

'You can't tell. Just because he's got a big house. You don't even know that it *is* his house. He might be just looking after it while the owners are away. You said it was all dust sheets.'

'It was. But he's not like a caretaker or anything. I'm sure it's his.'

'You *can't* be sure, Pearl. Anyway, what if it is? Owning a house doesn't stop anything. What's he doing by himself in a big house like that? Where's his wife? *Is* he married? What does he do for a living?'

'I don't know,' said Pearl slowly.

'Well, there you are. You know nothing about him. A strange man comes out of a big house and asks her to move in . . . ! Honestly! What's wrong with you, Pearl? It's madness. Tell her, Annette.'

'It wasn't quite like that,' said Annette. 'He did rescue her from those louts.'

'I know he did. And if that was all, we could just be grateful to him and there's an end of it. But it's the rest. If he were a normal decent man he wouldn't make such an offer even if it was genuine because he'd know it would look so terrible. Just suggesting it makes him suspect. You wouldn't go, would you, Annette?'

'No, I can't say I would,' admitted Annette. 'It does sound dicey, Pearl.'

Pearl knew it did. She had already received a similar reaction when she had first told the story to Jackie and Mick back at her old flat.

'He's a dirty old man, Pearl,' Jackie had said. 'He's on the lookout for something tasty and exotic, that's what it is. You want to be careful.'

Now Pearl pushed her cup away from her and shrugged at Annette.

'I have gone though,' she said.

Annette raised her brows, then pulled her mouth down in a half-admiring salute.

'What?' cried Marion, aghast. 'What was that? What did she say?'

'Pearl . . . ?' Annette invited her to speak.

'I already have moved in,' said Pearl nonchalantly.

'Oh Pearl.' Marion sat straight upright, her hands on the edge of the table and doom on her face. Then she leaned foward across the table. 'Well . . . go on.'

'Go on what?'

'Go on and tell us about it. You just can't leave it like that. What happened? What's he like?'

'Nothing happened. I've moved, that's all. I live there now.'

'Yes, but under what conditions do you live there? How does he behave?'

'What Marion wants to know,' said Annette, 'is are you actually living *with* him or just in part of his house, separately. She wants to know specifically which rooms you share, if any, and particularly which items of furniture you might be found on or in together.'

'Annette!' rebuked Marion.

'Deny it then.'

'I'm just concerned. You wouldn't have done it, and Pearl herself agreed it was a peculiar offer. Nobody could argue against that.'

'I'll tell you,' said Pearl. 'I've been there a couple of days. He gave me some keys, showed me the rooms and left me to it. I haven't seen him since.'

'And no – you know – innuendo or funny business?'

'Nothing at all. Come on, we'd better go back. Mr Drummond's getting up.'

Pearl stood, aware that Marion was pulling flabberghasted faces at Annette. What did she care? The decision was her own. There had been nobody at the flat when she returned after the attack. Sick and shaken, she had gone to bed and relived her terror throughout the night, churning in violent dreams, which shot her up through consciousness till she was almost awake. Then an angular face appeared; a quiet deliberate voice spoke. The fear and confusion gradually subsided and she was let down into a tentative calm.

In the morning Pearl was stiff and aching, her stomach sore from the boy's knee. At work Sadie immediately noticed.

'What's up, my old love?' she said as they changed into their overalls in the locker room. 'Not feeling too well today? Have you done yourself a mischief?'

Pearl told her, missing out the final invitation.

'Blimey,' said Sadie, stock-still as she listened. 'Blimey Norah. Oh my God. Oh Pearl,' and she put her arms round Pearl and hugged her. Pearl flinched. Sadie drew back.

'What they done to you?' she demanded. 'They done nothing more than what you said, did they?'

Pearl shook her head.

'They hurt you, though,' said Sadie. 'Just stay here a minute,' and she left the locker room, coming back with the Ward Sister to check that there was nothing worse than soreness and bruising.

'What a gentleman!' said Sadie suddenly. 'When you think what might have happened if it wasn't for him. It don't bear imagining.'

The story spread rapidly among the old ladies. Wherever she went on the ward, Pearl's hand was patted and sympathy offered from those who were capable of understanding what had occurred. The patients from outside understood only too well, many themselves living in fear of robbery and attack.

'They should hang them,' said Ethel, pulling at her hair. 'They get away with anything nowadays. Prison don't put them off. They've got colour television, all that. They're laughing. They should bring back hanging. That'd show them.'

'I'd have their balls off,' said Rose, twisting her mop in the cleaning-bucket.

'Thank God for that gentleman,' said Sadie.

Pearl went home and rang Clovis's number. There was no reply. Next day she bought a card which said Thank You and posted it to his address. She took a long time to choose it, going from shop to shop until she found something suitable. She finally picked one that looked like an old picture, and then still had to think of what to write in it. Should she mention the money? Not specifically, she decided, and put: 'I am very gratefull for your kindness last Tuesday, Pearl Thomas.'

Jackie and Mick were at the flat again. Pearl retold her story and they made a great play of staying with her all weekend, although Pearl was on duty on Sunday. Mick met her off the bus from work and insisted she went with them to a film. Pearl thought she might ring Clovis first.

'You want to be careful of him,' said Jackie. 'I know it's a good job he was there last week, I don't mean that, but you don't want to take it no further if you ask me.'

So Pearl didn't really have the chance.

The following Tuesday Pearl went to Duncan's night class and handed in her essay, written out again. It was a reminder of what had occurred but also a personal emblem of her successful effort. She had managed to write a proper essay, and had completed it, despite everything. With the dirty, crumpled copy thrown away and the clean copy presented, Pearl pushed the previous week aside and did not mention it to anyone there.

The local newspaper came out the next day. This week it was a working day for Pearl, so she bought her copies on the way to the hospital and went into the locker room for a quick look at the To Let columns after the patients had been given their breakfast. Yes, there were one or two possibles, she supposed, unenthusiastically. She'd give them a ring at lunchtime, although her previous attempts had suggested that most of the people with places to share were out during the day.

'Girl (mid 20s) for cosy ground-floor flat. Share room.'

The print seemed darker than the others and the advertisement leapt out at her. It was the same one, wasn't it, the one she had answered the previous week? So she hadn't been wrong about them. Unless maybe it wasn't the same advertisement. They were all fairly similar to each other. How could she find out? She herself couldn't telephone, she might be recognized from before. Sadie would, but her voice was too old. Rose. Rose could do it. Pearl went to find her in the sluices with her bucket.

'Do us a favour, Rose.'

'What?' said Rose, suspiciously.

'See this advert for a room? Ring them up as if you was interested and find out what the address is.'

'Why don't you do it yourself?'

'I think it's one I rang up last week. I just want to see if it's the same.'

Rose shrugged and put her bucket down. 'Got the money?'

'You don't have to do it straight away. I don't want to get you into trouble. Do it at break.'

'I'll go now,' said Rose. 'I don't mind. She'll just think I'm in the kazi. I could do with a change anyway.'

Pearl gave her the money and went to help Sadie tidy up the

linen store, piles of draw sheets and nighties that opened all the way down the back.

Rose stuck her head round the door. '49 Windlesham Grove,' she announced. 'All right?'

'Yes,' said Pearl. 'Thanks for doing it.'

'Was it the same address?'

'Yes, that's it.'

'Shame,' said Rose, and returned to the sluices.

'What was that about?' asked Sadie.

Pearl explained.

'Someone might have accepted and then dropped out,' said Sadie doubtfully.

'Maybe,' said Pearl. 'I've other ideas about it.'

'So you're still looking for somewhere to live?'

'Yes,' said Pearl, 'but I think I've found it.'

She rang Clovis as soon as she got home. At the other end, the receiver was lifted.

'Hello,' said Pearl. 'This is Pearl Thomas. You rescued me from a gang of boys last week.'

'Of course,' said Clovis with no trace of surprise. 'How are you now?'

'Fine,' said Pearl. 'I want to say thank you very much for helping me last week.'

'Not at all,' said Clovis. 'I'm glad it was no worse. And thank you for your card.'

'I hope you liked it.'

'Very much.'

What should she say now? How did you invite yourself to stay in a strange man's house?

You stopped thinking and did it, that's what. Like she did when she got herself enrolled for the night class.

'You know you said you had a spare room in your house, well, I still haven't found anywhere to live and if you don't mind I would like to take the room after all if it's convenient.'

'Of course. How nice!' No hesitation. Would a dirty old man say that?

'You were just talking about the room, weren't you? Nothing else?'

'Well, it has an adjoining bathroom. And do use the kitchen, unless it's too far away for you. You could cook in the room; it's quite large. There's some equipment somewhere. I'll look it out.'

He was talking about rooms. He must be respectable.

'When would you like to move in?' he was saying.

'I'm off from hospital this Sunday.'

'You're a nurse, then?'

'Sort of. Well, an orderly actually. We get a weekday off, and either a Saturday or Sunday. I'm off this Sunday.'

'Sunday should present no problems.'

'And would afternoon be convenient?'

'I'll be here all afternoon.'

'Right, well, thanks.' She didn't know what else to say.

'I'll look forward to seeing you on Sunday.'

Pearl rang off and crested a wave of happiness. She was safe. She had somewhere to stay. She could live and study undisturbed on her own. She hadn't seen the room, but what did it matter? It must be reasonable in a house like that and if it wasn't too comfortable at first, she could gradually buy things of her own if she had enough money left after the rent. The rent! It had never been mentioned. Dumbo, Pearl. What if it was too much?'

She redialled.

'Mr Fordingham. It's Pearl Thomas again. I'm sorry to disturb you but I forgot to enquire about the rent.'

'Rent?'

'Yes, I mean, I've made the arrangements with you for moving in but I never found out how much rent you were asking.'

'But I'm not expecting any rent.'

Pearl's heart sank. So he was a dirty old man.

'What are you expecting then?'

'I think you've misunderstood the situation . . . '

'I think I have,' interrupted Pearl.

' . . . It's a large house, most of it unused. You need somewhere to live. The room is there just the same whether you are in it or not. I need no rent.'

Pearl's mind did yet another about-turn. 'You can't give a room to someone free.'

'It's hardly *giving* the room. More like a loan, isn't it, for as long as you need it.'

'I can't do that.'

'Can't you? What do you suggest then?'

'I pay rent properly.'

'You don't have to.'

'Yes I do.'

'You haven't seen the room, although I think you'll like it. And there's no social life. It's very quiet here.'

'I want quiet.'

'As you wish. Do whatever makes you feel comfortable.'

'Right,' said Pearl. 'Well, I'll be there on Sunday. With my rent.'

Pearl put the telephone down and laughed at herself. Moving into a room she hadn't seen belonging to a man she didn't know and ordering him to charge her! What was she about? Only fair to pay rent, though. She'd pay the sort of price being asked for a room advertised in the paper. Better buy a rent book from the post office and do it properly.

Jackie was horrified.

'You out of your mind or something? I've given you my opinion. He's a dirty old man. He must be. Tell her, Mick. Tell her not to be so stupid.'

This time, Mick was not to be drawn.

'She's an adult, you know. She can make up her own mind. He might be quite a reasonable geezer. How can I tell? She's the one who's seen him.'

'Go with her then on Sunday. See if he's OK.'

'No, no. I can't do that,' said Mick. 'You don't want me hanging around when you turn up there, do you Pearl?'

Pearl certainly didn't. She was relieved that Mick's enthusiasm for protecting her had waned as he realized how soon he could be living in the flat. She wanted to make the move by herself. The results of her risky decision lay on the opposite bank and she needed to swim the river alone, bearing the sole responsibility for her new future.

'But how are you going to get your stuff over there?' pursued Jackie. 'You'll need a hand with that at least.'

'There's not a lot, is there?' said Pearl. 'It won't be much more than a couple of cases. I'll have a taxi.'

When it came to the event, Jackie and Mick were held up at Mick's over some negotiations with his ex-landlady. Pearl heaved her cases into the taxi, shut the door of the flat and posted the keys back through the letterbox for Mick. While she'd been living there, how her view of life had changed. She had plans now. She was moving off in a different direction.

The taxi pulled away. Pearl knew the route from bus journeys. They passed the parades of small shops and launderettes with flats above them, like her own had been, stairs leading up from the street door alongside the plate-glass window. They passed the quieter rows of terraced houses, bristling with estate agents' signs. Then the streets ended, the sky opened up and ahead stretched the Common. Its grass an early winter green, its trees standing quietly with their last few sparse leaves, the expanse seemed to be lying back, breathing.

The road ran along the edge of the Common. Opposite, set back, were the big houses. For Pearl they had always been part of a separate, different world, one that she scarcely contemplated as she passed on the bus, except to sense its otherness and know she had nothing to connect her with it.

Yet now the taxi turned through a gateway, along the drive and stopped by the white front door. Pearl hurried to unload her cases and pay the driver immediately so that it would be done and over with before Clovis might come out. She didn't pause to scrutinize the outside of the house or link it with what she remembered, but knocked and waited, just aware of the door, the gravel and grass, the low wall and high shrubs at the boundary with the road. The door opened.

'Good afternoon,' said Clovis. 'Let me help you in with those.' He reached over to take Pearl's cases.

Yes, she would have recognized him from her memory. The height, the grey hair and eyes, the boniness. They went into the hall – the massive vases, the table, the mirror. Oh, how she had been feeling the last time she saw those.

'Would you like some tea?' asked Clovis.

Pearl felt suddenly awkward. Again the strangeness, the absurdity of what she was doing came over her.

'No,' she said quickly. Then, 'Thank you.'

However, the refusal was accepted as easily as everything

else and instead he showed her the house.

He showed her the kitchen and told her how to use everything in it, then he took her up three flights of stairs to her room at the top of the house. He showed a cupboard on the landing, full of sheets and towels. She handed him her rent book and rent. He gave her a set of keys, and left her.

That was all. She had hardly seen him since, except for a few brief meetings in the hall or on the stairs, when he asked about her wellbeing.

After so many dire warnings, it would almost have been an anti-climax, had it not been that the room was so perfect. It was light, high up, with two large windows overlooking the Common. Behind a rattan screen in the corner was a tiny electric oven and some shelves with pans, plates and cutlery. There was a table, soft chairs, bed, wardrobe, chest-of-drawers and even a small television. Next door was her bathroom. Pearl was in bliss. She unpacked her clothes, notes, library books, bits of food and arranged them. She watched the sun sink over the Common, the streaks of coloured light seeming to fill the room. She reclined in her own bath. She had biscuits and coffee watching television.

Next day at the hospital, she told Sadie that she was renting a room from her rescuer.

'Every cloud . . . ' said Sadie. 'A bit of luck that – saved by a gentleman that lets out to lodgers.'

Pearl rang Jackie to tell her that she hadn't been molested yet, but Jackie didn't seem so worked up about it as before. Happy enough with Mick there, Pearl supposed.

By Tuesday, her living in the house seemed a delightful normality. True, she was alone, but only to pursue her plans undisturbed. She wallowed in the comfortable peace. During the night class break in the canteen she began to tell Annette and Marion the whole story. It was Clovis, of course, who caught their imagination. All glory for coming to Pearl's aid; all damnation for offering her a room; then all curiosity as to what was going on.

Pearl's life was going on. She grinned at Annette as they went back to the classroom and Duncan's lecture continued. Did Mr Drummond seem to be looking in her direction rather more than usual? No, he couldn't be. But he seemed to. There again. Was it her neck? Was something wrong with it? She felt round it as she wrote her notes. It seemed quite normal. She glanced up and Mr Drummond looked away. After that he talked mainly to the other side of the room. It must have been a coincidence. Anyway, so what? She'd got her first essay back and it wasn't at all bad, with a lot of helpful comments written on it. She'd start another tomorrow.

8

Philip walked back into the gym and thought about himself during the second part of his class as he followed the rhythmic sequence. Dear God, but he needed a perk. Nothing, not a thing, since well before the summer, and now too short of cash even to go to a West End studio regularly. He'd thought 'Tinderbox' was going to set him up, but no way. It was back to minor rep, then to signing on and that was all except for the occasional repeats or voice-overs. A has-been without having been. Nothing since before the summer. Sweet Jesus! And not even telling him about the Stables. Was it going to be down to this now – once a week Stage Dance in a cruddy suburban evening institute class taught by some old stager Cochrane girl, Billy Cotton Band Show floozy, God knows who, with the leading lights of the local amateur dramatics. Was that what he was down to – training with the Proscenium Players?

And no woman. Melanie up at the Citizens, spreading herself around, no doubt, and he wasn't even managing that. He'd tried the only one in the dance class worth having a go at, but oh my, the guilt, the anguish: should she tell her fiancé; should she leave her fiancé; how could she do this to her fiancé; just when she and her fiancé had nearly saved up enough for a house deposit; oh she was so confused; what was Philip doing to her; she would leave it all for him.

Dear, dear, what a performance.

'My love,' Philip had said. 'It cannot be. We must keep it as a beautiful memory, shared between us.'

Then he'd wiped away her tears very sincerely and tenderly, but she'd started up again so Philip had got out of it. Last week at class he'd drooped his eyelids at her, blown her a secret kiss, sighed, and thenceforth ignored her. She'd tried to corner him during the break. 'No, no, my love,' he'd repeated, holding her away from him. 'A memory,' and made sure he'd sat with Duncan in the canteen. She hadn't returned after the break, nor had she come this week, so perhaps he'd succeeded in getting rid of her. All he needed at the moment was some woman being intense.

Nevertheless he could do with a woman. No work, no money and no woman was too much. The black girl in Duncan's class. Pearl. Now that might be worth a try. She had definite edges to her, a certain self-containment that should rule out any histrionics. And anyway, cross-cultural relationships always had a certain cachet. Perhaps a manoeuvre was in order. Perhaps that evening. It might produce a perk.

Usually the dancers were among the last to leave the building, after changing, showering and packing away damp towels. He would need to be ready earlier so as to lie in wait for Pearl and encounter her accidentally. In which case he had better leave the class now.

He slipped out of his line to the front where Zora was demonstrating to those assembled how eyes-teeth could add panache to their movements.

'Sorry darling, must fly,' he breathed urgently. 'Super class. See you next week. Bye.'

Zora waved over her shoulder and went on eliciting style.

In the basement changing-rooms, Philip showered, packed away his damp towel and arranged himself in the mirror. Then he climbed the stairs and, taking up a position near the main doors, read the school notice board while awaiting his opportunity.

There were approaching clattering and voices. Philip looked round. Groups were coming along the ground-floor corridors, their classes over, and disappearing out into the night. More clattering from the stairs as people began to descend from the upper storey. Philip watched, primed for action, but didn't recognize any of them. Unless . . . Those two women, the older smiling politely at the pink-faced, rather sawneylooking man, the younger a couple of steps in front – weren't they the two who usually sat with Pearl in the canteen? Then Duncan's class must be out, Pearl would soon be following. He went a little way down the corridor, stopped, and watched the stairs again. There. There she came. Talking to Duncan. Close behind them hovered another man, as if anxious not to miss any gap which might occur in the conversation.

Philip strolled casually in their direction, alert to their movements, adjusting his accordingly. He paused by the notice board and placed his eyes on the list of games fixtures as they drew near. What was she saying?

' . . . only since Sunday.'

'It's not very important anyway,' Duncan replied. 'The University will send out forms nearer to the examination time, and provided you've got your correct address on there, that's what matters.'

Philip turned from the notice board into them.

'Hello Philip.'

'Well, hello Duncan,' said Philip in a surprised voice. 'And hello there,' to Pearl. 'I was just seeing if there was any amusement to be found in these notices.'

'What notices?' said Duncan. 'Oh, those. I shouldn't imagine so.'

The anxious man pushed closer and cleared his throat.

Pearl edged sideways. 'I'll be off, then, Mr Drummond,' she said. 'I just thought I was supposed to tell you.'

'Oh yes,' said Duncan. 'We might as well have it accurately on the register too. Till next week then. How was Dance, Philip?'

'Fine,' said Philip. 'I think that gentleman would like a word.'

'Merely a quick thought, Mr Drummond.'

'Yes,' said Duncan heavily, turning his attention. 'Yes, Mr Pontiff?'

Philip sped forward and reached the door just as Pearl arrived there.

'After you,' he said, and he held it open for her. 'Bye Duncan.'

The door swung back again and Duncan was lost with Mr Pontiff.

Philip kept pace with Pearl, smiled winsomely at her and opened with, 'You're a Psychologist, aren't you?'

'Nothing like that,' said Pearl. 'Only studying. I go to Mr Drummond's class.'

'And are you enjoying it?'

'Yes. It's very interesting.'

'I imagined you would,' returned Philip sagely. 'Duncan certainly knows his stuff.'

Having crossed the yard, they were slowing down by the gate.

'Which way now?' asked Philip.

Pearl looked up and down the road. 'I can't decide whether to catch a bus or walk,' she said. 'It's easy walking distance, but I don't like doing it much now.'

'You can't be too careful these dark evenings,' agreed Philip. 'There's no bus in sight, so if you like, I'll stroll along with you. I'm not in a hurry.'

'No, I'll go by bus,' said Pearl. 'Thanks.'

'Where do you have to get to?'

Pearl told him.

'By the Common!' exclaimed Philip. 'Well, there's a coincidence! That's where I was intending to go anyway. I'm dropping in on some friends over in that direction. So there you are. The decision is made. Lead on, Macduff.'

'All right,' said Pearl, and they turned up the hill.

'Yes,' repeated Philip, steering the conversation back. 'Duncan certainly knows his stuff. I keep telling him that our professions are very similar.'

'Are you a Psychologist too, then?' asked Pearl.

'Me? No – an actor.'

'Actor?' She was impressed, Philip could tell.

'You might have seen my telly series recently. "Tinderbox".'

'Oh, "Tinderbox".' Definitely impressed. 'No, I'm afraid I didn't. But a lot of people at work were watching it. They thought it was very good.'

'It had its following,' said Philip modestly. 'Or so the fan mail would have us believe. Sacks of it. Lovely, lovely people writing from all over. Despite that, though, telly isn't satisfying.'

'Isn't it?'

'No, my love, it isn't. It helps millions of the ordinary public to get to know you; don't think I'm knocking that for a moment. Not at all. It has its place. But my heart lies in live theatre.'

'You mean, plays on the stage?'

'Plays on the stage. That's why I haven't done another telly series. They look after you well, but it hasn't got the magic of the hushed auditorium.'

'So did you go back to the theatre?'

'Yes, I did. To Fortinbras.'

'I'm afraid I don't know where that it.'

'No, lovey – a role, a character in a play. Shakespeare.'

'I'm afraid I don't know much about acting.'

'Not many people do, even those who think they do. They see the glamour, but they don't know what goes on behind it. The glamour's there, of course it is. We all like the letters, the notices, being recognized in the street and so on. What most people don't realize is the amount of dedication it takes. It's a hard life, and you've got to be committed.'

'I suppose so.'

'Take me, for example. After all that, I'm filling in time doing Stage Dance here. Only temporarily, of course, but I'll tell you why and you'll see what I mean. It's because I've just turned down a lovely part. Iago. Smashing offer, but not right for me at this moment. They were wild to have me, begged me to reconsider. Yet I had to refuse. It's a hard thing to do, Pearl. believe me. You want to help your friends – you want work too. But you've got to be true to your gut instincts. Betray them, and you're lost.' He looked at her appealingly. 'Does that sound silly to you?'

'No,' said Pearl slowly. 'I do think that sometimes you've got to follow your own feelings, even when everyone else is against them.'

'Thank you,' said Philip humbly. 'I thought you'd understand.' He reached for her hand and gave it a little squeeze. Pearl took it back instantly and moved slightly further apart. Too fast, Philip. Back off a bit.

They had walked up the hill, past the row of houses beside the school, and had turned right at the crossroads. An occasional launderette, off licence or late-night supermarket was lit up. The other small shops were long closed. Now they were in the side-road by the reference library.

'Why don't you tell me to shut up,' he said suddenly.

'What?'

'We talk too much, we actors. It's another characteristic we have in common with teachers. I suppose it's the way we make our living. Take no notice and tell me about yourself. That's bound to be much more interesting.'

'I don't think it is,' said Pearl, embarrassed.

'I'll bet. Go on – tell me.'

'I don't know what to say.'

'Then I'll ask you. What do you do for a living?'

'I work in a hospital. St Luke's. With old people, old ladies actually.'

'Pearl, now that is a proper job. I'm quite ashamed. Going on and on about a selfish business like acting, and there you are, doing something really worthwhile.'

'You were very interesting about acting. I enjoyed listening to it.'

'Did you? Did you really? That makes me glad. You're very kind. Though of course you must be kind, to be a social worker.'

'I'm not a social worker as such,' corrected Pearl. 'In fact, that's why I'm going to Mr Drummond's classes. I want to be a social worker, and that's one of the qualifications that can get you on to the training.'

'I didn't know you needed special qualifications for the training.'

'I haven't got any others. I mucked around at school too much.'

'A lot of the brightest people do.'

'I don't know about that. A lot of people who don't get very far do, that's for certain.'

They were walking along the Common, on the house-side of the road. Opposite lay the dark space of grass and the darker bulk of trees rising to the sky, their tops picked out by the moon. It couldn't be far now. He ought to get on with it.

'There's something that might appeal to you,' he said. 'Black Mamba Collective are doing a show about the problems which black people in this country face at different ages. You know, elderly black people, professionals, schoolkids – the lot.'

'Oh yes.'

'It's a show I'd like to see, and I think you would too. Shall I get us some tickets?'

She didn't reply immediately.

'It's just your area, Pearl, with your background, experience of old people and your future in social work.'

'And being black.'

'Naturally. If it's a hard life for actors, it's desperately hard for black actors. Even in the supposedly liberal theatre they're restricted by conventions. It's all stereotype casting in white plays, you know. And not even much of that, either.'

'I can imagine.'

'Well then, you can see why they start a company on their own. You ought to give them your support.'

'So when is it on?'

'I can find out exactly and let you know. When would be best for you?'

'Well,' said Pearl, 'any time I suppose. Except Tuesdays: I don't want to miss my class.'

'I'll get it set up then. How can I contact you? Shall I ring you?'

'I don't know. I'm not sure. Perhaps . . . '

Why was she dragging it?

'Don't you want me to? Is there someone who wouldn't like it?'

'No, no, it's all right.'

So there was competition at home, was there? Might be just as well. That always provided a cast-iron reason for a speedy stringless exit if required.

Pearl had changed the subject. 'Where do your friends live?'

'Grove End Road,' he said. 'It's one of those on the other side of the Common. Do you know it?'

'No. I don't know over there very well. I haven't lived here long enough to know the different roads yet. Only the ones the bus goes on.'

'You've moved very recently, have you?'

'Sunday actually.'

She stopped by a gateway.

'This is it.'

Philip had not realized that she had meant quite literally by the Common. He looked up at the tall early-Victorian façade, disconcerted. A light was showing in the hall, and another softly on the first floor behind a balcony and long windows, their curtains undrawn. He could see a lamp, pictures, books. And he had envisaged her in a dingy flat or bed-sit like his, down one of the side-roads.

'You don't own all that, do you?'

'No such luck. I just rent a room at the top of the house.'

'How did you manage to find such a magnificent place? When I'm looking for somewhere I only ever find variations of dirty cupboards. If I can find anything at all.'

'I know what you mean. It's really depressing looking at flats.'

'So how did you find this?'

'Through a friend.'

'Privileged friends you have.'

Pearl did not respond. She merely said, almost abruptly, 'Good night then. Thank you for coming with me,' and began to walk down the drive. Philip caught her arm.

'Just a minute, Pearl.'

She stopped and half-turned.

He let his hand stay. 'Your telephone number,' he said entreatingly. 'Please.'

Pearl hesitated, then opened her bag. Philip wondered what she was doing. She groped around in it for a minute or two, then without saying anything, moved back on to the pavement to the light of the streetlamp. There she searched in the bag again and finally took out a small piece of card.

Don't say this woman has printed visiting-cards, thought Philip. What style; but Pearl didn't pass it to him. She merely held it up to the light and read a telephone number from it.

Absorbed by the proceedings, Philip was caught unprepared. His hand leapt for a biro and any bit of paper which might be in his pocket. Yes, an old bus ticket would do. Pearl repeated the number and Philip wrote it down, with difficulty, holding the bus ticket against the standard of the sodium light.

'Thank you,' he said simply. 'I'll ring you just as soon as I find out the details.'

'All right,' said Pearl. 'Good night then,' and turned to go again.

Philip caught her hand and brushed it with his lips. 'Good . . . night,' he murmured, lifting his eyes to hers.

Pearl was looking somewhat uncertain of what to do. Philip held on to the moment. Then he gently replaced her hand with a small sigh. When he looked up he had the rather unnerving impression that he had just been subjected to scrutiny. He put his head on one side, smiled and shrugged self-deprecatingly.

'See you,' said Pearl.

'*Arrivederci*,' said Philip.

He went further along the road to give her time to enter the house. He had no friends living at the other side of the Common and would have to walk back all the way they had just come in order to catch his bus.

Afer an appropriate interval, he turned round and retraced his steps towards Pearl's house. He loitered for a time at the gateway, looking up at the building. The fanlight was still glowing; the long first-floor windows were still uncurtained; apart from these, the place was in darkness. Then suddenly, high up, a yellow rectangle flashed through the night. Pearl's room? wondered Philip. And only Pearl's room?

There was neither house name nor number on the stone gate post. Stealthily, Philip made his way down the drive to the front door, placing his feet flat so as not to crunch the gravel. The number was high on the door, visible by the light from the hall. Seventeen. Right. He returned quietly to the gateway and stood a moment longer before becoming aware that he was under suspicious observation from a man and a woman at the nearby bus stop. Leaving the house, he walked with composure back down the road, wishing them good night as he passed. Name, telephone number, address. So far so good.

Nevertheless, as he reached the evening institute again, now also in darkness, caught the bus and let himself into his scruffy bed-sit in a house of scruffy bed-sits, he had further events to steer. The Black Mamba Collective, as far as he knew, did not exist outside his own improvisation. It would be easy enough to surmount this difficulty merely by saying regretfully that all the tickets had been sold. But how could he ensure that Pearl would nevertheless go out, minus the lure of an ethnic evening? What could act as a replacement? And when should he tell her? Philip boiled water for coffee in a pan on the single gas ring and sat by the electric fire to mull over the situation: Pearl, Pearl's house, his own empty present. He considered possible variations without perturbation. It was much more interesting than me and my fiancé. Or than nothing at all.

9

Next day Philip decided that a suitable arrangement would be to ring Pearl up and say that according to the telephone conversation he had had with the Black Mamba box office, there were plenty of tickets available. Consequently, he suggested, Pearl should name a convenient time and place, and he would collect the tickets from the theatre before meeting her. When the day came, however, he would arrive looking upset, saying that he'd just come from the box office and there were no tickets left after all. Word had got round about how good the show was and there had been a sudden rush to see it. He had remonstrated with the box-office attendant but to no avail. It was a sell-out. He would offer to take Pearl elsewhere and because she was already prepared for an outing and because he was disconsolate about the Black Mamba, she could hardly refuse. Then they could go somewhere else, perhaps to one of the films he wanted to see. He would be rather diffident and slow down his action. Last night he had probably been pushing it. He might draw back somewhat and be more remote for a short while. Or maybe that would be a better tactic for later, when he was more sure of her interest. Either way, he would not ring her immediately.

He bought brown rice at the supermarket, did his washing in the launderette, went up to an exhibition at the Photographers' Gallery.

The following morning, Philip received a letter from his

mother in Leamington, asking why he hadn't written recently and when he was going to visit her. He put it on the mantelpiece. He telephoned his agent from the coin box in the hall. No go. He ate a doner kebab, read the newspaper. Telephoned a friend he'd made in 'Tinderbox'. Was told by a flatmate that the friend was rehearsing. Did a few press-ups. Ran round the streets. Sweet Jesus. This was getting unbearable. It had to be Pearl. He telephoned her number.

The bell rang for quite some time without being answered. That's right, thought Philip; all one with the dismal pattern of the day. He was about to put the receiver down when it clicked, the ringing stopped and a male voice stated the number.

Who was the man?

Philip asked if he might speak to Pearl.

'I'm so sorry, but she isn't here at the moment,' said the voice. 'Would you like me to take a message?'

Of course she wasn't there. She'd be at the hospital, wouldn't she? He'd forgotten the basics of normal working life. Was the man connected to Pearl? He'd better tread carefully.

'I'm Miss Thomas's evening institute lecturer,' he said. ('Ah yes,' said the man. 'How do you do.') 'I meant to give her some information about next week's class. Foolishly, it never occurred to me that she'd be at work.'

'As far as I know she is,' said the man. 'Shall I ask her to contact you this evening?'

'It might be easier if I rang again,' said Philip, a new plan forming. 'Between seminars. Could you tell me what time she gets home?'

'I don't accurately know her movements,' apologized the man. (That didn't sound as if he was too closely involved with Pearl's life.) 'I think at about six.'

Philip thanked him and rang off.

Six o'clock. So she must finish about five. St Luke's, she'd said. He could get there in time. Should he present it as a deliberate meeting on his part, or a pleasant coincidence? The first. He'd used coincidence enough already.

Philip reached St Luke's at about four-thirty after a convoluted journey. It was a large general hospital occupying a square of land with an entrance from each of its surrounding roads. Philip approached what he supposed was the main gate, the one which was given in the telephone directory as the hospital's address. From here, a drive led off towards the various separate hospital buildings. A blue-and-white signpost indicated the departments, none of which was guessably Pearl's.

Philip went to the porter's lodge and enquired the whereabouts of the geriatric section.

'Which ward are you wanting?'

Philip described the characteristics of Pearl's ward, such as he knew them.

'Sounds to me,' said the porter, 'like Rosemary or Chervil.'

'They're called after herbs?'

'Nah. Girls' names. Anyway, squire, you're on the wrong road. Geriatrics is the other side. Your best way is down this road, turn left and left again. You can cut straight through, but it's not so easy if you don't know the way.'

Philip shot down the road and round two corners. There was the entrance, and there was the bus stop, with a bus drawing up, and the queue climbing aboard, and oh no, Pearl getting on the bus. What should he do? Chase after her? His plan hadn't allowed for this. Would it fit into his intended image? Perhaps, for today. He ran. Too late. The bus pulled away. 'Pearl!' he lamented, arms outstretched in the road, to the onlookers' entertainment. 'Pearl!'

'Yes?'

Philip whipped round. Pearl was standing behind him on the pavement, hand on hip, looking bemused.

What line should he take? He'd decided to make this a deliberate meeting and to ensure that a relationship was developing but at the same time not to be intrusive. The first of these was now inevitable anyway but the rest would have to be handled carefully. Perhaps he'd be light-hearted. He stepped back on to the pavement and tapped his head.

'I could have sworn you'd just got on that bus.'

'No,' said Pearl.

'Bye, Pearl. See you tomorrow.'

'Oh yes. Sorry. Bye Sadie.'

Pearl had been with an older woman. Intent on Pearl, he

hadn't noticed her companion, who left with a curious smile at Philip. This diversion gave Philip time to have second thoughts about the flattering remark he had been going to make in connection with Pearl's not being on the bus after all. He rejected it and pulled himself back to general friendliness.

'I'm sorry, Pearl, I didn't see you were with somebody. I hope she doesn't mind. It was such a surprise that you were standing behind me when I'd thought you were on the bus!'

'We work on the same ward, so if we're finishing at the same time we usually walk down together, but only to here anyway.'

"What's the name of your ward?'

'Cheryl. Why?'

'Cheryl!' enunciated Philip, satisfied.

'The female wards have girls' names. Why?'

'Pearl, are you in a hurry?'

'A hurry? Why?'

'Because I've got to apologize to you and I don't want to stand here doing it. Will you come for a drink while I tell you?'

'Why have you got to apologize to me?'

'Come for a drink and I'll tell you.'

Pearl looked at him (those long lashes) then widened her eyes (oh-oh) and nodded agreement.

'Where to?' asked Philip.

'I don't honestly know. I only come here to work and then go home again. I never walk about outside the hospital.'

'We'll find somewhere,' said Philip confidently, which they did. Round the corner of the hospital area, among a row of shops opposite, was a purple-and-gold wine bar called Corkers. Inside was purple and empty with etched mirrors and mock-Victorian iron-legged tables. Pearl sat on the edge of a chair and loosened her coat.

'What would you like?' asked Philip.

'Oh, I don't mind. You choose.'

Philip had to make a nice judgement. With his tight finances he had to be careful not to invest more than would be needed to create a desired effect. For some women it had to be a bottle with a good label; for Pearl, he surmised, such outlay was not warranted – one of the advantages with a simple lady and one that made Pearl a particularly acceptable object at the present. And yet she did live in that posh house – and yet he really was short of the readies.

He put two glasses of house red on the table and sat down opposite her.

Yes, she was striking. It came from the way her head was carried high on that long scoop-throated neck; from the fluid way she moved, although not relaxed at the moment, still with an economy of gesture. From his previous observations he knew of the bronze skin tinged with pink in the cheeks and noted now in the lamplight the sheen as it stretched over the definition of bone structure. The purple of the wine bar seemed to wrap them into an intimacy. Pearl sipped her drink and ran her fingers along the stem of the glass, her other hand beneath the table.

'My apology,' said Philip mellifluously.

'I don't know what you're apologizing for.' She looked up from her glass and smiled at him. Those eyes again. Full chiselled lips. Voluptuous purple in the air. Philip breathed deeply. Hold back. It won't work if you don't move gradually.

He cleared his throat. 'Because,' he said, 'I've let you down. I didn't manage to get any tickets for Black Mamba.'

'Oh,' Pearl seemed surprised. 'That doesn't matter.'

Too easily. She said it too easily. Philip would have preferred her to sound considerably more disappointed.

'I did think the show would interest you,' he said. 'I'm sorry.'

'It doesn't matter,' repeated Pearl. Then: 'It was nice of you to think of it.'

Philip held on. 'Will you come to something else instead?'

'No, no. Don't bother yourself.'

'To prove I'm forgiven?'

'There isn't anything to forgive.'

'Please.'

'Honestly. I don't mind. Really.'

'I'll feel bad if you refuse.'

Pearl looked at him hard. He looked back, mock pleading on his face. Suddenly she laughed. Ah – he had her.

'No you won't,' she said, but lightly.

'I will.'

Pearl took a drink. 'All right,' she said.

Philip sat up with a contented sigh. He raised his glass towards her. 'To forgiveness,' he said.

Pearl laughed again. He was winning. He put down his glass, folded his arms on the table top and leaned closer. 'So what's it going to be this time?'

Pearl cocked her head on one side.

'I mean, where would you like to go?' He was ready with the suggestions for when she said she didn't mind. She was hesitating. Right. Now, which was his first choice of film?

'On Saturday,' she said and stopped.

'Yes, Saturday,' he agreed. 'Would you like to . . . '

But Pearl had been in mid-sentence. '. . . evening, there's a concert of early music. I'd like to go to that.'

He stared in amazement. What an extraordinary mixture she was. Perhaps he should have bought a good wine after all. On the other hand, he was doing quite well with the glass of house red,so why worry?

'If you'd be interested,' she was adding.

Philip hurriedly rearranged his face. 'Why yes,' he said. 'Tell me more about it.'

'I don't know any more. I can find out though.'

'I'll do that,' said Philip, 'and ring you. Let's hope there are tickets this time.'

'I hope so,' said Pearl. 'It sounded nice.' She drained her glass.'More wine?' asked Philip.

Pearl shook her head. 'I'll have to go,' she said.

'So soon?'

'I shouldn't have stayed as long as this.'

'Are you supposed to be somewhere else?'

'I'm supposed to be working.'

'Working? Back at the hospital? I thought you'd finished for today.'

'Not that kind of work.' Pearl looked a little self-conscious. 'Studying. I've got an essay to write.'

'And can't it wait?'

'Not really.'

'For Duncan?'

'Mmm.' She was gathering her belongings, buttoning her coat.

'You're taking the course very seriously, aren't you?'

Pearl stiffened. 'I have to,' she said abruptly, 'if I want to get anywhere.'

Defuse it. 'I know, my love,' soothed Philip. 'I'm not needling you. Far from it. I respect your commitment. I hope Duncan appreciates it.'

'I'm doing it for myself.'

This was heading in the wrong direction. Philip tried to return to intimacy. 'What better person?' he said supportively; but Pearl was ready to go.

They went out into the dark of the early evening and made their way back to the hospital bus stop. Pearl walked quickly, but it *was* cold. Still, he ought to make sure he hadn't messed things up.

'Pearl,' he said earnestly. 'I wasn't getting at you about your course. Believe me. Please don't think I was.'

Pearl's pace slowed a little.

'I've got to do it properly,' she said at last. 'It's taken a long time for me to reach this point, and I can't afford to lose my chances.'

'I do understand, my love. Truly I do.'

They were outside the hospital again. Pearl pushed her lips over her teeth in a conciliatory smile.

'Thanks for the wine.'

'Thank *you* for coming with me.' Should he kiss her? Better not, yet. 'I'll find out about the concert.'

'Right,' said Pearl and smiled again.

It was tempting. Perhaps he could . . .

'Oh!' cried Pearl. 'It's mine!'

While his attention was on Pearl, a bus had arrived. Almost empty, it scarcely stopped to pick up its sole passenger. As it drove away he read the route on the back. He could catch it too. It wouldn't take him quite home, but it was going in his general direction. Should he run? Should he? No. He ought not to end as well as begin today's meeting with Pearl watching him chasing a bus. What a pity; if he'd been a bit more aware he could have gone part of the way with her.

It wasn't just early music, Philip discovered when he looked the concert up in the listings magazine. It was early *church* music. Byrd's Mass in B minor and other obscurities. Performed in a church, too, in Highgate.

What an unlikely venue for him. Not the sort of show he would have expected to attract a Pearl, either. However, she had chosen it and so they would go. This time. On future occasions the choice would be his.

In the morning he rang up and had some tickets set aside. In the evening he rang Pearl to tell her the arrangement. The well-bred male voice answered the telephone again, but Pearl was in. She spoke very briefly and sounded distant. Philip hoped it was just her manner. Increasingly Pearl fitted in with his present requirements. Their races and contrasting colouring would make them an arresting couple, yet her physical appearance was balanced by her gaucherie to pose no threat to him. Her caring job produced a pleasing aura of concern for humanity around him too, and the importance of her future career should prevent too much of an entanglement, making it easy for him to get away when he wanted to. Perfect.

They met outside the church. Philip was gratified to see that Pearl had arrived before him. He kissed her temperately on the cheek, led her into the church, found places in the filling pews and had time to display his knowledge of how many feet higher they were than the spire of St Paul's Cathedral, before the conductor called to attention the choir arrayed in the chancel.

Early church music – what a choice. He shifted his position in the hard pew and glanced at Pearl to see how she was taking it. Immediately he looked again. Pearl was enrapt. She gazed ahead, eyes fixed, lips slightly apart. The pulse beat in her throat and she breathed quickly. As the voices soared to a peak and then dropped, her head rose and moved back on that long neck and then relaxed down again. Sweet Jesus, thought Philip, she's being transported. Sensuousness radiated from her, with almost sensible heat. And this from early church music! Philip settled lower in his seat and watched her rhythmic bosom out of the corner of his eye, sucking on the inside of his mouth. He'd better get home with her quickly, before the effect wore off.

There was no interval. At the end, people began to shuffle

and move out, talking in hushed voices. Pearl sat glowing in the subdued church light.

'Well?' asked Philip softly, trying to keep her mood intact.

Pearl jumped as if shocked. 'I was miles away,' She laughed it off. The heady atmosphere had gone. 'I really enjoyed that. Did you like it?'

'Loved it,' said Philip.

He helped her on with her coat, then took her arm and ushered her into the aisle. Pearl paused by the door to do up her buttons. Small groups of the audience lingered, exchanging greetings and praising the performance.

'Oh,' said Pearl suddenly.

Philip followed the line of her eyes to where a tall, grey, distinguished-looking man was on the point of leaving his conversation with another man who was carrying a music case. They separated and raised hands in farewell, the smaller man turning to a new conversation, the grey man moving towards the door. He stopped, registered a pleasant surprise, inclined his head, and approached. He had seen Pearl.

'Hello,' said Pearl.

'Hello,' said the man. It was the voice which answered the telephone at Pearl's. 'What a coincidence.'

'Yes,' said Pearl. She looked flushed.

The man smiled at Philip.

'Sorry,' said Pearl hurriedly 'This is a friend, Philip, and this is Mr Fordingham who owns the house.'

'Clovis, please,' he said. 'How do you do?'

They shook hands. Good God, thought Philip. A rich smoothy. What kind of set-up is Pearl in? She seemed embarrassed and anxious to get away.

'I'm driving back,' Clovis was saying. 'Can I give you a lift? Home, or anywhere in that direction?'

Pearl was about to refuse, Philip could see. But if they went with him, Philip could investigate the situation, save their fares, and with a bit of luck get into Pearl's room.

'That's awfully kind of you,' he said in his formal voice. 'Yes, we'd be most grateful.'

'Good,' said Clovis. 'Shall we . . . ?' He stood back for Pearl, who silently preceded them out.

The car was parked round the corner. Philip gracefully held

the rear door open for Pearl and himself got into the front passenger seat.

'Did you enjoy the performance?' asked Clovis as they drove away.

'Loved it,' said Philip. 'Marvellous, wasn't it Pearl?'

'Yes,' said Pearl.

'Did you?'

'I thought it was good,' said Clovis. 'I gather the conductor wasn't altogether satisfied with the phrasing, but he has exceptionally high standards. I didn't notice anything seriously amiss.'

'But then a specialist is more aware of the subleties of his own area,' said Philip, establishing his credentials. 'I know I'm more critical in my own field.'

'Naturally,' agreed Clovis, 'I should imagine that some aspects of Psychology require considerable evaluation.'

'I'm not a Psychologist,' exclaimed Philip. 'At least, not in the academic sense. We all are in life, aren't we?'

'I do beg your pardon,' said Clovis. 'I assumed you were a Psychology lecturer. I don't know why.'

Philip could think of at least two reasons, both discomforting, the second highly perturbing. Clovis might have connected Philip's voice with the first telephone conversation when Philip had claimed to be Pearl's evening-class teacher. Unfortunate, but not disastrous. Much worse – perhaps Pearl was being approached by Duncan, too. Would Pearl do that? Play them both on the quiet? Jesus. The deviousness of women. He grew hot at the possibility. But with Duncan? Surely not. Duncan's mind would never flex to that. He'd had Pearl in his class for four weeks and was oblivious to her. Wasn't he?

'An actor,' Clovis was saying, presumably in response to an explanation from Pearl. 'How interesting. Oh, but Pearl, in that case – did your Psychology lecturer manage to contact you last week?'

'Mr Drummond?' said Pearl, puzzled. 'No. Contact me in what way?'

'He telephoned while you were at work. On Thursday, I think. He wouldn't leave a message but said he'd ring you later.'

'That's funny,' said Pearl. 'How did he know where to ring?'

'He'll have the number in the register,' said Philip.

'I don't think so. I told him my change of address, but I don't think I've ever given him a telephone number.'

'Pehaps you did it so automatically that you can't remember. A driver can never remember changing gears, can you Clovis?'

'Not usually,' said Clovis.

'Maybe.' Pearl sounded unconvinced. 'Anyway, I wonder what it was about?'

'I think I know,' said Philip quickly. So Duncan wasn't at it too. Nasty moment, though. 'His wife has been ill and he thought he might have to cancel a class.'

'Oh dear,' said Pearl. 'She must have been very ill if he thought last Thursday that he wouldn't be able to take the class next Tuesday.'

'He's very conscientious, you know Pearl,' said Philip. 'He was worried about it already at the last class. He was wondering whether to tell you all there so that he wouldn't have to let people down without warning. I suggested that he waited at least until the weekend, but he must have decided to inform everyone earlier after all.'

'Well, I hope it was nothing serious,' said Pearl. 'He *is* conscientious. I would never have known from last week that he was worried. He went on as normal. I hope she's better.'

'Yes, yes. She's fine now,' said Philip. 'I was talking to him yesterday. Completely recovered. Only a stomach bug or something. Actually Pearl, I wouldn't mention it to him if I were you. I think he feels now that he overreacted rather.'

'I won't,' said Pearl. 'And I'm glad it's nothing more. He's a good teacher. Some of the class weren't too sure at first, but everybody thinks so now. He really tries to explain things, on your essays as well.'

'Yes,' said Philip, full of generosity to a Duncan who didn't threaten his intentions. 'I expect he's quite inspirational.'

'It's not that really,' said Pearl. 'It's because he's clear. And he takes a lot of trouble with his marking.'

'He's very conscientious,' repeated Philip.

'I gather you know Pearl's lecturer fairly well,' joined Clovis.

'Yes. Not his wife though,' Philip put that in speedily, just in case, then laid the trail back towards himself. 'Duncan and I get on very well together. I always say our professions have much in common.'

'Teaching and acting?'

'Psychology and acting. In both we're trying to understand people, to discover what makes them behave the way they do.'

'Ah yes.'

'For an actor it's essential to understand. You must know the reasons for your character's actions. You must know what he's thinking when he's not speaking. You must come to know every facet. It's very challenging. Ultimately, you know many things about him which don't directly come into the play. Perhaps what he had for breakfast, how many children, what he likes to read . . .'

'So the process goes further than discovering motives for the behaviour given within the text to creating other behaviours and characteristics which lie beyond it. A powerful position, to be creating people.'

'Powerful and very exciting. Often at the beginning you're quite frightened because there's so much you don't know. Then gradually you find small clues – you see a pair of shoes, for example, that seem to suit him, or the sort of place he might live in.'

'I take it you were trained in the Method school of acting?'

They were near the Common now. Soon the journey would be over and he would be in the house with Pearl. He hadn't been formally trained at all. In the sixth form he'd pinned his future on drama school and failed every audition. Unable to face the job in the bank that his parents were so relieved about, with day release to sit the professional exams, he'd hitched to London, joined a squat, got in on fringe theatre, read. That was how he'd started. He'd been in and out of work over the years. Very often out, but not noticeably at any great disadvantage to most of the people he came across from the prestigious drama academies.

'I think,' he said, 'that you develop your own techniques.'

'Yes indeed,' said Clovis. He turned the car through his gateway and halted on the gravel before the house.

They got out of the car, Pearl's movements seeming

reluctant. Clovis unlocked the front door and stood back for her to pass into the lighted hall. Philip followed close behind. He saw a large room, tall Chinese vases, the mellow wood of old floors and banisters, a reflection of himself in a framed mirror.

Clovis smiled gently.

'I'll leave you to continue your evening,' he said. 'Good night, Pearl. Good night, Philip. It was a most interesting conversation.'

'Thank you for the lift,' said Pearl.

'My pleasure.' Clovis disappeared into the back of the house.

Pearl remained where she was, by the hall table. She glanced up at Philip, but that was all.

'Pearl,' said Philip, 'I'd love some coffee. Please.'

Pearl nodded. 'I'm right at the top,' she said.

Philip followed her up the stairs.

10

Duncan put down the chalk and rubbed his hands together.

'So that's Attribution Theory,' he said. 'The ways in which we infer, or attribute, reasons, motives for someone's behaviour. We'll pause there for a moment, and take up those points again after the break.'

There was the usual yawning and stretching as people relaxed from concentration and remorseless notetaking, followed by the scraping, shuffling and hum of conversation as some members departed to the canteen and the non-migratory section took out their thermos flasks and biscuits.

Mr Pontiff's path converged with Duncan's at the classroom door.

'I'd be obliged by another of our little discussions, Mr Drummond, if you have a moment. I didn't wish to take up valuable teaching time, particularly since I'm aware that not everybody enjoys going into matters in the depth that I do. May I?'

This was not a request so much as a statement of intent. Duncan continued his route downstairs to the canteen, resigned to the inevitable.

'If I might hearken back to our very first meeting this term. You may remember that the content of your lecture made a great impression on me.'

'Yes, I remember,' said Duncan.

'You very kindly guided me to an institution where I might find the means of investigating the topic further.'

'The University Library.'

'Yes. I have subsequently spent many rewarding hours there. A veritable temple of human knowledge. That I must thank you for too.'

Duncan nodded.

'However, to the matter in hand. On reading more, I find that the approach you delineated so clearly in that first lecture is not indisputable. The objectivity of scientific interpretation, for example, seems to be a matter of some controversy. I was reminded of this by the content of your present lecture. Am I correct in thinking that there are those who would consider the scientific enterprise to be more akin to the sort of attribution process you have just been describing than to an unbiased quest?'

'You must never forget,' said Duncan, 'that in any area of academic interest there are bound to be different interpretations, contending theories. This is a sign of strength. Without dispute an issue is intellectually dead.'

He paused by the canteen door for a moment, peering at Mr Pontiff eagle-eyed for emphasis, then gesturing him in to join the queue first.

Mr Pontiff examined his small change. 'Controversy is certainly productive,' he agreed. 'When governed by the proper spirit of enquiry, of course, not when it degenerates into mere haranguing. Do you take tea or coffee, Mr Drummond? Allow me.'

'Tea,' said Duncan, 'thank you.'

'It was the evaluation of these various approaches that concerned me, rather than anxiety as to their existence. Which has the greater standing in academic circles?'

'Oh, the one I dealt with at the outset,' said Duncan immediately. 'Our time is limited. I select the most important aspects for my lectures.'

'Ah yes,' said Mr Pontiff. 'Two teas, please.'

He handed one to Duncan, who thanked him again and began to turn away.

'You won't join us? I do so relish our discussions.'

Duncan shook his head regretfully. 'I've a standing arrangement with an old friend here. You know how it is – the only regular chance we get of meeting is during the break.'

'Ah, the busy academic life.' Mr Pontiff sighed sympathetically over its demands. Duncan sighed too in concurrence and made for Philip's table.

'Well, congratulations. You've managed to avoid the limpet.' Philip grinned at Duncan and raised his cup in a mock toast.

'He's a very keen student,' explained Duncan with furrowed brow. 'He finds the lectures enthralling and always has more to discuss than there's time for in class. In fact, the students would prefer me to sit with them now, but they'd question me so much that it would be like continuing to teach, and I do need the break.'

He gazed wearily into his tea then up at Philip. Philip was looking across the room – and quickly back again.

'Sorry?' said Philip. 'What were you saying?'

'I was saying,' repeated Duncan, 'how I need to get away from the students in the break. They're very pleasant and do their best but it's quite draining to be giving yourself all the time.'

'I know,' said Philip. His eyes flitted again.

'Yes, it must be the same in the theatre. Anyway, it's probably better that they sit together and get properly acquainted with each other. Actually, Philip, how is it that you're always by yourself in the break? Don't the rest of the class come out?'

'They do. Unfortunately. I was stuck with them the first week. There's a gang of them now over there and some more at the other side. I avoid them like you avoid the limpet.'

'What's wrong with them?'

'Suburban amateurs, Duncan. I don't want to start pulling the old professional but between ourselves there is no self-obsessiveness, no vanity like that of the mediocre amateur. And when they discover that they have a professional in their midst, half of them become terribly condescending, don't you know, and offhand: "Of course, I could have made a career in theatre, but I decided against it, darling. It's so indulgent." Alternatively they assume you have Lew Grade's ear and constantly pursue you for advice and a way in. Both are very irksome. Why should I suffer that tediousness merely because we've chosen the same movement teacher? You know,

Duncan, apart from the basic civilities of general social exchange, I believe more and more in being selective in friendship. I prefer to spend my breaks with you.'

Duncan glowed with friendship. 'I must say that I always enjoy them too. When you're heavily involved in research and teaching, as I am, it does tend to become your entire world and its very refreshing to hear from the outside, from a rather glamorous outside too.'

Philip's eyes returned. 'And with the insecurities of my occupation – what's going to happen next, where I'll be or what I'll be doing, Heaven knows – it's reassuring to be in touch with a more regular way of life, not to mention the intellectual stimulation.'

They smiled at each other. Duncan felt impelled to further gestures of amity. 'We should get together more often,' he said. 'Why don't you come round for a meal some time? This weekend if you're free.'

'What a lovely idea,' approved Philip.

'Can you make it this weekend?'

'I should think I could squeeze it in. I'd certainly like to. There's just one problem. I'm expecting a friend. Would it be very presumptuous of me to bring her along too?'

'Not at all,' said Duncan, warming to his own hospitality. 'Anyone you like. It'll be nice for Roz to have another girl to talk to. Would Saturday or Sunday suit you best?'

'Ah,' Philip pulled up short. 'Now that I'm not sure about. I don't know if anything has been fixed already. Can I come back to you on it?'

'By all means,' said Duncan. 'It won't make any difference to us. Roz will be cooking anyway.'

'Lucky man.'

'Am I?'

'To have a Roz who'll be cooking anyway. If I were to invite you over to eat I'd have to be very strict about the date. There wouldn't be anything to eat unless I made a special effort. Your way is so much more relaxed, so much more natural, don't you think?'

Duncan thought. Philip's eyes wandered.

'I haven't considered it much.'

'You probably don't realize it, Duncan, because you're used

to it. People who haven't a family life appreciate its comforts more.'

'Does that include you?' Duncan was surprised. 'I always imagined you actor types valued your freedom above anything else. The ones you hear about don't have much of a domestic image attached to their private lives.'

'Media hype, Duncan. Actors of all people need that security. Imagine now, Duncan, never knowing when or where you're going to have work next, never being sure that you *are* going to have work. And if you are working you're with a group of people who've been brought together only temporarily. For a few weeks you can't get away from each other. It can be suffocating, but it grips you. The show welds you together. Then that suddenly disintegrates when the run ends, and you start up again with a different group. Very exciting, but so spasmodic. You need the permanence of a stable relationship to stop your life being a series of incidents.' Philip became oratorial. 'Anyway, what are the great themes of art? Aren't they human relationships, conflict, love and its effects? The cycle of the generations? Aren't they?'

'Yes,' said Duncan uncertainly.

'So what meaning can art, the theatre, have without life? Life is the primary experience.'

'Isn't acting your life? Isn't that what matters most to you, like my subject does to me?'

'But Duncan, those aren't the basics. They may enrich life, our own and other people's, we hope. But they're derivative, secondary. The vital primary experiences occur within the home.'

'Mmm.' Philip's thesis had dispossessed Duncan in one area, and rapidly promoted another. There wasn't time to follow it up. 'I'd better get back to derivative Psychology. We've taken too long a break.'

'My fault. I went over the top a bit there. Sorry, old mate.'

'A novel approach,' said Duncan. 'We can talk about it again at the weekend.'

'Will do,' said Philip. 'I'll give you a bell to say when. Oh – I'd better have your number.'

Duncan wrote it with his Parker ballpoint on Philip's copy of the *Stage*.

'See you later then.'

'Looking forward to it.'

Duncan walked briskly back to the classroom. He liked to keep the breaks to the stipulated length and didn't want to be late himself, even if he had to wait for the others to come up from the canteen. The non-migratory group were brushing away crumbs, shaking the drops from cups before reassembling their vacuum flasks.

'They's enjoying their break today,' chuckled the capacious black woman, Mrs Albert, packing her shopping-bag with thermos and plastic box.

Mr Patel folded his *Telegraph*. Duncan picked up his chalk and looked incipient. There were clattering and chattering along the corridor as the others arrived. On seeing Duncan ready by the board, they sped to their desks a little abashed.

'Our apologies,' said Mr Pontiff.

Duncan cleared his throat and spoke. The class secretary's pencil flew across her shorthand notebook. Mr O'Connell wrote laboriously in green felt tip. Mr Pontiff smiled, frowned, nodded, exclaimed 'Ah!' silently. Miss Thomas looked thoughtful. The clock jogged on.

'A suitable stopping-place,' announced Duncan finally. 'Thank you very much. And don't forget to keep up with your essays.'

Mr Pontiff was uncharacteristically the first to be ready to go. He slipped out to the front where Duncan was initialling the register, and bent low to his side.

'I won't keep you,' he said. 'I know you must be anxious to get back to your wife. But it was particularly appreciated that you were here this evening.'

'I'm glad you enjoyed it,' said Duncan.

'Good night,' said Mr Pontiff. 'I hope your wife remains well.'

'Yes thank you,' said Duncan. 'Good night.'

'How is your dear wife now, Mr Drummond?' Mr O'Connell's pink face examined him mournfully.

'She's very well, thank you,' replied Duncan, tidying papers. 'Oughtn't she to be?'

'Well, you never know. Sometimes things take a funny turn. I'm glad they haven't though. Good night to you.'

'Good night.'
'Good night Mr Drummond.'
'Night.'
'Bye.'
'See you next week.'
'I almost forgot to collect the register!' Mrs Hewitt the class secretary dashed back in. 'Though I expect you'd have kept it for the week, wouldn't you?' She put it carefully into her bag and smiled as she crossed to the door again. 'Good night Mr Drummond. I'm glad everything's all right at home.'

Duncan finished packing up. What an odd obsession with his domestic life there had been this evening, one way or another. Had he said something to the students which might have triggered it off? He couldn't remember doing so. Had they overheard Philip during the break? Surely not. They were sitting too far away. That had been unexpected in itself: Philip undermining the status of his own vocation as well as Duncan's in praise of the family. You would have thought that having no ties would be an advantage if prospects were as insecure as Philip constantly made out. Risks wouldn't matter so much if you weren't responsible for others. Still, raunchy old Philip envious of him and Roz! That was nice. It was cheering to discover that something you never particularly thought about was highly desirable to an experienced freewheeler like Philip.

He switched off the lights.

Actually, now he thought about it, it was quite pleasant to be going back to the flat and Roz. It was a solid seam of life that lay there reliably and so enabled him to apply his energy to work. Philip had a point.

Was that him there? Waiting at the bottom of the stairs? If so, he'd disappeared quickly. Probably not.

Duncan stepped out into the schoolyard. Brrr. A cold night. He hoped supper would be ready when he got home.

11

Pearl sat by the bed and fed evening mince to Tilly. The old lady ate with an alarming speed, machine-like. She sat motionless, propped up on pillows, unreacting until the spoon touched her lips. Then her jaw snapped open, her tongue shot forth and cradled the underside of the spoon while a mobile top lip scooped the food inside. Two twists of the chin, a jerky swallow, and Tilly was back to first position. By this means she would down a bowl of mince and mashed peas, followed by a bowl of rice pudding, her pace never slackening, her method never varying, her expression never registering any sensation.

The quality of the meat had already been well discussed in the ambulatory patients' dining-room, and its source speculated on, for an article in one of the daily newspapers had given rise to concern by describing how diseased and cancerous beef had found its way into a famous chain of butchers. The patients peered at the grey slices on their plates, prodding them suspiciously with their forks. A few ate only the vegetables. Ethel was not one of them.

'They've always got to make a scare about something, these papers,' she declared. 'It'll take more than that to put me off my dinners. I wouldn't give them the pleasure. You leaving that piece, Beatty? Shall I help you with it?'

Sadie had been asking Pearl how she was getting on with her night class and, while she spooned the mince into Tilly, Pearl reflected on the change in her life since she had started the course. New thoughts, new home, new types of people.

Mostly she felt exhilarated, at times overwhelmed, but she had the familiar routine of the ward to stabilize her, and her ambitions to pursue. She could already see how she had progressed. Rebelling in children's homes, truanting and disrupting lessons at school, a hair's breadth away from worse possibilities. From there to a council hostel supervised by social workers, and a job filling shelves, later at the check-out, in a supermarket. Boring, boring. There must be something better to do. A romantic vision of life-and-death dramas led her to apply to the hospital, where she was taken on to the geriatric ward, not what she'd intended by life and death. Nevertheless, after the initial shock of those empty bodies, her sense of lifespan adjusted and she pictured herself too in an inevitable old age. Looking back over her own life from that viewpoint, what would she feel she had really achieved? Would she have messed about all the time? Frittered herself away? She couldn't use her origins as an excuse for ever. Sadie had contributed to the effect too. By assuming that Pearl was sensible and reliable, Sadie had helped her to become so. The next step had been moving into Jackie's flat, independent and responsible for herself. Then as she got used to her steady life, and her precarious institutional childhood receded, Pearl needed something more again. She found it at the dentist in a magazine article about social workers and how demanding the job was. A lot of the kids were leading the social workers a right dance. Pearl ought to be up to those tricks, having once perpetrated so many of them herself.

She put down the empty mince bowl and started again with the rice pudding and Tilly's snapping jaw.

Pearl was on the second shift, doing the evening meal and bedtime. It wasn't a very late shift even so, for events in the ward's daily timetable took place earlier than their counterparts in the outside world. Nevertheless, second shift on Tuesdays would have prevented Pearl attending night class on alternate weeks had she not managed to fix a permanent swop with another orderly, each doing one second shift during a week of first shifts and so providing the other with a free evening. Being able to make such arrangements was the great advantage of working on a non-urgent ward. In the same way Pearl had taken her day off yesterday, Wednesday, instead of the rostered Monday to let Sadie stay longer at her daughter's.

Pearl had been in the library again. A couple of years ago, she would have thought anybody was crazy to spend a precious day off swotting. Jackie obviously thought that now. Yet it was so satisfying. She knew she was accomplishing something important and moving gradually nearer and nearer to a way of life that would suit her. She wasn't entirely at ease in her new situations yet. Although she loved her room at the top of the house, with its privacy and independence, it was still somebody else's house, a kind of house she was not used to, a house not intended for shared amenities. She felt awkward, for example, about using the telephone, going out to a call box to ring Jackie and sounding, she was sure, stiff and artificial when someone rang her, even though she was alone in the hall. She found that she hesitated to give people her telephone number. Mr Fordingham – Clovis – himself always behaved as if she had unquestioned right. He treated her with total acceptance. Actually, she couldn't make him out at all. What did he do? He spent a lot of time in that first-floor room. There was another telephone inside – a separate line. She'd heard it ring. Often music came out, occasionally voices, but he obviously lived alone, leaving most of the house unused. Of how he lived there was no indication.

Yet the house itself felt right, its atmosphere created by the sorts of things Pearl was becoming increasingly drawn towards and wanting to bring into her own life. That was how she had known about the early-music concert; from a leaflet lying on the hall table. It had intrigued her – its connection with the mysterious Clovis had also added to its appeal – but she could have no inkling of what the music would do to her. She had been taken over. She had soared and plunged and thrilled. She had sensed the existence of other, non-earthly forms of knowing. Her spine tingled at the memory. What would Jackie have thought about that? If Pearl said, 'I had a fantastic time last Saturday night, Jackie. I went to a performance of early religious music. In a church.' Jackie's idea of a good Saturday night was composed of very earthly forms of knowing. 'I went with a television actor.' That bit would get her going, though.

Pearl put down the pudding bowl and took up the cup of

tepid tea. She placed it at Tilly's mouth. Tip, back, swallow. Tip, back, swallow. Tip, back, swallow.

Philip was another one she wasn't sure what to make of. For different reasons. Why should he be interested in her? A television actor, and a proper serious theatre actor too. Shakespeare and such. He had discussed his ideas about acting with Mr Fordingham. She didn't know anything about those things. She didn't know anything about anything much just yet, although she was beginning to learn fast and one day she definitely would have the knowledge and experience to talk of her ideas and theories and interpretations and all those intellectual things. She would.

She wiped Tilly's mouth and settled her back on the pillows. Why didn't Philip have a girlfriend who was like that already? He was good-looking with it. So why was he bothering about her?

She wheeled the trolley round the beds and collected the used dishes.

She couldn't help but be flattered by Philip's attentions, although sometimes it all seemed too much. That was probably her own fault, through her inexperience of such people. She wasn't used to ways of talking and behaving like his and she didn't always know what to say or do in return.

Well – in some respects. It was clear enough what he wanted her to do on Saturday night after the music. She'd been so embarrassed standing there with him in Mr Fordingham's hall not knowing whether it would be all right to ask him to her room, wondering what Mr Fordingham was thinking, wondering what Philip was thinking, wondering if it would be mannerless to show him straight to the front door.

He'd taken her out of the quandary by inviting himself. When they got up to her room, he'd been most enthusiastic, wandering around, exclaiming, gazing out across the darkened Common while she made the coffee. As they drank it, he asked her about Clovis and how she came to be living there.

Her description of what had happened that night at the bus stop aroused him.

'That bus stop outside?' he said pointing to the window.

'He asked you just like that?'

'You'd never met him before?'

'Were you suspicious of his motives?'

'And he wasn't trying it on?'

'Weren't you scared?'

'My poor Pearl,' he said, putting his arms around her. 'Poor, poor Pearl.'

Of course, he had gone on from there except that, well, she hadn't really wanted to. She'd already been like that ages ago, not knowing people properly before, but doing it anyway if that was what happened; and eventually doing it got to be nothing. So one day she decided not to bother any more. It was just as easy not to and why should she? She belonged to herself. Then later on her life had begun to change.

That Saturday night was the nearest she'd been for years. Philip had spent a long time working up to it, very skilfully she had to admit, and it seemed ungrateful not to after all that effort and getting the tickets for the music and everything. It felt nice too, of course, but then he suddenly started whispering in her ear, 'Pearl, Pearl. My Pearl. You belong to me. My own Pearl.'

Nobody was going to start taking her over like that. She belonged to herself. She might go permanent shares with someone eventually; she would have lent herself out even that night. But she wasn't going to be claimed.

She didn't get angry so much as lose interest in the proceedings. She waited for a brief lull to disentangle herself. And Philip – well, very peculiar. He didn't get angry either, though he had a case for it. After he'd sorted himself out he went respectful, going on about how unusual it was nowadays: she must forgive him for his assumptions.

Apparently he'd put a completely different meaning to her behaviour.

'As chaste as unsunn'd snow,' he murmured, kissing her hand.

She could hardly tell him in detail how inaccurate he was, especially since that was over long ago, and it might be a bit insulting to him. Instead she began to explain about belonging to herself. He interpreted this as if she was trying to defend her behaviour and wanted her to know that it wasn't necessary.

'To thine own self be true,' he said. 'Everybody has to live their own truth, Pearl. I respect you for maintaining the truth of your unique selfhood.'

By that time he'd missed his last bus. It was a long walk, he said. He would go if that was what she wanted. If he could stay the night, though, he would sleep on the floor, in the bath, wherever she decided.

Pearl didn't want him to stay. She loved lying in bed at night, feeling the room surrounding her and the quiet of the Common opposite. Some nights she had been able to see the moon through the window and would leave the curtains undrawn. Yet it would be mean to refuse him.

They made his bed on the floor. Their preparations for the night were very discreet.

'Good night, my love,' he said and kissed her gently on the forehead before they climbed into their respective sleeping arrangements. In the morning, he'd left the house early with Pearl when she went to work. Actually, he'd been very nice. Pearl wondered if she would come to regret her image of protected virginity.

'Penny for them,' called one of the livelier old ladies from her bed as Pearl pushed the trolley out of the ward to the kitchen. Sadie helped her unload it into the food lift.

'I've got the dayroom settled,' she said, 'in front of the TV. I should think we could have a bit of a sit-down after this.'

They joined the patients in the day room.

'You look thoughtful today, Pearl,' said Beatty.

'She is thoughtful,' said Sadie. 'She's got her studies to think about.'

'You don't want to overdo it, Pearl,' said Ethel. 'Here, sit down. Take your weight off. You work hard enough with us lot.'

'It's true,' said Beatty. 'She's a jewel.'

'Course she's a jewel,' said Sadie. 'She's a Pearl.'

'Cor blimey. Hear that, girls? "She's a jewel," says Beatty. "Course she is," says Sadie. "She's a Pearl."'

'You've got to be quick to work here,' said Sadie.

At night class on Tuesday, Philip had been sitting in the canteen as usual when Pearl's group had entered for their break. He beckoned her over to his table and pulled comically sad faces when she shook her head and sat with her classmates.

She couldn't suddenly leave them now and go off with Philip. Anyway, Mr Drummond always sat there. He did again. They were soon deep in discussion. Pearl could see them out of the corner of her eye. She could also see that Philip was looking across at her. She jumped her glance away.

When Mr Drummond stood up to go, so did the Psychology group. So did Philip. He made a detour to catch her arm as she left, and breathe, 'Meet me. Afterwards.'

Pearl nodded and caught up with the others in the corridor.

'Aha. In with the in-crowd,' said Annette. 'Pearl knows Mr Drummond's handsome pal.'

'Only slightly.'

'He fancies you, though, doesn't he? How about that, Marion? Romance is in the air.'

'I think it's very nice,' said Marion. 'I always like it when a special friendship develops on these courses. It often does, you know.'

'Oh yes,' agreed Mr O'Connell. 'Life's rich tapestry. We get it all at night class, to be sure.'

'Actually,' deflected Pearl, 'we almost didn't have a class tonight. Mr Drummond's wife has been ill. He began ringing round us to cancel it.'

'Really?' said Mr Pontiff. 'I received no call from him.'

'Nor me,' said Marion, 'and I'm the secretary.'

'You might have been out,' said Pearl. 'I was. I only got a message. Then she got better quickly so that would be why he didn't ring again.'

'Still, it must have been bad if he felt he had to cancel the class,' said Marion. 'I wonder what it was.'

'Stomach bug, I think,' said Pearl, but Marion was already scuttling into the classroom where Mr Drummond was waiting by the blackboard. They had dawdled too long.

Pearl had known that she would see Philip tonight. But her insides had lurched unexpectedly in the canteen and her eyes were pulled constantly in his direction. That wasn't what she was coming to class for. She was being distracted. And what about meeting him afterwards? He would come in for coffee. Then what? Should she maintain her image? In any case, it was late already. If he missed his bus and stayed again, even like before, he'd be there in the morning. And tomorrow was her day off. She was going to start another essay. He had nothing particular to hurry to, she was sure. Would her essay get written?

She was doodling on her file paper instead of making notes. That was Philip distracting her. Now. Concentrate on what Mr Drummond was saying. That was what she was there for. The other could wait and see.

At the end of the class, Philip was not ready by the door. Nor was he in the entrance hall downstairs, nor outside the building. Right. Priorities, Pearl. She walked across the yard with Annette and caught the bus straight home.

It was still strange at that bus stop by the Common with its associations – flat, Clovis Fordingham, Philip, home. It looked as if Mr Fordingham was out, although he always left the hall light on – was it out of consideration for her? – and she felt secure in her room even when completely alone in the house.

As she started up the stairs, the telephone rang. Philip? So quickly? What if it was an important message for Mr Fordingham? That would probably come in on the other line. Philip? What would she say to him? Better not to disturb her essay day. She left it to ring and carried on up the stairs.

Philip rang on the Wednesday night, but he didn't mention Tuesday. Hadn't he waited for her after class? When he'd gone out of his way to ask her? She felt slightly hurt. Wasn't he really interested after all?

When was her day off this weekend? asked Philip. Sunday? Oh good. He was going to friends for lunch. Could she come too? She could? Wonderful! Where should he meet her?

'Evening all!' An ambulance man stuck his head round the dayroom door. 'Look at that, Sid. Cushy number for some, isn't it? Lolling around watching telly. Some of us have to work for our wages.'

'They work hard enough,' said Ethel.

'Not like us. They don't know the meaning of it. Do you Sadie, my old love?'

'I know the meaning of cheeky,' said Sadie, along with Pearl helping stiff arms into coat sleeves. 'Ready ladies? Your chauffeur awaits your pleasure.'

'He should be so lucky,' said Ethel, shuffling out.

'Now who's cheeky?' cried Sid.

The out-patients were taken off home. Each night at this time the room seemed to Pearl suddenly empty and quiet despite the laughter from the television, the live-in patients shrunken and forlorn.

Sadie looked at her. 'Come on,' she said. 'We'd better do the drinks. Beatty's right, you aren't half thoughtful today. You sickening for something?'

'I hope not,' said Pearl.

12

She'd peeled the potatoes, done the vegetables. The meat was in the oven, the batter resting, pie and cream in the fridge. Soup in the pan. What else? The last-minute rush of gravy and dishing up. That couldn't be done in advance. Set the table for a traditional Sunday lunch.

At least she'd discovered in time which meal they were coming to. Duncan hadn't mentioned it at all until Thursday evening, and then didn't give any specific details.

'You must have some idea, Duncan,' she'd said.

'It'll be Saturday or Sunday some time. Don't worry about it.'

'I'm not worried. It would just be easier to organize if I knew.'

'There's nothing to organize.'

'Isn't there?'

'Relax, Roz. He'll ring up and say when they're coming.'

Which he had, on the Friday morning while Roz was at school. Duncan had forgotten to tell her until Saturday morning when she'd come back from shopping. Next time round she'd be a man. Mustn't be too hard on him, though. His mind was always filled with his work. And it didn't actually make much difference. She'd bought enough food for two big meals, so she'd be covered whatever happened.

'Can I do anything to help?' came from behind the newspaper in the other part of the room.

'I think everything's done for the moment, thanks,' said

Roz, running her eye over the table. 'I'll go and get changed now. What shall I wear?'

'Don't make such an event out of it Roz.' Duncan put down the papers. 'Take it in your stride. Philip likes a natural, homely atmosphere. That's what he's missing out on.'

'Yes, but I don't want to be all floury and greasy.' Roz went into the bathroom and began to wash.

The bathroom door opened.

'Is it a roast?'

'Yes.'

'Is that all?'

'Well, there's the vegetables and Yorkshire pudding. Then we're having soup to start with, and apple pie for afterwards. There's cheese too, if anybody wants it. Won't it be enough?'

'It'll be enough. But couldn't you have done something a bit more unusual?'

'What do you mean?' Roz turned to Duncan, her face covered with soap.

'He is an actor, you know. She probably is too. He's been around a lot. A roast is rather an ordinary meal to give them.'

'You keep saying he likes a natural, homely atmosphere. You said he felt the lack of ordinary family life. You said I had to be relaxed and normal.'

'You could still have cooked something less run-of-the-mill; couldn't you have done a foreign dish or something?'

'You don't like foreign food!'

'We never have it.'

'We never have it because you don't like it.' Roz turned back to the wash basin.

'I used not to. That was a long time ago, Roz. I probably would now. Tastes change.'

'Well, it's too late to do anything about it today, Duncan. I'm sorry. If you'd told me this before, I could have cooked something completely different. Now it's too late.'

Roz stuck her head over the basin and rinsed her face. The bathroom door opened and closed sharply. Duncan had gone out. Roz reached for a towel and sighed. How was she supposed to know what Duncan would prefer it he didn't say? Especially when it was contrary to what she might reasonably expect. She wasn't clairvoyant. Honestly. Men. Never satisfied. Her mother was right. 'Do your best and never expect any appreciation,' she'd advised her newly engaged daughter. 'They only notice something when they don't like it. You have to humour them. That's the secret of a successful marriage.'

Roz was quite willing to humour Duncan over this Philip person. It was so unlike Duncan to invite anyone home. He always said they stopped him working, or thinking, or relaxing. When she used to have her friends round, from school or the year she'd done badminton, he'd always spread out more books and papers and kept looking resentfully at them as they talked. It was impossible to counteract such an un-welcome so she met them elsewhere, if at all.

And now this sudden concern over Philip, the food, the atmosphere, the constant reminder to relax, which was difficult to do when trying to carry out the other requirements. Roz felt both intrigued and apprehensive as she changed her clothes in the bedroom. What had she to wear that would have satisfied the demands of a non-run-of-the-mill meal in combination with a natural ordinariness of proceedings? Nothing; that was the short answer. She'd just have to wear the dress that she would have worn as a matter of course had it been a less confusing occasion. In any case, she carried her natural ordinariness of appearance with her, regardlesss of clothes. She peered at herself in the mirror. Shoulder-length mousey hair, light-brown eyes, unremarkable features: a run-of-the-mill face. She'd got used to it.

She went back into the living-area where Duncan appeared to be rearranging the objects which were scattered over the bureau. The various sections of the Sunday newspaper were dropped on the floor, some inside-out, their pages slipping. Roz began to straighten and fold them and place them in a neat pile on the coffee table.

'Roz,' groaned Duncan. 'Leave them alone, can't you?'

The bell rang. Duncan leapt. 'I'll go.' He shot off.

Roz walked round the furniture. Feet trod the lino on the stairs outside. The flat door was opened. 'Straight ahead,' called Duncan's voice. Feet plodded down the short passage, past the bedroom and bathroom on left and right, to the kitchen door. It pushed open hesitantly.

'Hello,' said Roz. 'Do come in.'

'Hello,' said the young woman.

She looked rather put-out, thought Roz. That wasn't very actressy, was it? Her manner wasn't actressy either, although she was undoubtedly handsome with those large dark eyes, the bronze complexion and her hair drawn back from an oval face. Her clothes were quite conventional too, the sort of style that Roz might herself wear. Roz, who had expected to feel immediately diminished, felt immediately more at ease.

Slightly behind was, presumably, Philip, and right behind him, Duncan. Who also looked disconcerted. How odd. What could be the cause? Had Duncan not expected Philip's girlfriend to be black? Had she observed his reaction and been hurt by it? But Duncan was remarkable for how little he registered about even obvious physical characteristics. He neither noticed nor cared usually. Why should he now?

They were clustered in the kitchen and Duncan was making introductions. Pearl and Roz smiled at each other. And Philip . . . So taken up had she been with the curious aspects of the situation that she had scarcely attended to Philip. Yet how could she have overlooked him? Golden smile, even teeth, fair hair, blue eyes. A charming manner. What an attractive couple he and Pearl made.

'This is Roz.'

'The illustrious Roz,' he pronounced. 'I've heard a lot about you, Roz.'

Had he really? From Duncan? She didn't think he ever talked about her.

'Quite some lady.'

So her mother was wrong. You did get appreciated occasionally, even if you heard about it only second-hand. She glanced fondly at Duncan, taller than Philip, so darkly intense in comparison, then back.

'I've heard a lot about you too.'

That didn't surprise him in the same way, of course not. He was someone who would always be talked about, she imagined.

'Let's move round,' said Duncan, gesturing to the other part of the room. 'It's more comfortable.'

'Shall I take your outdoor things?' said Roz.

Pearl removed her coat. Philip unwound his long scarf and gave Roz his jacket. She took them away into the bedroom. When she returned Duncan was pouring wine, and Philip was opening a second bottle and talking about the contents of a third. Pearl was sitting forward on the sofa. Roz joined her. She hoped Duncan had not inadvertently hurt Pearl. What could she say to make her feel better? Roz never felt confident about small talk. She'd try though.

She smiled at Pearl. Pearl smiled back. Pearl sipped her wine.

You asked people about their work. They would always talk about that.

'What are you working on at the moment?' she enquired.

Pearl looked nonplussed. 'Sorry. I'm not sure what you mean,' she said.

'Oh sorry. I'm probably not using the correct terms. I meant are you in a play?'

'Oh.' Pearl's face cleared. 'No. I don't do that.'

'You don't do plays?'

'No. Not me.' She laughed as if amused by the suggestion.

She didn't do plays. So what did she do? She couldn't be, could she, something like a stripper? Could she? Would Philip have brought a stripper to lunch? Perhaps she was being narrow-minded.

'I'm the actor, for my sins,' smiled Philip.

'Yes, I know. I thought Pearl was too.'

'Miss Thomas is in my night class, stated Duncan peremptorily.

So that was it, Roz thought. Duncan hadn't realized there was anything between Philip and Pearl. Naturally, he'd be surprised to see her today. And she'd be embarrassed by his surprise. Why hadn't Philip told Duncan it was Pearl he was bringing? Perhaps he assumed Duncan knew. Perhaps it would have been obvious to anyone but Duncan. He didn't bother about such things.

'That's nice,' said Roz. 'How are you getting on?'

'Well, I think I'm improving.' Pearl looked modestly into her wine glass. 'It's very interesting. I didn't know anything about it before. Your husband is very good at explaining. Are you a psychologist too?'

'Me? No. I teach juniors.'

'So you teach everything.'

'Just about.'

'Do you like that?'

'Oh yes. I'm not clever enough to be a specialist like Duncan. Even if I were brainier, I'd prefer the variety.'

Pearl shook her head disbelievingly. 'You must be clever to be a teacher. You can't do it without qualifications. That's why I'm going to night classes.'

'To be a teacher?'

'A social worker. If I prove I can cope with this course I'm more likely to be accepted for training. When you're older they're sometimes less strict about having a lot of exam passes. Because of your experience.'

'Have you got that sort of experience?'

'You could say so. And I work with geriatrics during the day, in a hospital – St Luke's.'

'Isn't that very depressing?'

'It was when I started. Terrible. You get used to it.' Pearl described to Roz how she had reacted at first and how she felt now. They gradually settled back into the sofa as they talked.

Philip seemed to want to listen to them too.

'Roz,' Duncan broke in eventually when she was about to tell Pearl what the children at school were like. 'Roz, are we going to get any food?'

Roz jumped up.

'Can I help?' offered Pearl.

'It's nearly ready,' said Roz. 'It only needs a light under the vegetables, and the bits to finish off. Come and talk to me, if you like.'

The meal was a great success, despite Duncan's qualms. Roz couldn't have asked for more appreciative eaters. Wrong again, Mother.

'This is marvellous, Roz,' said Philip. 'A proper Sunday lunch. Do you know, I'm so pleased that there's this renewed interest in traditional British food. For years, every time you went out to eat, the cook felt obliged to produce some esoteric foreign dish, as if anything else wasn't to be contemplated. There were some super treats of course, but our own food heritage was sadly neglected. I'm all for this revival. Bless you.'

'It's the sort of thing you don't make when you're by yourself,' said Pearl. 'And a roast dinner cooked in an institution never tastes the same, does it? This is lovely.'

'Absolutely delicious,' from Philip again.

Even Duncan. 'Very nice, love.'

Well, that was an epoch-making comment. What a rewarding occasion it was turning out to be.

They finished eating and Roz suggested that they went back to their sofa and armchairs while she made some coffee. The men moved through.

'While you make the coffee, I'll wash up,' said Pearl.

'No, no, Pearl. I'll do it later.'

'No. It's not fair to leave you with it.'

'I don't mind. I didn't expect anyone else to do it.'

'I'll start now,' said Pearl. 'I can get some of it done at least.'

She began to take the pans out of the sink.

'Come on, Duncan,' said Philip from round the corner. 'We can't leave it for the girls.'

'Sit down, sit down,' said Duncan.

'We can't sit down while they're washing up.'

'Yes we can. Why not? There isn't enough room in the kitchen. We'd only be in the way.'

'Witness,' called Philip, 'my loves, that I did try.'

'I don't expect anyone to do it,' repeated Roz. 'That's you too, Pearl. Really.'

Pearl shook her head.

'Aren't women marvellous,' said Philip. 'They're so capable. You're marvellous, girls, did you know that? Don't you agree, Duncan?'

'Oh yes.'

'It always amazes me how much they're able to juggle simultaneously. Completely different aspects of life.'

'Yes?'

'Take our two there. Working all day, running households, caring for others, attending night classes, cooking for friends. Done without batting an eyelid. They take themselves for granted. I think it's quite awesome.'

'Oh yes.'

Roz put on the kettle. Pearl squirted washing-up liquid

into the sink and turned on the taps.

'There was a woman I knew on a show a year or two ago. Freelance designer. Three kids. On her own – her old man had left her. Must have been having a bad time financially. And yet, you know, you could drop in any time day or night, and she'd give you a drink or a meal, or sit and listen to you sounding off about the traumas of the show. Marvellous. How do they do it?'

'I suppose theatre life must be different anyway. Less structured than most other occupations.'

'An illusion, Duncan. It's very disciplined. The less structure there appears to be, the more discipline is involved, especially self-discipline. No, I think it's that women are closer to, what shall I say, the essences of life.'

Roz set out cups and saucers. Pearl stacked the wet dishes in the drainer.

'How do you mean?'

'I mean, what it ultimately boils down to without the frippery. I mean the nitty-gritty events of life on which everything else is based – food, shelter, birth, death, relationships.'

'What you were talking about on Tuesday.'

'I did go on, didn't I? I'm going on again too.'

'We said then that we'd talk about it further today.'

'As long as I'm not boring you . . . '

Roz started to dry the dishes. Pearl scrubbed the meat tin.

'I should leave it to soak,' said Roz, in a low voice so as not to disturb the conversation.

' . . . No. I think that being in touch with those rhythms of life for so long gives women the edge over men when they do enter the public arena. It enables them to have a holistic view of a situation. We men tend to see only the public, more superficial aspects, whereas women automatically see it in relation to that essence I was talking about. That's why we have underestimated women for so long, keeping them out of the sphere of influence of public events, but placating those awesome abilities by a sort of religious reverence. It's a conspiracy of male fear.'

'Oh,' said Duncan.

'Aren't you awed by all that's involved in womanhood?'

Roz waited for Duncan's reply. This wasn't the sort of topic Duncan usually gave a moment's thought to, she was sure.

'What is involved in womanhood?'

'All the things I've just been talking about.'

'Well, you know, I leave that sort of stuff to Roz.'

Roz carried the coffee in on a tray.

'You're very pro-woman,' she said, handing a cup to Philip.

'I am indeed. In the struggle for equality I'm right there – you bet.'

'I've poured yours Pearl,' called Roz, 'so leave the dishes now. And thanks very much.'

Pearl came round from the kitchen end and took up her former position on the sofa.

'How's the research progressing, Duncan?' asked Philip. 'What exactly is your line of enquiry?'

'Cognitive styles.'

'Meaning?'

'Different people have different ways of solving problems. You can classify them as various styles. Some are probably aspects of personality.'

'It sounds fascinating.'

'People don't realize the amount of sheer hard grind that goes into fascinating research.'

'Exactly what I was saying earlier about underlying discipline.'

'It certainly takes a lot of discipline to keep up the initial impetus in research. Particularly when you're contantly fragmented by other considerations – marking, teaching and so on.'

Duncan sighed.

'Tell me more about your plans,' said Roz quietly to Pearl.

'About becoming a social worker? There's not much more to add. They'll sometimes accept you for training without the normal school qualifications if they think you're suitable. One way to show you're suitable is to do some sort of course first to prove you can cope with lectures and essays and so on. That's why I'm doing Mr Drummond's class. Also the more practical experience you've had the more chance there is of being accepted, say working with old people or in a handicapped club.'

'Even ordinary children?'

'I should think so. A lot of women do it after raising their own children. That counts. I'm banking on the geriatrics.'

'You could come into school with me one day,' suggested Roz. 'More than once if you like. You could help with some groups and it would be an extra to put on your form.'

'Could I? Would I be allowed?'

'I don't see why not. I'd have to ask the headmistress beforehand but she's not likely to refuse when she knows the reason. Shall I ask her?

'Please,' said Pearl. 'That would be really good. Thanks.'

'Will you be able to take the time?'

'No problem. We have to work one day each weekend so we get one weekday free instead. I can always swop days so I could come whenever you want.'

'I'll ask tomorrow then.'

' . . . males, females, introverts, extraverts, various IQ bands,' intoned Duncan.

'More coffee?' asked Roz of Pearl.

'Actually Roz, we'd better be on our way,' replied Philip. 'You need some Sunday to yourselves, especially you, Roz, with all that cooking.'

'It was nothing; don't rush off,' said Roz, but Philip was moving rapidly. Coats were fetched, thanks repeated, Pearl's telephone number given, goodbyes returned.

Duncan and Roz went down to the front door to see them out.

13

After they'd left, Duncan dropped into the sofa and picked up the newspaper again. It seemed to have gone well, much better than he would have imagined under the circumstances, much better than he'd thought when he opened the door and saw Miss Thomas standing there.

Philip might have spelled it out to him. Certainly there had been that business about her neck the other week but it was a big step from ogling a girl to turning up with her, particularly when the girl was his student. Philip should have prepared him.

It took a real mental bend for someone who was firmly fitted into life as your student suddenly to become an intimate of your friend. It completely disordered an established perspective. Readjusting in two minutes between the doorstep and the kitchen was most arduous.

Her name, for example. 'Miss Thomas' she was in class, as Philip well knew. You couldn't use that to a girl your friend brought to lunch. But the name 'Pearl' wasn't part of Duncan's relationship with her by any means, a relationship which maintained distance. Yet if he got used to calling her Pearl over lunch, how could he distance her again in class? He'd solved the problem by avoiding using any name. In fact, if he thought about it, he hadn't talked to her directly a great deal. Roz and she had been nattering away. Most of his own conversation had been discussion with Philip.

Surprisingly similar, he and Philip, in their approach to

their work. Quite a serious-minded fellow, although you'd never have guessed so at first. Even then, not too proud to show his respect for the academic; envying Duncan's marriage and homelife too. Duncan had managed to keep that favoured image going, he was sure. A roast was just the thing after all.

Apparently tradition was fashionable. Roz couldn't have known that. She was hardly one of the *beau monde*.

On the whole, a pleasing afternoon. Nevertheless, he preferred it in retrospect rather than in actuality. He liked a quiet house with his time his own.

He leaned back into the sofa. Another glance through the newspapers and then he'd go on with his work.

'Roz, any chance of a drink of tea?'

Roz had taken to Pearl. To decide what you wanted from life and then deliberately set out to achieve it – Roz admired that. She had no doubt that Pearl would eventually get what she wanted. There was a quietly purposeful air about her even when she did something mundane, like the washing up. Roz had noticed it occasionally in a pupil. There were children who didn't push themselves forward nor strive to influence others, although often they did become models for their classmates. They rarely made a fuss, just got on with the matter in hand. They were self-contained, methodical, unflashy. Roz gained the same impression from Pearl, despite her good looks.

Duncan had that sense of direction too. Of course, he hadn't had to start again from scratch in the way Pearl was doing, but he'd always known what he wanted next; moving from office worker to teacher to university to research. It must be nice to have that clarity of purpose.

'Roz, any chance of a drink of tea?'

'As soon as I've washed up these cups.'

She'd never had any sense of purpose beyond coping with the immediate state of affairs. She'd drifted through school, usually doing reasonably well, never doing very well; being fairly popular in a wishy-washy way but never being chosen for any important role. She'd specialized in the subjects for which she'd received her best exam grades. In the sixth form the girls were divided into the university group and the teachers' college group. She was put into the latter and so unquestioningly applied for college. Her father was proud she'd got so far. Her mother said teaching was a good job for a woman. It gave you some experience of children before you left to have your own.

Drift, drift. Into the first school to accept her. Where she'd met Duncan and had lived the vicarious fulfilment of his plans. Where she'd been ever since.

'Tea,' she announced to the newspaper.

'Right,' said Duncan.

Roz sat down. 'It went quite well, didn't it?' she said.

Duncan lowered the paper. 'Surely you're not worrying about it, even now?'

'Just thinking about it. I like Pearl.'

'Good.' Duncan reached for his tea.

'You weren't expecting Philip's girlfriend to be her, were you?'

'It's up to Philip who he has as a girlfriend,' said Duncan shortly.

'Yes, but you didn't expect it to be Pearl, did you?'

'I was surprised, that was all. He never said who it was.'

'Perhaps he thought you knew.'

'Perhaps. It's hardly important.'

Roz took a drink. 'I'm going to arrange for her to come into school one day.'

'Are you? What on earth for?'

'She wants to be a social worker, you know.'

'So?'

'She's more likely to be accepted on to a course if she's got varied experience of working with people. She works with the elderly now, and some experience with children too might help.'

'Elderly! More like the living dead.'

'It did sound depressing. She doesn't seem to mind though. Philip's a charmer, isn't he?'

'He's rather more than a charmer, Roz. We frequently have a serious discussion, and he can come up with some stimulating thoughts. Well – you heard what he had to say today about women. Quite a new line.'

'I'm not sure about that,' said Roz.

'What do you mean? Of all topics you girls must have found that interesting.'

'I mean what he said wasn't new. They weren't his own ideas, although obviously he said them in his own way.'

'I've never heard them before.'

'It's not the sort of thing you're usually interested in. You've probably always skipped anything to do with it.'

'Are you saying that you already knew the points he was making?'

'Well, yes. More or less.'

'You've kept this very quiet, Roz. Why don't you use the ideas in discussions then?'

'We do sometimes.'

'We? Who's we?'

'At work.'

'You mean you and your colleagues sit around at school having serious discussions! I don't remember many when I was there.'

'It's not all the time. Caroline Harris usually starts this one up.'

'Who's Caroline Harris?'

'Oh Duncan,' reproachfully.

'How do I know who's there now?'

'She's one of the teachers. She's very involved in the women's movement.'

'The women's movement! Well, she has Philip's support.'

'I don't think she'd agree with everything that Philip said.'

'Aha. Dissent. Where do you stand on the matter?'

'You know me. I'm just interested in what people have to say in general. I'm not very good at taking sides. There are a lot of different views. Like most topics, I suppose.'

'I must say, Roz, I hadn't realized you were so in touch with the cognoscenti.'

'I'm not, am I?'

'Oh, I don't know. This hidden knowledge on feminism, not to mention what it's fashionable to eat nowadays.'

'Stop it, you're tickling me.'

'Clever girl, our Roz, on the sly.'

'I know you've always thought that.'

'Hey, but Roz, the meal was nice you know. It really was. Well done.'

Roz warmed with pleasure. Wrong yet again, Mum.

Duncan went back behind the newspaper.

Pearl wondered if Mr Drummond hadn't known either. From the questions Roz had asked at first, it was obvious that she at least had expected an actress. So probably Mr Drummond had as well. How embarrassing it had been, and for Mr Drummond to, if he'd thought she was going to be someone else. He couldn't have been as bothered as she was. It was different for a teacher. Nevertheless, she could tell he was having the same problem over names. 'Mr Drummond.' 'Miss Thomas.' How could you turn that all at once into 'Duncan', 'Pearl'? They'd taken the same way out, she'd noticed, avoiding naming each other. Philip teased her about it afterwards. It's only a name, he'd said. But there was more to it than that. Maybe not for him. He'd immediately used the name 'Clovis' when they were coming back from the music, while she always dithered between that and 'Mr Fordingham' even in her thoughts, despite Mr Fordingham himself – Clovis – asking her to use his first name.

Why hadn't Philip told her who his friend was?

Because, he said, you wouldn't have wanted to go.

Very probably.

Roz had been nice. Treated her just like any friend, so it was easy to think of her as Roz. Pearl had been filled with apprehension going up the stairs of that flat, wondering how Mrs Drummond would react to her husband's uninvited student. She needn't have worried. Actually the flat wasn't much to sing about. Only one step up from where Pearl used to live. No. Be fair. Better than that. It was a converted house in a quieter area. But they were very cramped, especially with all those books and papers lying around. You'd have expected Mr Drummond to want more space. Roz too.

Pearl wondered if Roz really would arrange for her to visit the school. It would certainly be an addition to her application form if she could put that she'd worked with, say, slow readers. Roz didn't seem to be the sort who would make an offer and not mean it.

The visit had turned out quite well despite Pearl's

predicament. Also she couldn't help but feel reassured by the fact that Philip had taken her, as a guest, to Mr Drummond's, the lecturer, his friend. He hadn't been ashamed of her low educational attainment nor her lack of social knowledge. Maybe she wasn't so very out of place in such settings as she'd thought.

Philip seemed perfectly happy about the visit. After leaving the Drummonds they'd gone for tea in the café of a local fringe theatre that Philip knew about. In a converted church. She was becoming quite an attender. They walked to the house across the Common where they stopped to watch the bonfire being built for the Guy Fawkes display that week. He told her how he and a friend had been caught trying to make fireworks in the chemistry lab at school and had been hauled out on to the platform in Assembly to make an example of them. He said it merely made them into heroes. She told him about their Bonfire Nights in the Children's Home, how it was the girls' job to distract the wardens so that the boys' jumping-over-the-bonfire dare could take place. How she was the only girl who used to do it.

Then he knew she'd been brought up in Homes and asked her about it. Very delicately, she thought. They went indoors and upstairs and Philip asked her what had happened to the other children in the Homes. She didn't know. When you were moved around, you stopped trying to keep in touch. Actually you soon stopped yourself getting too close to anyone. It wasn't worth the upset when you were separated, and you usually were, one way or another.

That seemed to affect him, although she hadn't said it for that reason. It had distressed her a long time ago, then it just became a fact. Philip said life owed her some compensation. He seemed to imply that he could be part of it. This time he wasn't proprietorial.

When they'd been walking down the drive to the house, they'd looked up at the long lighted window to see Clovis sitting there. Philip had raised his arm, but Clovis remained as he was. Philip said, 'He looks a bit eerie stuck up there in the dark, gazing out.'

'He often sits like that,' said Pearl.

'What's he doing?'

'I don't know,' said Pearl. 'He's a strange man. But very kind. I owe a lot to him.'

At her side now, Philip stirred. It was only a single bed.

Beds I have known, thought Philip. Shared or not. In digs, boarding-houses, bed-sits, flats. On floors. In the bath. Now with Pearl.

He'd been right. Success with her depended on not being too insistent. She was an independent creature and had her own way to go. That was fine by him in the long run. Meanwhile the affair was developing well. What an intriguing girl Pearl was turning out to be. Her looks had attracted him first, the air of unassuming autonomy, added to which was the undeniable frisson of her race. Yet everything he found out about her added further depth. Tonight, for example, her upbringing in Children's Homes was simply implicit in exchanged memories of Bonfire Nights. She wouldn't have said more had he not directly questioned her. Yet it wasn't as if she was trying to hide her past. She seemed to have accepted and assimilated it. If it was relevant, she would tell; otherwise, deal with her present and future.

These present circumstances had their eccentricity. This guy Clovis, literally picking her up off the street and installing her in his elegant house. Without ulterior motive, so Pearl claimed. Living alone in a few rooms. Sitting in the window at night, staring out over the Common, unheeding. Was he slightly crazed? Not according to his behaviour after the concert. It had been a most civilized return journey.

Philip's relationship with Pearl had progressed since that evening. He'd enjoyed taking her with him today. It had certainly rattled Duncan. Philip grinned at the image of Duncan's rapid sequence of expressions when he opened the door: the conscious smile of hospitality immobilized, staggering, then being heaved back into position. How could Philip possibly have resisted? A good bloke, Duncan, but rather fuddy-duddy. He could do with a bit of research into physical style as well as cognitive. That way he might find his students more rewarding.

His Roz was a sweetie. Not entirely insipid either. She'd

been almost provocative in her comment about his being pro-woman, the more effective in its artlessness. And there she was pulling in the readies all day as well as providing a full service for Duncan. The lucky bugger.

But not for Philip himself. He wouldn't want Duncan's lifestyle even if it were a possibility. The romantic vision of domestic bliss was alluring and he liked quoting it. The reality was an inescapable bore. No.He shifted his position and felt Pearl's bare skin. No. This was what he wanted for now.

14

Philip and Pearl went to the bonfire on the Common. There were gingerbread men, toffee apples and a spectacular fireworks display. As the sky shimmered and inverted chrysanthemums of light hung in the night, the well-heeled young parents of the area gave exaggerated ooohs and aahs, while their children and other people gazed up open-mouthed, exclaiming with delight at the sparkling tendrils plummeting through space. Later that week they saw an Algerian film in a cinema club, and Philip explained to her why it was good.

They had agreed to keep to the established procedure at the evening institute the following Tuesday. Pearl wondered if Philip and Mr Drummond talked about her during the break. She herself did not make any reference to the lunch, and Mr Drummond maintained his usual professional distance. Philip waited for Pearl after class and invited his friend for a drink with them, but Duncan excused himself.

It was as though Sunday had never occurred. Except that Roz rang up.

Roz had not encountered any difficulty in arranging for Pearl to visit the school. Miss Elyce saw such a provision as part of her function; Mr Hill referred to Pearl as 'Roz's trainee do-gooder' but raised no objections; Caroline and Martin eagerly volunteered their slower children for Pearl's attention, although it had been decided that on a first visit she would be better to stay with Roz all day.

'If she turns out to be any good, she can have my class and

I'll take early retirement,' offered Tod.

'You don't need to be any good nowadays,' said Mr Hill sourly. 'We can only live in hope till next term and pray for a considerably more effective selection strategy. There can hardly be a shortage of applicants.'

This was a reference to Paula, who had given in her notice and was disintegrating. She was white-faced and black-eyed and her class rampaged. She refused all attempted help and rarely came into the staff room. Roz and Caroline would go to see her in the breaks. She would fend them off with some forced occupation.

Yes, perfectly all right, she'd say brightly. Just rather busy. No thanks, she didn't drink much tea. If they didn't mind she'd carry on.

Sometimes they resolutely stayed in her classroom throughout the break, talking lightly while trying to draw Paula in. If only she would accept their friendship, they might be able to give her more support. Paula would not budge. She ignored their conversation and continued with her contrived task, answering them politely but briefly only when it was unavoidable.

She gave in her notice with no other job to go to. What was she going to do? they asked, spending break in her classroom again.

Something would turn up, she said nonchalantly.

But what? Jobs were scarce. What would she live on?

Paula stared ahead. Her face grew taut, her jaw stiffened.

'I don't bloody care,' she said through closed teeth. 'Just let me get out. Right? Anything's better than this. If I never work again it's better than this. Christ!' Her head jerked and her voice grew. 'How I hate this place. I hate it. I hate it.' She quivered with tension, then crumpled on the desk, sobbing.

Next morning Paula was absent and not answering the telephone. She came in the day after, brightly brittle and rejecting as before. Then she was away again. In and out; her attendance continued erratic. Her class would be temporarily shared out. Supply teachers came and went. Miss Elyce had her in the office for long private talks, to no avail.

Roz explained this to Pearl on the journey to school. Pearl found the situation telling.

'It's so odd to me,' she said, 'to be hearing it from the other side now. When you're a child you expect the adults to be in charge. It's like a law of nature. And you either obey because they're stronger or you try to cause as much trouble as possible. But you never think of them caring personally. You might make them angry at the time but you never think of your behaviour affecting their life. I suppose you never really believed that they had a life apart from the one with you.'

'Paula's class has some nice children in it. I'm sure they don't realize what they're doing to her.'

'I was terrible at school.'

'I don't believe you.'

'I was. I'm being honest with you. We didn't care. One teacher kept crying in class and we thought it was really funny. We despised her for it too. I can hardly imagine it now.'

'Neither can I.'

'It's true, though. It's peculiar looking back, because although she was crying and we knew things must be bad to make a teacher cry in front of us, even then I didn't consider I'd hurt her personally. It was as if none of us were real people with feelings. It was a sort of a game. Against authority, I suppose.'

'And so you'd won?'

'We thought we had. But you don't win in the end, because you don't learn anything. That's why I'm having to do night classes, isn't it?'

'You're keeping up, aren't you, with the course?'

'I think so. I think I understand it. But there's a lot I do wrong just because I don't know. Take apostrophes. They were always being corrected in my essays and I didn't know when to use them. I thought you put them before every s, but they kept being changed, so I got a book out of the library to learn punctuation and spelling rules. If I hadn't messed around at school, I wouldn't have had to do that now, would I? I'd have known.'

'Perhaps,' said Roz. 'But you'll be able to draw on that experience as a social worker.'

'That's my only justification,' said Pearl.

It was one of Paula's away days. Roz couldn't help feeling

relieved. To keep her class going smoothly against the fracas at the other side of the partition required extra effort and she could do without that when she'd got Pearl too. Miss Elyce took Paula's children for a lesson in the hall after assembly, by which time the supply teacher had arrived.

Actually, Roz felt by the end of the day, Pearl could almost have taken over Paula's class there and then, if she'd known what to teach. That aura of hers which had so impressed Roz also made the children treat her seriously. Pearl observed lessons for the first part of the morning, then had small groups for reading and number work. Roz noticed Pearl's unforced control and the way the children accepted her guidance. So easy for some people. How long had it taken Roz herself to achieve? Why couldn't Paula? Miss Elyce, passing through, commented favourably. Later Roz heard Lotty quoting to another child what 'the coloured teacher said'.

'Are you in a hurry to go home?' asked Pearl as they waited by the bus stop after school.

'Not particularly. Why?'

'Have you time to come back to my place for a cup of tea?'

'Plenty of time. Duncan's up at the University today. I never know when to expect him.'

They got off the bus before Roz's usual stop and walked some way through side-streets until they reached the Common.

'Here we are,' said Pearl. 'I must tell you in advance that I only rent a bit of it.'

'Pearl, what a house!'

'I know. Aren't I the lucky one?'

She unlocked the door and let them into the lighted hall. Beautiful objects – mirrors, pictures, vases, tables – and emerging from the back of the house, a tall, refined, rather melancholy figure.

'Oh, Mr Fordingham.'

'Please – Clovis.'

Pearl introduced him to Roz.

'How do you do.' He shook hands. They all stood looking willing. Pearl seemed to be making a decision.

'We're about to have some tea, Clovis,' she said steadily. 'Would you like to join us?'

Clovis raised his hands slightly. He was going to make an excuse, Roz could tell.

Then, 'Thank you,' he said simply. 'I will.'

They followed Pearl to the top of the house. She opened her door and switched on a lamp. Roz entered. Furniture, belongings, books glowed in the mellow light. Shadowy beyond them, angled walls enclosed Pearl's own domain. In the comfort of these surroundings, Pearl was building her future. And she had more unintruded upon space to do it than Roz had.

'It's a lovely room, Pearl.'

'I think so too.'

'Do you? I am glad,' said Clovis. He didn't sit down until Pearl asked him to.

Pearl was behind the screen, filling the kettle.

Clovis turned to Roz. 'Do you work with Pearl?' he asked.

'No. I'm a teacher.'

'Are you? What sort of teacher?'

'A very good one,' came from behind the screen.

'I'm sure,' said Clovis gravely.

Roz blushed. 'I teach in a Junior School,' she said. 'Pearl has been visiting us for the day.'

'To get some experience,' explained Pearl, issuing forth with a plate of biscuits and disappearing again, 'to support my application for social-work training.'

'A very good idea,' said Clovis. 'Is that why you're doing Psychology too?'

'That's right.'

'How is the Psychology course?'

'I'm enjoying it.' Pearl carried out two cups of tea and went back for her own. 'Here's some sugar. Actually, Roz is married to my Psychology lecturer.'

'Really?' Clovis smiled at Roz. 'Did you know each other beforehand?'

'No,' said Roz. 'We met through,' she paused, 'that connection.'

'It seems we've all been teaching today,' said Clovis.

'Are you a teacher too?'

Roz knew why Pearl was surprised. It was hard to imagine Clovis in a classroom.

'I am.'

'Where do you work?'

'At the Academy.' Pearl looked none the wiser. 'It's a music college.'

'So that's why there's so much music here.'

'I hope it doesn't disturb you.'

'Oh no.' Pearl hurriedly dismissed any impression that she might be complaining. 'I like it. Sometimes it's you playing, isn't it? Even I can tell when it's a piano, but there's another instrument too.'

'The cello.'

'It sounds lovely.'

'That's my main teaching.' He inclined again towards Roz. 'I see most of my students individually. I doubt that I'd be up to the demands of your classes.'

'Pearl would be,' said Roz. 'She's got a natural ability. Duncan, my husband, must have it too. I had to learn gradually from my mistakes. Now I'm averagely competent.'

'Not according to Pearl.'

What a graceful shape he makes, thought Roz, as Pearl described her day to Clovis. That long body twined in the chair. The hands large but delicate. Honed features. Does he let all his house? Has he fallen on hard times? His clothes were very good: his trousers well cut; his sweater cashmere, she was sure. A button off his shirt cuff. The conversation went on around her. Standing up. He was leaving. Thanking Pearl for the tea. Saying goodbye to Roz. She was smiling in return.

Pearl looked pleased. 'I'm glad I asked him,' she said confidentially as his footsteps descended the stairs. 'It was taking a plunge because I only see him occasionally. I even have to leave the rent out on the hall table for him sometimes.'

'Do you see much of the other tenants?'

'There aren't any. Only me.'

'What about his family?'

Pearl shook her head. 'A cleaning-lady comes in.'

'You live on your own here? Just the two of you?'

'You'll think it's even more peculiar when I tell you how it happened. Want to hear?'

'Go on,' said Roz.

Philip returned from the launderette and walked over the afternoon post. Two for him. Leamington and Glasgow, so no mystery about either sender. He went into his room, dumped the plastic carrier of washed clothes on the bed, made a mug of coffee and sat down to read his letters. Leamington: the usual: news of people he hadn't seen for years, and when was he going to visit? He put it on one side. Glasgow: Melanie packing each line with longing. What did that imply? The end of some Glaswegian affair? Ah, she had a few days free next week. She could come to London on Sunday and stay till Thursday. How about it?

Very interesting. Did this signify a romantic débâcle up there, or was Melanie merely keeping old irons in the fire? Either way, she was blithely taking for granted his continuing presence, assuming he would be available as and when it suited her. Not this one, sweetheart. Not quite.

Sure, she could come to London and stay with him. She was a vivacious lady and would be fun to have around. But she'd better drop any notion that he was just waiting on her convenience. She'd have to learn that his world didn't revolve around her whims.

Sunday to Thursday. How much of that should he spend with Pearl and leave Melanie dangling? Not too much. She might well go off and find someone else to occupy herself with. Just enough to discountenance her, to be a little disparaging. Just a little.

He'd leave it till the last moment to ring her in Glasgow. Saturday. If she was out, so much the better. A mere message would appear nicely unconcerned. Meet her off the train on Sunday. Pearl's day off. They'd agreed to go out. No matter, he could defer Pearl. Tell her – what? His eyes lighted on the other letter. Tell her he was going to Leamington to visit his mother. Have a good run with Melanie till Tuesday. See Pearl as usual on Tuesday after night class. Be vague to Melanie about what he was doing but make her expect him later in the evening. Spend the night with Pearl. Return to discomfited Melanie next day. Laugh at Melanie – call her crypto-conventional. That should make her wild. Possibly bed Melanie again. Put her on the train north next day. Continue with Pearl.

Which was where he was due now. Take a toothbrush. A few clean clothes. Collect takeaway Chinese en route? No, too early. They could go out later on.

'Oh.' Pearl jumped as Philip crept up from behind. 'I didn't hear you. How did you get in?'

'Clovis,' said Philip. 'So I thought I'd sneak along and surprise you. Empty tea cups? Is this a secret cell of the Women's Institute?'

Pearl began to clear away. 'Roz came back after school. We bumped into Mr – Clovis – and I asked him to come up as well. He did too.'

'So you enjoyed your school visit?'

'I really did. I've only ever been in school before as a pupil. An unco-operative one at that. But I took a few groups today, small ones. I didn't know how you're meant to deal with them, so I just did what seemed common sense. It couldn't have been too bad because Roz said I could become a teacher if I wanted.'

'Do you want?'

'No, but I'm going again and it's nice to know you didn't make a mockery of yourself. Roz heard one child call me "the coloured teacher", telling another what I'd been saying to them.'

'A black kid?'

'White. Or grey, poor little thing. Pasty and not too clean.'

'What had you been teaching them?'

Pearl laughed. 'I was hearing them read. I wouldn't know how to give a proper lesson.'

'You could tell them about black culture. Draw on your own knowledge.'

'I haven't got any knowledge about black culture.'

'You're black, Pearl, aren't you?'

'But I don't know anything about black culture. I'm only just beginning to find out about any sort of culture.'

'Pearl, look, sit down,' said Philip. 'Think. Now this is only a suggestion because I care about you. Yes? You don't have to accept it. But if you really are as ignorant as you say about your racial heritage, ought you not to be finding out?

The black experience is pulsating, Pearl, throbbing with life and pride. Black theatre, literature, dance, art – there's an explosion of talented awareness. Look, I'm white and I'm telling you how exciting it is. Why aren't you getting in there? Never mind about white culture, my love. Never mind about early church music. What about negro spirituals? The blues? What about the ancient rhythms of Africa? These are what made you, Pearl. What made you black.'

Pearl sat motionless, searching his face. Philip held her gaze. She turned her head away, pressing a knuckle to her mouth. Ah, he'd made her think. He kept the silence. She turned back.

'My mother was Welsh,' she said quietly. 'Thomas – that's her name.'

'A Welsh Thomas? I'd assumed it was West Indian. A vestige of the plantations, like Benjamin or Albert or Job.'

'No.'

'You were born in Wales then?' For the moment, Philip's curiosity overcame his zeal.

'No.'

'Did your father live in Wales?'

'Africa.'

'So how . . . ?'

'She came to London. They were students. She got pregnant. I think she went on with her studies afterwards. Good on her.'

Philip leaned forward intently. 'Aren't you bitter, Pearl? Don't you resent her for ditching you?'

Pearl rubbed her forehead. 'I don't know,' she said slowly. 'Sometimes, I suppose. I don't want to. By the time I found out, I was old enough to realize what it must have done to her. I used to imagine what might have happened if she'd kept me. But that's just fairy-tale.'

'You could trace her.'

'No.' Pearl shook her head adamantly. 'Never. Leave her be.' She took a deep breath and returned to a measured tone. 'So I'm white as well as black. It's equal in me.'

Philip's ardour reignited. 'It isn't, though, is it Pearl? Your heredity may be both, but what about your experience? What does society say? What did that kid at school call you – "the coloured teacher". That's society's image, Pearl. Your experience isn't white.'

'It's not black either, Philip. Not in the way you mean it. I don't feel part of this black culture you talk about. I can't pretend I do.'

'How can you say that? You don't know anything about it. You said so. Don't reject it, Pearl, just to concentrate on wriggling into a place in white society. Don't betray your colour.'

Pearl flinched.

Philip regretted going so far. He got up and crouched by her chair, taking her hand in his. 'Pearl, Pearl. I've offended you. I didn't mean to.'

'I'm not offended,' said Pearl in a flat voice.

'It was none of my business, Pearl. Tell me I'm presumptuous. Tell me I've no right. Tell me to shut up. Just don't tell me to go away. Please – Pearl.'

'You're entitled to your opinion.'

'You're entitled not to listen to it.'

'So where's my Chinese takeaway?' said Pearl.

15

They went for their Chinese meal and talked about other matters most of the time, but Pearl was very disturbed. For the rest of the week as she fed and changed the bed patients, as she chatted in the dayroom or joked with Sadie and Rose, she recalled other comments Philip had sometimes made and heard again his most recent words.

She was glad he was going to visit his mother that Sunday. It would give her a chance to think through what he had said without interruption, before he could say anything else to confuse her further.

She started Sunday by trying to read up on some background for her next Psychology topic. It was hopeless. She couldn't build mental walls this time as she had before in the library to keep out the preying of prejudice. This time the issue was too fundamental to the person she thought she had become and the life she was planning. What was the point of knowing her Psychology topic if what Philip said was true and her decisions were the wrong ones, made for the wrong reasons? She stood by her window, staring out to where the bare branches cracked the grey sky over the Common. Then she left her room and the house and crossed the road to walk and think.

People were exercising dogs and children. A game of football was in progress. Where the land dropped suddenly and formed a bank, boys were leaping their bikes over the edge, outdoing each other. Pearl paced the paths, her thoughts pounding, becoming increasingly confused, two phrases only ringing clear through the jumble: 'betray your colour' came Philip's voice; 'wriggling into white society'.

'Pearl?'

Clovis. Watching the path, watching her feet, not lifting her head up far enough to see who owned any passing legs, she hadn't noticed him approaching.

'Pearl, is there something wrong?'

She was crying. Only four times had she met Clovis properly and on two of these she'd cried. What would he think? What was wrong with her? She wasn't a weepy sort of person. Was she? How could you know what you were or why you were doing things?

'He says I'm betraying my colour,' her thoughts said aloud.

'He?'

'Philip. Am I?'

Clovis looked at her gravely. 'Let's go home,' he said, 'and talk about it.'

Pearl had walked almost in a circle. They cut through the remaining stretch of Common, crossed the road and entered the house. Up the stairs to the first floor.

Clovis opened the door. 'Please . . .' he said, indicating a chair.

She was inside Clovis's own room.

She noticed the piano first, a dark grand piano backed into a corner, the lid up, the keyboard open. The walls on either side were full of books. Leaning against a chair in front of the far window was the cello. The room ran the length of the house, the two windows at the front giving a less aerial version of Pearl's own view. By one there was a kneehole desk, stacked with papers. The other went down to the floor and led on to the small balcony. Drawn up to it was a buttonbacked chair facing outwards to the Common. In the middle of the room were a sofa and more chairs on one of which Pearl was now sitting. The walls were almost hidden by pictures, books and records. And records. Lined up in rows. Pearl had never seen so many outside a shop.

Clovis was pouring drinks at a side table. Pearl took off her coat and laid it across her knees. Clovis took the coat, gave her a glass and sat down opposite.

'Why did he say that?' As if the conversation had continued

without lapse.

Pearl groped in her tangled feelings for a strand to pull out. 'For a start, I don't know anything about black culture.'

'A lot of white people don't know much about white culture.'

'No, but I don't know much about any kind of culture. But I was beginning to find out. Philip thinks I'm going the wrong way.'

Clovis rocked his glass gently. 'What is the wrong way?'

'Well, take that music up in Highgate. Where you were too. That was so, so . . .' She gazed past Clovis to the cello and the leaves moving in the November sky outside. 'It transformed everything. You flew above where you usually are. And afterwards, even looking at the programme, you can remember it a bit in the words. Like Kyry.'

'Kyrie.'

'Kyrie. It still makes me go tingly. Does that sound silly?'

'Far from it,' said Clovis. 'Doesn't it make Philip tingle?'

'I don't know. It's not that so much. I think he thinks it would be all right for him to tingle but not for me.'

'Why on earth not?'

'Because . . . When I first said I'd like to go, he looked taken aback. But I thought it was because he didn't expect someone like me to be interested in such things. Which was fair enough because it was new for me. Now I think he'd think it better if I was involved in reggae or gospel, you know, something really black. He'd have quite liked it if I'd jumped up and shouted "Praise the Lord" in the middle of that Kyrie.'

Clovis's mouth twitched. 'You don't like reggae?'

'I like it. It's a different sort of like though, isn't it? I mean, you like music. You play lovely things. I'd like to know more about that kind of music. I want to know what makes it hurt.'

'You sound quite sure about what you want. Why has Philip's opinion worried you so much?'

Why had it? Because it was hard to be completely confident about your choices, especially when they concerned matters in which you hadn't much experience.

'Because part of me thinks he might be right. I haven't met people before who know about plays and music and reading. Other people know different things, I realize that, but I was just beginning to find out a whole new world and I thought at last I knew how to start going about my life. Then someone who knows so much more tells me I've got it wrong. It's broken everything up again. Maybe I ought to be finding out about African music and all that instead.'

'But?'

'But I can't feel any connection. It's an ought rather than a want. I feel guilty that it is only an ought. From what Philip says, it's very important to other people, so it ought to be to me too. I mean, I am black. Only I haven't had a black life that way. I was brought up in Homes, you see. I'm black and I'm white. My mother was white, but my main problem was that nobody wanted me enough. As we were growing up, there were both black and white ones of us left over. More black, I suppose. People prefer to adopt little white children. We knew we weren't wanted so we made ourselves unwantable. We hurt people before they could hurt us. We rejected people so that it wouldn't matter as much when they rejected us. We even did it to each other. So I never really belonged anywhere and I never felt any particular allegiance. Philip says that's all the more reason to go for my black roots, because I don't feel I have any.'

'He thinks you'd find some.'

'I suppose so. Only I'd just got to see my life straightening out in a completely different way. And that's got confused again. I was intending to become a social worker. I'm sure Philip thinks that's wrong too.'

Clovis raised his eyebrows. 'What could he object to in that?'

'There's a little girl called Lotty in Roz's class. She's white. I don't know if they've got a social worker, but she comes from a poor family. Philip would say that if you help Lotty you make sure that there'll be a constant supply of new Lotties being produced because all social workers do is prop up the unfairness of society. He's said before that they paper over the cracks so it looks better but nothing's actually changed. He thinks if the system collapsed there would be a chance of building something better next time.'

'And what do you think?'

'I think he might be right. At least about papering over cracks. That's the problem. I can always see what he means. I wouldn't care otherwise. What he says sounds right, but I can't feel it for me. I think things ought to change but I don't know anything about politics. I'm not going to be doing it myself, so what should I do while waiting for society to change? Tell Lotty to lump it? What would you do if you were me, Mr Fordingham?'

'Clovis.'

'Clovis.'

'I don't know that I'm qualified to give that advice.'

'Why not?'

'I'm not black.'

Pearl looked at him, a silver-grey person.

'No,' she said with a laugh. 'No, you're not. Neither is Philip,' she added.

'That had crossed my mind.'

'And I'm asking you.'

Clovis stood up and went to the shelves along the wall. Pearl wondered what was happening.

'Listen,' said Clovis.

He sat down again, leaning back in his chair, fingertips pressed to each other against his mouth.

Pearl listened to an eerie rumble as the world was created, suspense mounting until voices flashed, 'Let there be light.'

Clovis turned off the tape.

'What do you think?'

'It made me tingle, just like the Kyrie.'

'Ian Hall wrote it,' said Clovis. 'He's black; from Guyana, I believe. He does know about steel bands, and jazz and African music. He's also classically trained. He knows about church organs and choirs and ecclesiastical music too. He brings those influences together in his work.'

'You're telling me that I ought to be studying African things.'

'I'm not black, Pearl.'

'You keep saying that, but I want to know what you think'.

'I think,' said Clovis, slowly, 'that he, Ian Hall, produces something which is from his own experiences. From black cultures and from white, in his case. It's his own response to what's been around him in life. I think you ought to make your own response to what's going on around you, and you're the only one who can do that. Somebody outside can't tell you what you ought to feel.'

'This Ian Hall, he's combining things. I can't.'

'Why not?'

'I've nothing to combine. I don't know anything about African music or black anything. That's the point.'

'He combines his own experiences, and it's through music because that's his interest and his genius. You have your own experiences. You know what it's like not to grow up in a family. What it's like to be on your own. What it's like to have to make yourself.'

'So . . . ?'

'So you're an individual. You work within your own experiences. You haven't betrayed anything as far as I can see. You might, though, if you do something which doesn't feel right to you, just because somebody else thinks you should.'

'My feeling might be wrong.'

'Philip might be wrong. I might be wrong.'

'But you think I was right, before?'

'You sounded very clear about what you wanted. Suppose later on you change your mind. Does it matter? You'll have learnt something in the process, even if it's only what you didn't want to be. You may need the experience in order to make up your mind. You can only act on the experience you've had so far. You can only do what seems right for you as you are.'

'Philip keeps saying that you should be true to your own feelings.'

'You could quote it back to him. Anyway, your decision to become a social worker doesn't mean that you're irrevocably cut off from becoming more involved in black affairs later on. They're not mutually exclusive.'

'They didn't seem so before. Betrayal – it's a hard word though. You think you're going on OK then suddenly something trips you up. It's hard to have faith in yourself continuously. It all suddenly goes.'

'Yes,' said Clovis. 'It all suddenly goes.'

'Could I hear that music again?'

Clovis put the tape back on. Its distinctive sounds filled the room. Pearl wondered what her mother was doing at that moment. She wondered whether her mother ever thought about her.

16

'It all suddenly goes.' Clovis waited in his car at the traffic lights, thinking of Pearl again as he had several times in the weeks since that conversation.

How difficult it must be for her. Yet she had emerged from her past with a sense of direction which Philip's outpourings had only temporarily shaken, he felt certain. She was a remarkable mixture of toughness and sensitivity. He had been astounded to see her at the Byrd Mass, then had assumed this was under Philip's influence. On the contrary. It had been her idea and she was the one who had 'tingled'. She had tingled too to the Ian Hall; that had been obvious.

The traffic lights changed.

'It all suddenly goes.' Oh yes. Here he was, driving back from a drink with colleagues after late tuition at the Academy. His tutee was a talented young woman, hopeful and still trusting that life would produce what she deserved in exchange for her dedication.

So had he been at that age, lugging his cello on the bus between home and class against the barrage of comments jocular and ribald: 'Too big to get under your chin innit?' 'Fancy getting your legs round her.' He used to respond in those days with a wearily crooked eyebrow.

After school he had won a scholarship to the Academy and from there had begun to build a career as a soloist, travelling first around Britain, then Europe. He was fulfilled in every aspect of his life; the future could only blossom. And then – it all suddenly goes. Oh yes.

He drove up the hill by Lixbury School. Lixbury? Wasn't that where Pearl did her evening class, where Roz's husband taught, where Philip danced? A hive of activity. Each window glowed with the light of nocturnal education. Clovis drove past.

Inside Lixbury Institute, it was break time for Psychology and Stage Dance. Philip took his feet off the canteen chair as Duncan approached with his cup of tea.

'Another week,' said Duncan by way of greeting as he sat down.

'Like that, is it?'

Duncan pinched the inner corners of his eyes between thumb and forefinger. 'You know the feeling. On and on. One week runs into the next.'

'Rather samey.'

'You've got it. I expect you must feel like that as well, being out of work for so long.'

Philip bridled. 'It hasn't been *so* long. Theatre isn't like an ordinary job. You need to recuperate after a show until the next right offer comes along, otherwise you'd get on to a commercial treadmill and never have space to grow artistically.'

'I'm on a very uncommercial treadmill.'

'You are morose tonight, Duncan. Whereas I'm full of good news.'

'What's that?'

'I'm auditioning for Magus.'

'Is that the name of a play?'

'It's a company, Duncan. A touring company. A very good touring company, in fact.'

'That's terrific,' said Duncan genuinely. 'Do you think you'll get it?'

'Oh yes. If I want it.'

'You might not?'

'I never commit myself until after the auditions, when I've had chance to assess the working atmosphere.'

'But the chances are you'll be involved in something again soon?'

'If not Magus, then another venture. That's one of the joys of theatre: there's always a new challenge round the corner. It stops you getting stale.'

Duncan was very stale. The novelty of extra-mural teaching had worn off and it was with monotonous regularity that he intoned information, printed psychological jargon on the blackboard, answered the students' questions and wrote comments on essays. His research was equally in a rut – too far from the beginning to be fresh, too far from the end to be satisfying. He ought to make an appointment to see Professor Reece again but the meeting would be only a valueless formality and he'd have to slog on by himself as before.

'Not to worry, Duncan,' consoled Philip. 'It's nearly the end of term. At least there's the Christmas break to look forward to.'

'Do you look forward to Christmas?'

'Me? No. Dreadful few days. It's only bearable if you're in panto.'

'So why should I look forward to it?'

'Oh dear, Duncan. It's different for you. I have to be penned up in Leamington. You're married.'

'Which gives me a choice of two places to be penned up in – her parents or mine.'

'You don't have to be penned up with them. You could be with Roz in your own home. Chestnuts roasting in an open fire, children's faces all aglow.'

'I don't like chestnuts. And we haven't any children.'

'That's easily changed, Duncan my old mate. Have children. You've left it too late for this Christmas, but you could make an arrangement for the future. You could have proper family Christmases. Professor Drummond, *père de famille.* That's what I'd be doing, given half the chance.'

'Not just yet, Philip. I've got to finish my thesis. Children are very disruptive.'

'Life's very disruptive. What about Roz? Wouldn't she like to have a family?'

'Roz wouldn't mind.'

'From what I've seen of Roz, she'd cope with any hassle herself. It wouldn't interfere with your other plans. I don't know what you're waiting for, Duncan. You've been saying how samey your life has become. You can change that without any upset. I really envy you.'

Duncan pinched the corners of his eyes again.

Philip leaned towards him over the table. 'Look, I'm only going to be in Leamington for a few days over Christmas. When you come back from your jollifications, give us a tinkle and we'll have a night out to get over it.'

'Sounds like a good idea.'

'I'm full of them.'

Duncan drank the rest of his tea while Philip described some of the antics that had been required at previous auditions. After the break he went back to his classroom to find that the conversation of the non-migratory students was running along similar lines to the earlier part of Philip's.

Mrs Albert was showing off a huge and brilliantly pink stuffed animal. 'What do you think of this one, Mr Drummond?' she enquired proudly.

'Very colourful.'

'A Christmas present for my new granddaughter.'

Granddaughter!

Mrs Baptiste, her friend, cackled delightedly at Duncan. 'She don't look the age for it. How many you raised, Eva?'

'Eight. Eight and two for my sister.'

'Me five. All sturdy baby. They big now.'

'Have you any children, Mr Patel?' asked Duncan, stirred by this fecundity.

'Oh yes. Two sons, one daughter. Children are the blessing of God.'

'You need children for Christmas. You need them to spoil.'

'Christmas isn't Christmas without them.'

'You have kids Mr Drummond?'

'No. No, not yet.' Duncan felt he was making an incriminating admission.

'You have some. You see the difference.'

Duncan returned quickly to the blackboard, not wanting to court public discussion of his procreation, especially now that the rest of the group were back. He drew and explained a flowchart of Deci's motivational cycle, dealt with queries, fobbed off Mr Pontiff yet again.

He had been reminded of Christmases when he was a small child and still a believer. He could remember waking up at first light on Christmas morning and just being able to distinguish the lumpy tube hanging from the foot of the bed. He crawled out over the bedclothes to unhook it and scrambled back. It was very cold in the room. You could see yourself breathe, and the inside of the window used to be covered with frost patterns. In bed he made an igloo out of the pillows and eiderdown, crouching within it, trying to let in enough light to unpack the stocking while simultaneously keeping himself covered up, shivering at his lack of success. Where was Roy during this operation? Duncan couldn't remember. Older, wiser, probably still asleep. They used to dress in bed on those winter mornings. Having had the foresight to leave their clothes as close by as possible, they would shoot a hand out through the frosty air to drag them in for a warming before the contortions of putting them on. In his stocking there had been a clown puppet, a model aeroplane, other toys probably, as well as the apple, the orange, the coin right in the toe. On the chest of drawers were a few crumbs left from the mince-pie oblation. Each Christmas Eve he would will himself to stay awake and catch a glimpse, holding his eyes open and singing carols over and over in his head.

Duncan left the Institute and cycled off down the hill. That magic disappeared from life as you grew older. Did people regain it later through their own children? Could it alleviate such monotony as his at the present? It might. Roz would be pleased. She'd been getting pretty broody at the beginning of term. And Philip was right. The practical organization would be down to Roz. It needn't interfere with his progress in any way.

He used to go fishing with his father sometimes. He and Roy. Sitting on the canal bank with the chimneys behind them and slow water in front. Dad didn't say much. He didn't help academically but he hadn't stood in Duncan's way either. Duncan's children would go to university, carrying on from school, the straightforward way. He'd talk to them intelligently from an early age, answer their questions in detail, foster a critical awareness. They would look up to him, respect his intellect, emulate him. He would take a modest pride in their achievements. 'What a gifted family!' people would say.

He arrived at his gate, dismounted, pushed the bicycle up

the path and into the hall, climbed the stairs to the flat. Roz was at the oven. The table was set, her exercise books and biros placed to one side. She looked rather happy as she turned to him. Good. They'd have the meal first and then he'd tell her what he'd decided. Roz served the food. While they ate he talked about the evening's lecture, half listened to anecdotes from school. Mr Pontiff; Paula; Mr Hill; some child called Lotty. He finished his chop.

Then: 'And guess what, Duncan?'

Was this a pudding night or a biscuit night? He cast around for clues.

'What about?' Tolerantly. This was family life.

'I'm going to apply for a deputy headship.'

Roz? A deputy headship? Now?

'Isn't that rather over-ambitious, Roz?'

'I'd have thought so too not long ago. Actually it wasn't my idea.'

'Whose idea was it then?'

'I think it was Tod originally, but then the others joined in. It's advertised in *Contact*. Pond Street School, about three bus stops further on. I thought he was joking, but Mr Hill agreed with him and said I ought.'

'It's an enormous career leap.'

'That's what I said. Mr Hill said that the Pond Street children were similar to ours and that I'd done a great deal for our school and so I ought not to be put off applying.'

'Doesn't Tod want it himself?'

'Apparently not. Martin's desperate for promotion but he wants to move nearer home and this post's even further so he's not interested. Everyone said I should try. I felt very nice.'

'I'm sure you did. All the same, I think you're overstretching yourself. Don't you, Roz – being realistic?'

'I did. But I've been thinking about it all evening and, you know, I *could* do it. There'd be a lot of extra work, especially at first, but yes, I can imagine myself doing it.'

'You're going to have extra work anyway, Roz.'

'Am I? Why?'

'Because we're going to start a family . . . '

Well, that had winded her. A better proposition than uncertain deputy headships.

' . . . so you needn't bother about anything else.'

'What do you mean, I needn't bother about anything else?'

'You won't have time, with a baby to look after.'

'Where did this baby come from all of a sudden?'

'Roz, don't you know where babies come from?' Roguish, a bit of a lad.

Roz wasn't laughing. 'You know what I mean.'

'You wanted a baby before, Roz. Now we'll have one. You've more chance of achieving that than the deputy headship.'

'Thank you.'

'Haven't you? In any case, you couldn't take on a demanding new job as well as a new baby.'

'Couldn't I?'

'No. You wouldn't do either properly.'

Roz aligned the salt and pepper pots.

'If I give up work, Duncan, how are we going to live?'

No, no.

'I didn't say you'd give up work completely, Roz. You're putting words into my mouth. I was merely pointing out that it would be too much for you to take on a responsible new job as well. It's different for you to carry on with your old job. You're familiar with it; it doesn't require much of you; you can let it tick over.'

'If I'm out working, who's looking after the baby?'

'You're being very belligerent.'

'I'm not being belligerent, Duncan, I'm being practical. I can't be in two places at once. If I'm at school, I can't be at home looking after the baby, so someone else has to. If I'm at home looking after the baby, I can't earn money, so someone else has to.'

'All right, all right. There's no need to talk as if I were in your remedial group. I did think this was something you'd be pleased about for once.'

'Oh, I am pleased, Duncan, but it's out of the blue. I'd started thinking about life along completely different lines. And there are so many decisions that would have to be made.'

'What do you suggest?'

Roz examined the pepper pot. 'The easiest would be for me to give up teaching and stay at home with the baby.'

'We need the money, as you yourself said.'

'Would you get a full-time job?'

'Roz – my thesis. How would I possibly finish it?'

'Then I'll work and you stay at home with the baby.'

Duncan shied. 'How will I finish my thesis then? Be reasonable Roz.'

She put down the pepper pot. 'It's your turn to provide some solutions.'

Duncan drew on his limited knowledge of social facilities. 'Aren't there women who look after other people's babies while they're at work?'

'Child-minders.'

'Exactly.'

'You have to pay them, Duncan.'

'Can't we afford it?'

'Not in our present circumstances.'

It seemed insoluble. Duncan felt deflated.

Roz was looking downcast too. Then: 'I can think of one possibility,' she said tentatively. 'if you took on some more extra-mural classes next year, we could manage it.'

'I really don't want to waste too much time teaching.'

'It wouldn't need too much time. Just some.'

'I'm not very happy about that, Roz.'

'What's the alternative?'

Duncan couldn't think of any. A few hours wouldn't make much difference to his schedule.

'All right. I'll compromise,' he said generously. 'Are we actually in agreement now?'

'I think so,' said Roz.

She was looking at him incredulously. Duncan himself felt as if he had stepped into a new world and only just met her.

'So you won't bother about the deputy headship?' he said, to get back to familiar ground.

Roz's gaze shifted. 'We'll see,' she said.

17

Philip hoped against hope that he would be offered a place with Magus. To be working again; to leave behind Zora's class of pretentious eyes-teeth enthusiasts and return to the real world of theatre; to regain confidence in his professional skills; to have an income again, temporary and paltry though it might be: a hair's breadth separated his present public category from that which was truly his. In the dividing hair's breadth lay the audition. What if he was rejected? Stamped back into the herd of also-rans. He clenched his teeth. Such a possibility was not to be contemplated. He must think positively.

One decision that would have to be made was about his base. If he gave up his bedsit, he would lose his tangible link with London. Except for Leamington, which he discounted because it was not in London, he would have nothing to consider himself attached to, no fixed point. To keep the room, though, as a means of maintaining his connection with London and its potential opportunites, would be a continual drain on the mingy income he was glorying in.

He knew what the solution was: move in with Pearl. She could look after any possessions which he didn't want to take with him, handle his mail, be there with her cosy room as and when needed.

He waited for her after their evening classes and they walked together back to the Common. The night was clear and crisp. He walked with an arm around her, sometimes two, told her about Magus, made an event of rubbing her back warm, pointed out the stars, sharp and inscrutable over the Common, and Clovis sitting in his first-floor window.

They went up to Pearl's room. Philip watched with affection as Pearl switched on lamps and drew up chairs.

'Pearl, Pearl, if you only knew,' he sighed.

'Knew what?'

'What you've brought into my life.'

Pearl sat down without saying anything.

Having set the tone, Philip went on: 'It gets more and more difficult.' He waited.

Pearl then said: 'What does?'

'Leaving you each time, my love.'

'But you'll be moving away soon.'

'If I accept it, yes.'

'You're likely to accept it, aren't you?'

Philip stared into his coffee for an appropriate interval, then looked up at her, his head still lowered. 'Leaving you gets more and more difficult,' he repeated softly.

Pearl frowned. 'You can't not accept it because of that, Philip.'

'No, I suppose not,' – resigned.

There was a pause which Pearl didn't seem predisposed to fill.

Philip started up again. 'Knowing that I may be away for quite long patches makes me feel all the more that I want to be with you as much as possible, to make the most of what time we have together.'

'We do spend quite a lot of time together.'

'But I'm always leaving you. I spend so much of it travelling across London from my place to yours and back again, time which could be ours. It's such a waste. And if I do tour, I'll be in London only for the occasional few days – am I going to spend those touring too, from there to here?'

Pearl did not reply. She ought to have taken her cue by now.

He'd have to be more blatant. 'You know what I'm getting at, don't you?'

'Yes.'

That was all.

'I'm suggesting I move in here with you.'

'Yes.'

'Don't jump at the idea, will you?'

Pearl bit her lower lip. 'I don't think it would be fair to Clovis,' she said finally.

'Clovis? What's he got to do with it?'

'It's his house, it's his room.'

'As far as he's concerned, it's your room while you're living here.'

'I wouldn't want to impose on him. I wouldn't want to take advantage of him. I think it would be rude. Anyway, I'd feel rude.'

'Then let's ask him if he minds. It's easy enough. I'll ask him now. He's in his room – we saw him there.'

Philip got up and strode purposefully to the door past Pearl.

She grabbed his hand. 'Don't Philip.'

'Why not? If that's all you're worried about?'

'It isn't.'

'Aha!' Philip turned back. Then he stood silently a moment or two, his face growing increasingly morose. 'You don't want me, Pearl, do you? That's what it is. Clovis is just an excuse. You don't want to be with me.' His shoulders sagged.

'Philip, I've got to work.'

'Who hasn't?'

'I mean study. I've got to study.'

'I know you have. I'm not going to stop you. I admire you for it. You know I do.'

'No you don't.'

Philip strode back to a position in front of Pearl. 'Whatever gave you that idea?'

'You did. I'm studying to become a social worker. You said in no uncertain terms that I ought not to be doing it. I ought to be learning about black culture instead. I ought not to be wriggling my way into white society. That's what you said.'

Philip dropped to his knees by Pearl's chair. 'Pearl, Pearl. I worried that you might have misunderstood me. I didn't mean it in that way. Why should I talk to you like that? It would be most presumptuous. It's not for me to tell you what to do with your life.'

'No, it isn't.'

'You've completely misinterpreted what I was saying.'

'What were you saying?'

'I was trying to act as a sounding-board, to make you think carefully about your decisions, not to tell you what to decide. So many people leap into things without analysing whether it's what they really want.'

Pearl wasn't replying again.

'Don't you believe me?'

'That wasn't how it came over.'

'That's what worried me afterwards: had I been too strong? I was intending to play devil's advocate to help you to crystallize your reasons.'

'What made you think they needed crystallizing?'

'Obviously they didn't. What I said had no effect on your decisions – because you knew they were correct for you. You have retained the same intention as before to become a social worker. Quite correctly. You didn't need me to focus you.'

He knelt up in front of her and folded his arms on her knees, boyish and appealing.

'It was kindly meant, Pearl. Because I care. Don't resent that. Please. I couldn't bear it.'

He reached for her hand and kissed it.

'Oh well,' said Pearl uncertainly.

He left the matter there. There was more to be gained by letting the proposition grow by itself in Pearl's mind, especially since she kicked at any hint of being cornered. Yet later in the night, as he lay awake running over the conversation in his head, other aspects of the situation occurred to him. For a start, one reason that he wasn't asleep was this single bed with the two of them lying together like lashed planks. It could be exchanged for a double bed, but there were other considerations too. Pearl was very committed to her self-improvement. Highly creditable but potentially heavy going if you were in its company all the time. And it would be difficult to gain much light relief from other sources if he were actually living with Pearl. There might well be a by-product of unavoidable monogamy, which he was loath to accept. Melanie, for example, was unquestionably a gutsy lady. He had enjoyed those days juggling her and Pearl, and Melanie had been none the worse for it. He wouldn't be able to do that it he were sharing Pearl's room, and he wouldn't want to miss out on other visits from Melanie when it suited him. Then there were the new people he might meet with Magus, members of the company itself and those attached to the various venues. In all probability there would be contacts he would wish to follow up and renew from time to time. Living cheek by jowl with Pearl must cramp his lifestyle. He was glad he had not pressed her further.

The night lay quiet in the house. Pearl slept. Somewhere Clovis slept. In the other rooms was no one. That was it! He would inveigle Clovis into letting him have one of the other rooms. Clovis wouldn't mind. After all, it had been at his own suggestion that Pearl had moved in. Clovis would never accept rent for it while Philip was away on tour: Philip would argue that out with him just enough for window-dressing and then be forced to submit to Clovis's generosity. He would be near enough to Pearl for his own convenience, but distant enough to be able to follow his independent interests with a little manoeuvring. Wonderful. He'd better nab Clovis as soon as possible.

Pearl was on the early shift next day. After she had gone, Philip spread out into the breadth of bed and slept on. He woke up, breakfasted, bathed in some of Pearl's foam and washed his hair. It was lunchtime. He gathered up his belongings to leave, pausing to knock on Clovis's door as he passed, then calling down the corridor from the hall to the back of the house. He must be alone. What an opportunity to explore! The front door rattled. Philip sprang back so that by the time Clovis entered the house he was in the middle of the hall.

'Ah!' Clovis jumped somewhat. 'Good morning, Philip.'

'Hello there. How are you, Clovis?'

'Very well, thank you. And you?'

Philip planted his lines quickly. 'Making choices.'

'Not unpleasant ones, I hope?'

'By no means. Very exciting.'

'Good, good.' Clovis contemplated quietly for a while, then geared himself again. 'Well, I trust you'll come to the right decisions.' He appeared to be about to move away.

Philip continued at once. 'Actually, I was wanting to have a quick word with you, when you had a minute.'

'Of course,' said Clovis. 'I'm expecting a colleague any moment, I fear. Would you rather we met again later?'

If Clovis hadn't much time and was thinking of something else, he might be more amenable.

'No, no. It will only take a minute. I can explain now, if you don't mind.'

'Please do,' said Clovis.

Philip spoke quietly and earnestly. 'I'm deciding whether or not to accept a place with a touring company, which would mean I'd be away from London most of the time.'

'Congratulations,' said Clovis.

'Now, Clovis, please, don't feel obliged in any way or put in a difficult position. I want you to give me an honest answer.'

Clovis waited.

'To be frank, the problem is going to be accommodation, Clovis. It's an excellent company' (he deliberately didn't say its name), 'but it has a limited budget and can't pay its actors well. It would be impossible for me to keep on my present room in addition to paying for digs on tour. What I'm asking, Clovis – and be at liberty to refuse me – what I'm asking is to be able to use one of your spare rooms.'

'You mean you'd like to move in here?'

'Yes.'

'Have you discussed this with Pearl?'

'Oh, I didn't mean to move in with Pearl.' Philip's eyes widened. 'I meant to have my own room.' He took a new tack. 'You can't blame me for noticing what you have and comparing our positions. Naturally I'm prepared to make sacrifices for the sake of my profession – I expect I always will have to – but a little help would be greatly appreciated.'

Clovis listened impassively. Then he said again, 'I think this should be discussed with Pearl.'

Philip felt irritated, but masked it with a puzzled frown. 'Why with Pearl? Surely it's your house. Pearl is only another tenant. Isn't she?'

Either Clovis did not notice or he ignored the implication. 'Pearl came to live here first. I should prefer her to be involved in any such changes. If Pearl's happy with the arrangements, then so am I.'

Why should Pearl be vested with such powers over him? Philip couldn't afford to let his indignation show. 'I'm sure Pearl will be most happy,' he stated.

'Discuss it with her. If she has no objections then she can let me know and you can go ahead.'

'Thank you.'

'Not at all. If you'll excuse me now, I must locate some papers before my colleague arrives.'

He went upstairs and Philip left the house, feeling less triumphant than he had expected. His annoyance gradually dissipated on the way home, however. He'd as good as got what he wanted. He could manage Pearl easily enough and there was no immediate rush to finalize his accommodation. For the time being, he'd concentrate on his audition.

18

Pearl always worked over Christmas. There were two reasons. The altruistic one was generally followed throughout the hospital: that it was fairer to give this time to the people with families, especially to those who had small children. The second, personal, reason was that it was pleasanter to be on the ward than to be at home by herself. The staff were full of jollity, ready to find any source of hilarity. Someone dressed up as Santa Claus with a sack of milk-chocolate soft centres and talcum powder donated by the Rotary Club. Any of the non-resident patients could come in as usual, and social services referred several who would otherwise have been alone. There was a proper Christmas dinner and a sing-song.

Clovis had enquired solicitously what Pearl would be doing then. He himself was going to be away for a couple of days but asked Pearl to join him for a drink on Boxing Day evening when he returned. Pearl was glad to accept. This Christmas season removed from her several of the features of her new life, and she could easily feel that she had gone into abeyance. The first term of night classes was completed, and Roz's school had broken up so there were no more visits that year. She and Duncan were spending most of the holidays with their families out of London. Philip was visiting his mother in Leamington. With Clovis away too, she might easily feel marooned, almost in her old life, as if she had been living an illusion, a feeling which could be exacerbated by having so far to go to achieve her aims, while those near to her were visibly progressing. Roz had applied for a deputy headship, which in Pearl's opinion she well deserved. She had brought the form for Clovis to check, apologetically explaining that she didn't want to ask Duncan since he was so absorbed in his own work. As for Philip, he had decided to accept the offer from Magus. Rehearsals in London started after Christmas, then he went on tour. Fortunately he had not raised again the question of moving in with Pearl, for the more she thought about it, the less favourably did she view the suggestion. She'd learnt a lot during the time she'd known Philip, but he was to be taken in small doses, not as a constant companion. And no matter how he'd denied it afterwards, he had tried to argue against her getting herself educated and becoming a social worker. He'd changed his tune to suit the occasion. You couldn't rely on someone who did that.

She felt a pang of loneliness on Christmas Day, coming back from the hospital to an empty house, even though she'd left the light burning in the hall so that she wouldn't have to face darkness too. Everywhere on the journey back there were Christmas trees in windows, coloured lights, and paper streamers decorating front rooms. Pearl imagined the people indoors relaxing and laughing together. Families. Belonging. The streets were quiet as the lone bus rattled along, its crew anxious to get home and join in the festivities.

On Boxing Day evening, the light was shining upstairs. Pearl did not bother going up to her own room but knocked directly on Clovis's door.

He opened with an uncharacteristic flourish. 'Happy Christmas,' he said.

'And to you.' She hesitated. 'You did ask me to come, didn't you?'

'I did indeed.'

Music was playing. Clovis lowered the volume, gave her a chair, poured drinks. Beyond the long windows, a yellow moon hung over the Common. The piano was open, the cello leaning against it.

'How was work?' asked Clovis, sitting down.

Pearl described the ward's activities. 'Did you enjoy your Christmas?' she finished, shyly.

'Thank you, yes. I was staying with some friends whom I

haven't seen for a good few years. It was a generous invitation.' He rocked his wine glass ruminatively, then added, 'Picking up dropped threads isn't easy after so long.'

It sounded like a thought spoken aloud. Pearl sat quietly, watching. He looked up and said in a different, conversational tone, 'Philip didn't stay in London for Christmas?'

'No. He's gone to his mother's in Leamington. He won't be in London much now. He's got a part with a touring company.'

'So he did accept it.'

Pearl was surprised. 'You knew about it?'

'Not in detail. He mentioned it when he came to see me about the room. Which company is it?'

The question flew past Pearl, her attention caught by what came before.

'What room?'

'He'd like to move in here. Hasn't he discussed it with you?'

He'd been to ask Clovis about moving in! What cheek! Without telling her! Sneaking around behind her back.

'What did he say?'

Clovis raised his eyebrows. 'He compared our relative positions, he described the problems of finance and accommodation when touring and he pointed out that there were rooms here which weren't being used. As there are.'

So he hadn't asked about moving in with Pearl, as she had immediately assumed. He'd been after a room for himself. Certainly that would be better than having him sharing with her, but how dare he go and accost Clovis! Had he no decency? She felt it reflected on her. 'As there are,' said Clovis.

She straightened her lip. Philip had won.

'You said yes.'

'No. That decision is yours.'

Incredulous. 'Mine?'

'Yours.'

'But it's your house, Mr Fordingham.'

'Clovis.'

' – Clovis – it's not for me to say.'

'You live here. You would be the person most affected.'

Her decision. What should she say? There was room; Clovis didn't mind either way; it would suit Philip to have a permanent address in London; actors didn't have much money. And yet – this last incident repelled her. Why did it? She had the benefit of living here; what right had she to exclude Philip?

'It's entirely up to you,' reiterated Clovis. 'Think it over.'

Clovis had asked her to live there; Philip was pushing himself forward. That was the difference. Except Clovis might have offered first had he known Philip's situation.

'Clovis,' said Pearl slowly. 'Why do you do it?'

'Do what?'

'Let people come and live in your house. It's not your job; you aren't a landlord. You didn't want to take rent from me, and I was a complete stranger. It's not, well, normal. Everybody warned me against coming.'

Clovis smiled. 'I suppose they would.' He put down his glass and placed the tips of his fingers together, thumbs against pursed lips.

Then he dropped his hands. 'I suppose you could say it's the effect of radically changed circumstances. I've only recently come back to this country and my life is very different from the way it was before I left. My old preoccupations have gone, I'm not gripped by any new ones, so why not live simply, doing what the immediate situation seems to demand, when it demands it? You needed somewhere to live; I could provide somewhere to live. Hey presto.' He spread his hands in a magician's gesture.

There was a lot hinted at, thought Pearl. What aspect was safest to pursue?

'You haven't lived in this house very long?'

'I've lived here nearly all my life. The house was let to tenants while I was away. You see – I have been a landlord. When the tenants returned to their own country, I returned to mine.'

'What country did you go to?'

'America.'

'Did your work take you there?'

His mouth twisted. 'Not in the way you mean. I taught there – music – much the same as I do now.'

'Had you been abroad before?'

Again that twisting. A pause before answering. 'I was born

abroad. In India. My father died just before Independence, and my mother brought me back to England straight away. My father's was a long-standing colonial family, but my mother went out only because she married him. This is her house. Her father was living in it at the time and we joined him here.'

'You've lived here ever since?'

'More or less.'

Pearl laughed. 'You know, there's always someone who asks me if I miss the sunshine and coconuts although I've lived here all my life. Nobody would dream of asking you, but you're the one with the tropical memories.'

'Very vague ones. I was only about five or six when we left. They're mainly impressions of heat and colour. Baked colours: yellows, ochres and rust; white *kurtas* and bright saris. I can remember lying beneath a ceiling fan – at least, I suppose I was lying beneath it – that's the angle I remember it from. Round and round, whirring. A clammy dampness that must have been monsoon time – sheets and clothes feeling sticky. I may have other memories or they may be stories I was told later. My mother loved India itself although she loathed the life of a memsahib.'

'Did you like America?'

A strange expression came over Clovis's face. Again he paused.

'It made me drive,' he said eventually.

Drive? What a peculiar reply.

'One must drive in such a car-orientated society.'

'I'm glad you do drive now,' said Pearl vehemently. 'If you couldn't, I don't know what the gang might have done to me that evening.'

Again, Clovis's face seemed to be responding to an inner sequence of thought. He stroked his throat silently, then switched subject. 'How are your plans going? What stage are you up to now?'

'Same as before, really. I'm just concentrating on the Psychology course at the moment.'

'Is it coming along well?'

'I'm getting a lot better. I mean, I'm not good or anything. But I know how to go about writing an essay now. And I'm used to looking things up in the library and picking bits from different books. I expect most people started off being able to do that, but for me it's progress.'

'So have you begun to apply for social-work courses yet?'

'Oh no,' said Pearl. 'I haven't anything to put on a form. Unless I pass the exam in the summer.'

'Your hospital experience. Your visits to Roz's school. Your evening classes.'

'It's not much, though, is it?'

'I think it would be enough. It's well worth trying for next year. Don't you want to?'

'I wouldn't know where to try. I mean, I don't know what colleges to apply for; I don't know the sort of courses the different places put on; I don't know how to apply. I haven't investigated any of that yet.'

'It shouldn't present much of a problem. I can help there.'

'Can you? Do you know about social-work courses?'

'Not specifically. But I know about applying for Higher Education in general and how you can find out about your courses. You'd need to apply early for a grant too.'

'I can't ask you to help me.'

'Why not?'

'It's too much trouble.'

'No trouble, provided that you'd like me to. I don't want to push you into decisions if you don't feel ready to make them yet.'

She could be ready to decide, if she knew what she was deciding – and Clovis could help her acquire that information. She could apply for next year. The gap between her present and future selves contracted sharply. She might be nearer to her future than she realized. In the coming autumn she might be a proper student, studying full-time at a proper college, on her way to a profession. Even if she didn't make it this time, she'd have learned how to go about it better for her next attempt. Initially she'd felt doubtful about being able to cope with her present Psychology course; but she was coping. She could learn to cope with applications and interviews too. She could learn to cope with a more difficult course.

'I'm ready,' she said.

She felt ready, too, to cope with Philip. He rang up the following evening and arrived not long afterwards. Pearl opened the front door, having been poised on the stairs waiting for the knock so as to prevent him from meeting Clovis first.

'Pearl!' he stood on the doorstep, head on one side, smiling his golden smile. Pearl led him up the stairs.

Once in her room he took both her hands, looked her up and down, then kissed her open palms. 'How I've longed for you,' he said and began planting more kisses over her face.

'Did you have a nice time?' asked Pearl.

'It made my mother happy, poor darling, and that's what it's all about. For myself, I'd rather have stayed here and had Christmas with you.'

'Except that I always work over Christmas.'

'I know, my love; you're very unselfish.'

'I quite enjoy it.'

'We'll make up for it, though. We'll have our own Christmas celebrations, very special ones. Just for us.'

He sat, pulling her gently down with him. 'The one good thing about being away from someone you care about deeply is the delights of the reunion.'

'You're going to be away a lot soon,' said Pearl, balancing on him.

'Don't worry about it, dear heart. While I'm away, just keep thinking of what it will be like when I'm back again.'

'I've been thinking about that already.'

'Good girl. We're strong enough together to survive a separation. And in the meantime, we'll both be growing. We'll have more to give each other from our new experiences. Each time I come back, our relationship will be richer.'

Pearl didn't reply.

'Don't worry,' he repeated, shaking her gently. 'It'll be all right. In fact it's the best way for people like us with aims in our lives. And while we're on the subject, Pearl, I've solved our other problem too.'

'Which problem?'

'My accommodation. I'm going to move in here, but into the house, not into your room. I'll have my own room. We'll be here together, but also free in our independent spheres.'

'You've discussed this with Clovis?'

'Well of course, my love. I could hardly do it without his knowing.'

'When did this happen?' Pearl wanted to hear what it sounded like coming from Philip – and to test her own reactions again.

'Oh, some time before Christmas.'

'You didn't say anything to me about it.'

'It was in converstaion, my love. Between Clovis and me. We were chatting about the theatre and Magus and the problems of touring. And he offered me a room here, as a base.'

'*He* suggested it?'

'And naturally I was delighted. As you were when you moved in, weren't you?'

'Yes I was.'

'This must be a delight to you, too. This way we can be together yet leave space for each other. It must be good for you too, Pearl.'

'Except that I'm not delighted.' Pearl got up and stood, hands on hips, frowning down at Philip. 'I said before that I thought it was wrong to exploit Clovis's kindness. You've gone ahead regardless.'

'What an exaggeration. It's hardly exploitation, Pearl. He's giving me a room, that's all. He has several available, you may have noticed. He has a great deal available to him. It's not going to hurt him to have us cashing in on it. That's not exploitation. Any exploitation around must have come from his family in the past. You don't get his advantages without milking somebody somewhere along the line.'

'That's a different matter. It's past and it's not personal.'

'You moved in like a shot.'

'That was his idea. I didn't think he owed it to me.'

'He doesn't *owe* it to me, my sweet.'

'That's what you just about said.'

Philip got up and put his hands on Pearl's shoulders. 'Pearl, he's happy with the idea. You're the one who's making the fuss. It's no problem to him, why is it to you? When we talked about it before, I could tell you didn't want me to move in with you. And yes, it did hurt me. Then I realized you were right. A relationship like ours doesn't depend on being together all the time, and we both have things to do with our lives. This ideal solution comes up, and I thought you'd be as delighted as I am. Why aren't you, Pearl? It's very hurtful to me.'

Pearl walked away and stood with her back to him by the window overlooking the Common. 'Leave me alone, Philip.'

'It's got to be discussed some time, Pearl. There's no point in shelving it.'

'I mean, leave *me* alone. Go away please. I want to be by myself.'

'That's terrific, isn't it? I haven't seen you for days. I ring up and schlep all the way over here, yet again, and now you tell me you want to be by yourself. You might have told me on the telephone you were in that sort of mood.'

'It's not a mood. I mean – leave me permanently. I want to go back to being on my own.'

He was at her side, hand on arm. 'Come on, Pearl. It doesn't have to be like this. We can sort something out.'

'I have sorted something out. This is it.'

'Why Pearl? It's been so good. What's happened?'

'I'm better by myself. Thank you all the same.'

'I don't want to leave you.' He began nuzzling.

Pearl pushed him away with annoyance.

Philip backed off. 'Sweet Jesus, doesn't she pout.'

'You swear too much.'

'Ay me. That Puritan streak again.'

'Goodbye.'

'Goodbye to you. Let me know when you recover. There's no point in staying with you when you're in this mood.'

'There's no point in staying at all.'

She didn't move away from the window until she saw him going down the drive and out of the gateway.

So what if it was selfish? She didn't want him mucking up her plans and that was that.

19

He was back in London. What an escape. Back to his books, his bureau, the peacefulness of the flat. The best part of a week had been spent with his family over Christmas, then on to Roz's parents, the Latimers. It was a nice judgement which was the more trying of the two: his own family's blinkered lack of appreciation of his way of life, or the other lot's sickly pseudo-understanding. Probably the latter, though that ranking might be an order-effect produced by his already feeling the strain of the visit to his own family. Both had seemed much worse this year. A couple of days with the Latimers had just about finished him off. He had resorted to being convincingly struck by an important new idea connected with his research, and had used this as an excuse to make a getaway. Roz was still with them, being filial.

What did he care now, at a distance, what they said or thought? Why should it irk him anyway? Yet it had, when he was trapped with them.

'I can't see that it's of any use,' said his brother, a builder. 'Be honest now – at the end of the day where's all that education got you? No offence like, but look at you. Examination passes up and down your arms. Years and years of studying. Still at it. And what you got to show for it? No offence, but you've got no job, you've a flat which, if I'm not mistaken, you pay rent for, and your wife has to go out to work. Now look at me. I'm not boasting, like. I'm just saying for example. I've not got exams but I've got a good solid trade.

I work hard and it pays off. We've never wanted, even when we went Council, and now look what we've got. Our own house – first occupants. Fitted kitchen, carpets, curtains, the lot. Lovely furniture. New car and we'll get one for our Terry when he passes his test. My wife's a lady of leisure, aren't you, love? I can provide for my family like a man should, and I do it to a high standard too. It's a contrast, Duncan, you've got to admit it.'

'Everybody's different, Roy,' said his father peaceably. 'We've never had much by way of possessions, have we, Mother, but we've been happy.'

'We have that,' said his mother. 'And it's nice to have a scholar in the family.'

But it was Roy who was taking them on holiday next summer, to Ibiza, fully paid for.

'I think education's important,' said his sister Maureen. 'That's why we took out that scheme for school fees, so they can go to a good school instead of the Comprehensive. They don't learn them nothing there, and you need a good education nowadays to get a job. It's not like it used to be.'

'I'm with you there,' said Roy. 'Up to a point. I'm not saying education's no good. I'm just saying you can go too far with it and not get anywhere, if you take my meaning.'

'You don't stand much chance without some qualifications in this day and age. I want the best for my children and I don't mind who knows it.'

Those children. Two of Maureen's – garrulous, whiney, junior-school-age girls – and monosyllabic Terry. Fighting for control over the television, walking around with blaring cassettes, lounging with their feet up, demanding and being given instant attention.

To remember that before Christmas he'd been quite swayed towards the imagined pleasures of family life. He must have been more tired than he'd noticed.

It was quieter at the Latimers': a genteel, oppressive quiet. Roz's parents let it be known that they weren't upset that Christmas itself had been spent with Duncan's side this year. They fully accepted the need to share these occasions out. It was a pity, though. It hadn't seemed like Christmas being on their own. That was the disadvantage of having only one child.

Mr and Mrs Drummond senior must have enjoyed immensely the presence of all three children, not to mention the grandchildren. Such a pleasure in grandchildren. Pass those serviettes, Rosamund dear. Now Duncan, tell us about your research. It must be so exciting to contribute to our understanding of human nature. We're very proud of you.

He had not really been struck with new ideas for his research. He only wished he had. Spacious as it felt to be back in the London flat, he wasn't any the more attracted to his thesis. It lay heavy over his present and seized up his brain with tedium whenever he approached his bureau. He dealt with this by avoidance. He needed a break, a real one, not a taxing experience like Christmas. He sat with his back to the bureau, reading John Le Carré.

The first day on his own was bliss, the second and third less so. Although he had spent much of the last few years by himself in the daytime, there had always been Roz in the morning and evening. Without that framework he felt strangely uncorseted. He would have liked to look up and see Roz leaning over her marking or unrolling her wallchart of the Voyages of Discovery. There was a vacuum where she ought to be, and she would be away for a few more days. The afternoon spread on into the evening with no cut-off point. He was beginning to rattle round in his freedom, neither enjoying his solitude nor making use of it.

He should call some friends and arrange to meet. But who? He had been so involved in his work that he had lost contact with the people he'd known at college and university, and had not replaced them with new friendships. Except Philip. Philip had said that he'd be around soon after Christmas. Philip had suggested they get together before the new term. He rang Philip.

'Hello there,' said Philip's voice. 'Do you know, you were on my mind?'

'Was I?' said Duncan, pleased. 'What a coincidence.'

'I was thinking how we said we'd be in touch, and that I must see if you'd come back yet. How was it? Did you have a good Christmas?'

'Yes thanks,' said Duncan. 'You?'

A groan came down the line. 'Not my time of year, I'm

afraid. Very constricting. I got away as soon as I could.'

'I know what you mean,' said Duncan. 'I only said I had a good time out of habit. Actually, I got away early too.'

'Good to be back, isn't it?'

'You said it.'

'How's Roz? Does she enjoy it?'

'She's still with her parents. I came back on my own. I couldn't take any more.'

'So you're a free agent for a while?'

'I suppose I am.'

'We'd better make the most of it. Where do you want to go?'

'A pub would suit me.'

'To start with. Then what?'

Duncan laughed. 'I'm a man of modest needs.'

'I wish I was. Right – pub, then party.'

'I don't know that I'm up to a party.'

'On your own in the big bad city? You're up to anything, mate. I'll come round to your place, shall I?'

They arrived at the party well after closing-time, Duncan's initial reluctance attenuated by several hours of ale and Philip. It was held in the East End in a large terraced house. The windows were open, the door ajar and sounds of music, voices and laughter cascaded out on to the street as Duncan paid the minicab driver. Philip pushed open the front door with difficulty against the bodies packing the hall.

'Philip! How sweet of you to come!' It was a dark-haired woman in a bright red dress.

'Wouldn't have missed it for the world.' Philip embraced her. 'How are you, darling? You're looking wonderful. Meet Duncan, an old dear friend of mine. Duncan, this is Sophie. You're at her and her old man's housewarming.'

'Hello Duncan. Nice to meet you. Are you in the business too?'

'No, no,' said Duncan.

'Very wise. And nice to find someone here who isn't. It gets so incestuous. You're very welcome. Now, Philip, what do you think of it?'

'Incest?'

'The house, darling.'

'Super. Absolutely super. So much detail left. Just look at that plasterwork. Luscious. Look, Duncan.'

Duncan looked up at a ceiling festooned with bunches of pock-marked grapes.

'We're picking it out,' said Sophie. 'There are years and years of distemper up there. They'd almost flattened it. What a job though. Up a ladder, poking away at a ceiling, the bits dropping in your eyes.'

'A right little Michelangelo.'

'How long did it take him?'

'Four years, wasn't it?'

'Blimey, don't tell Will. Half an hour's his limit. I know who'll end up doing it all. Ah, there he is – Will!'

She stretched out an arm to a large hairy man carrying several glasses of wine.

'Philip!' he exclaimed. 'Good to see you! Hang on a mo while I get rid of these to the punters.' He pushed his way backwards into the party and emerged a few minutes later having off-loaded the drinks. He put an arm round Philip and shook his hand. 'Good to see you,' he said warmly.

'You too,' said Philip and introduced Duncan.

Will shook his hand warmly too. 'Has Sophie been telling you how we've sentenced ourselves to hard labour? We must have been crazy to take it on.'

'Not with so much potential,' said Philip. 'It's going to be wonderful when you've finished.'

'So much of it is undoing what those before have done. Unboxing the staircase, putting back the cornices, taking the formica off. Dear God, you wouldn't believe what people do. Have you heard about the fireplace?'

'I haven't got on to that yet,' said Sophie.

'Come and look,' said Will.

They squeezed into the other half of the double room.

'These are ours,' shouted Will as they passed the folding doors between the two halves. 'They'd been replaced by a stud partition, but luckily the architrave was still there. We pinched the doors off a skip in the next street. Stripping well, aren't they?'

They arrived at the fireplace.

'Just look at that,' said Will.

Duncan looked. It was metal with tiles and a carved wooden surround.

'That's beautiful,' said Philip. 'Really lovely. Where did you find it? It must have cost a fortune.'

Will laughed gleefully. 'It was here,' he said. 'All boxed in again.'

'There was this wooden excrescence,' said Sophie, 'coming out of the wall. I said, "Come on Will, we've got to get rid of that," and he says, "It'll be covering up a fireplace."'

'But I expected it to be one of those fifties jobs,' said Will. 'You know – Chez Nous with the horse brasses. Not this. It only needed a new firebrick. Amazing, isn't it?'

'If you do find any fifties fireplaces,' said Philip, 'you should hang on to them. Seriously. I mean, store them somewhere. It must be the next revival.'

'Ah, revivals,' said Will. 'That reminds me. Anabel's here. Have you seen her?'

Philip rounded his lips. 'OK. Thanks, Will.'

'You should get some food,' said Sophie, 'while there are a few fragments left. I've been slaving away for hours. I need you to appreciate it.'

'I'm sure we will,' said Philip. 'Coming Duncan?'

There wasn't much left. They took what remains there were over to a space by the pinched stripped doors.

'Hello Philip,' said a cool female voice.

'Anabel!' cried Philip. 'How are you my love? It seems an age.'

'Does it?' said Anabel.

'Meet Duncan,' said Philip.

'Hello Duncan,' said Anabel.

'And what have you been up to?' said Philip.

'Not much.'

'Not much!' echoed a small balding man who was leaning against the doors, holding a whisky bottle. 'Same old story everywhere, isn't it? It's a risky business when times are good. When they're bad – nothing.'

Philip nodded gravely.

'Have a drink,' said the man, waving his bottle. 'Where's

your glasses? Down to plastic cups, are we? Never mind. Hold them out, I'll fill them up.'

Their cups were still partially full of wine.

'Chuck it away,' said the man. 'You don't want that when there's the real stuff on offer. I always bring my own to parties nowadays.'

'You drink it yourself then,' said Anabel.

'There's plenty more, sweetheart. Don't worry about that. Look –' Another bottle was stuffed in his inside jacket pocket 'Come on, my old mate, let's have your cup.'

'I'm all right, thanks,' said Duncan.

'You'll be righter still soon.'

He took Duncan's wine, crouched down and poured it through a crack in the floorboards.

'There,' he said, filling the cup with whisky. 'Next please.'

Philip finished his wine and handed over the cup.

'Good lad,' said the man. 'I'm George, by the way.'

They said their names.

George filled Anabel's cup. 'To Lady Fortune,' he said. 'May she turn the wheel up.'

They drank to Lady Fortune.

'So what are we all doing here?' said George. 'What's the connection?'

'"Tinderbox,"' said Philip.

'That's right,' said the man, with recognition. 'I thought you were a familiar face. You too, eh?' to Anabel. 'You?' he looked suspiciously at Duncan.

'No,' said Duncan. 'I'm a friend of Philip's.'

George stared at his feet. 'And I'm a friend of Will's,' he said. 'We were at RADA together. I got the Best Actor award in our year, and I've never been heard of since. None of us thought much of Will's chances and he's on the up and up. It's a whorey old business.'

'That's the way it goes,' said Philip.

'Have you had much work since "Tinderbox?"'

'I haven't had many offers to attract me recently but I – '

'That's one way of putting it.'

'Oonagh!' called Philip suddenly over their heads. 'Would you excuse me, George. I've just seen someone I must have a word with.'

George waved his hand. 'Nice chap, though, Will. Couldn't happen to a better fellow. In fact, they're a lovely couple. Even the kids. Where are the kids? Are they locked away upstairs somewhere?'

'They're staying with friends,' said Anabel.

'Lovely house,' continued George. 'At least, it will be when it's finished. I couldn't do it, though. All this picking out of moulding and what have you. Dear God. Paper it over, I say. Preferably pay someone else to do it. Lovely fireplace over there. Did you notice it?'

'I'll look now,' said Anabel, and left.

'Costs a lot,' said George, refilling his glass. 'More?'

Duncan shook his head.

'A place like this costs a lot. Even if you do it yourself. It's the film, you know.'

Duncan didn't know.

'Film. That's where the money is. That's where this house came from. A minor part in *Contour Man* and you can move house. That's the secret.'

'I haven't seen that film.'

'It's not been released yet. They should name the house after it. Better than Still Owen. Couldn't happen to a nicer bloke, though. Have another drink. No? Must have a slash. Won't be long.'

Duncan took George's place against the folded doors and looked round the room. A bare room, full of laughter, gestures, demonstrations and rounded voices.

'Have you heard about Chad?' came from a very young group nearby. Nobody had.

'You'll never believe it. Chad – wait for it – Chad is training to be an accountant. I know. I know. Incredible but true. Says he's fed up of being skint, he's going where the money is; stuff art.'

'It's a loss. He was very talented. We were both with Artsmobile a couple of years ago, and he was really something.'

'I didn't know you'd been with Artsmobile.'

'God yes. But I try not to think about it too much.'

'Bad as that?'

'They're all right. But you play such cruddy places. One

night we were out in the sticks with an ASM who didn't know his A from his E. I storm off stage after my moment of glory and this guy's only put a pile of stacking-chairs right in my exit. I storm straight into them, metal ones, an' all. There's this almighty crash, my leg's cut open, I twist my ankle. They're on stage trying to pretend nothing's happening and I've got to hobble back on with my pants torn and blood dripping down me. Cor dear. There's how many unemployed and they take on nurdles like that one.'

Philip and Anabel were talking at the other side of the room. Philip waved, said something to Anabel and began to squeeze his way back to Duncan. Halfway across he was hooked into another group. Duncan joined them. Two conversations were taking place simultaneously.

'Used them as extras,' someone was saying earnestly. 'Paid them a pittance. Tom objected at one point but he just said that it was a lot more to them in comparison with their standard of living and he never lacked volunteers. Totally unscrupulous. His much-vaunted third-world idealism is a complete sham.'

'It's creeping gentrification,' went the other conversation. 'This house was a multi-occupancy before. Everyone keeps going on about the amount of work in redoing it, but what about the poor sods who were living here before? Where do they go when they're winkled out? What happens to the poor when affluence decides it likes their neighbourhood?'

Groups merged, groups disintegrated, groups reconstituted. Philip embraced many women and some men. Anabel came back. Philip went away. A new film was discussed. Anabel and Duncan were the remaining group.

Duncan made an effort. 'You know Philip from "Tinderbox"?' he said.

'Yes,' said Anabel, looking out into the room.

'I'm afraid I didn't follow it regularly.'

'Never mind.'

'Did you have a good part?'

'Reasonable.' She continued to look outwards.

Duncan tried the other conversation. 'This house will be nice when it's finished.'

'So everyone keeps saying.'

'Don't you like it?'

'I just think it's an extremely boring topic of conversation.'

'So do I,' agreed Duncan wholeheartedly.

Anabel turned to him for the first time, scrutinizing.

'Have you known Philip long?' she asked eventually.

'Not long. No. A few months.'

'But you're friends? You see each other quite regularly?'

'Yes. At least weekly. We both – '

'That's nice.' She smiled at Duncan, a delightful smile which transformed her sullen aggression. She held Duncan's inner elbow. 'Will you wait here for me, Duncan? I won't be a minute. I'm just going to the loo, but I'll be back.'

She gave Duncan her plastic cup and disappeared.

George came by. 'Two cups now,' he said. 'Good lad. Fill them up.'

'I think there was wine in that one,' objected Duncan, unable to stop him pouring out more whisky.

'Grape and grain,' said George. 'And more for you too, Philip old pal. It was Philip, wasn't it? How about you, darling?'

Philip had brought over Oonagh, his latest lady. 'One minute,' he said to her. 'I must have a word with Duncan here.'

His lady smiled at Duncan.

'Anabel,' said Philip to Duncan.

Duncan waited for more.

'That's Anabel you were talking to.'

'Yes.'

'Be kind to her, Duncan. That's what I wanted to say to you. She's been having a hard time recently and she needs some kindness. Be good to her – eh?'

'I'll try,' said Duncan doubtfully. 'But she's not very communicative.'

'Don't let that put you off. It's only a defence. She needs kindness. Ah, she's coming back. Hello Anabel. See you Duncan. We're going over the hall for a boogie.'

'For a what?' asked Duncan of Anabel, wondering if it were a euphemism.

'A boogie. A dance. Let's go too.'

She took the plastic cups from him and put them by the

skirting-board.

'I'm no good at dancing,' protested Duncan.

'There won't be any room for anyone to be good at it. Come on. Bye George.'

The room across the hall was dimly lit and full of varieties of dancing. Duncan stepped from one foot to the other as rhythmically as he could. Music, darkness, swaying. He felt loose-limbed and floating-brained. They had danced near to Philip and Ooonagh. Anabel was very close, under his chest it seemed. Her mouth was moving. She was saying something.

'Sorry, I can't hear you,' said Duncan, still changing his weight from foot to foot.

Anabel's mouth moved again.

Duncan beamed down at her. 'Sorry.' He moved his shoulders in time with his feet.

Anabel stopped dancing and put her hands on his arms to hold him stationary. Then she stretched her mouth up to his ear and said, 'It's too hot and noisy in here. Let's find somewhere quieter where we can talk.'

She took him by the hand. Duncan lolloped after. They bumped into Philip and Oonagh as they passed, but Anabel didn't seem to notice. She led him up the uncarpeted, unboxed stairs. A row of doors led off the landing. A queue indicated the bathroom. Behind another door, a small tight cluster of people was crouched on the floor, their attention on a white packet. Anabel closed the door again. The next room contained the guests' coats, piled on bed, chairs and dressing-table. A girl was rummaging through them, crying. The next was a dumping-ground. There was no light, and that from the sodium lamp outside revealed packed cardboard boxes, plastic sacks, plant pots, a stringless guitar.

Anabel found two cushions and put them against a filing-cabinet. The beat of the music below throbbed up through the floor. Anabel's hair glowed against the curtainless window. Duncan rested his head backwards. Anabel put hers on his shoulder. Duncan felt mindless, liquid.

'Who are you?' said Anabel softly.

'Me? I'm Duncan.' His tongue moved reluctantly, as if he were talking through semi-sleep.

'Duncan, tell me how you know Philip.'

She was stroking his leg. Nice.

'I'm very comfortable,' said Duncan. 'I like it better in this room.'

'With me?'

'Yes.' He could stay like this for ever.

Anabel began to undo his shirt.

20

As soon as you're back at school, thought Roz, it's as though the holidays had never existed. There was always such a build-up to Christmas, what with carol concerts and nativity plays and parties and painting Christmas cards. Then everyone went away home luxuriating in the long free stretch ahead which, once you arrived at the other side of it, seemed to vanish into nothing.

The holiday hadn't been exactly a holiday anyway. That first part with Duncan's family involved continual references to their lack of home, possessions, trips abroad, children. Did his family feel threatened by Duncan's academic achievements, using the jibes and comparisons to protect themselves? Or did they just seize any opportunity to gloat over their own material success?

'Your wife has to go out to work.' Has to go out to work! Was that all they could say about Roz's career? She had not realized until then quite how much she extended into her job. Yet she also knew that her life must be easier were she not the sole financer. The comments scalded her twice: because they were right to some degree, and because they were right for the wrong reasons.

So she had been torn; part of her galled by what Duncan's brother and sister said, part of her wishing that Duncan would be a little influenced in their direction. She had kept these divisions clamped together and held down under an amenable façade, both because she wasn't naturally an explosive person, and for the sake of Duncan's parents, whom she liked. Mainly, though, it was to counteract Duncan himself who was becoming increasingly touchy.

She had tried to discuss it with him on the train journey to her own parents, but he had been unforthcoming. Staying at her parents hadn't improved matters. After a couple of days Duncan had been struck with ideas crucial to his thesis and had scarpered back to London. Roz doubted the authenticity of his excuse and was again divided by her reactions. She envied the unbespoke days he was going to; she was peeved with him for not sticking it out with her parents – she'd done it for him so it was only fair that he should pull his weight in return; she was also relieved. It had been hard work for her having to fill in his silences and answer pleasantly for him so as to minimize the effects of his boredom and irritation. Since he wasn't being sociable, it was easier for her to do her bit without him. He had been heading towards an outburst and she was at least grateful that he had gone before the situation got any worse.

A partly-this, partly-that holiday; the parts in conflict, and the conflict exacerbated by the dilemma with which she had started off: deputy headship versus baby. Of course, the dichotomy wasn't really so clear-cut, logically she knew that. A lot of other factors were involved. She'd thought through the various permutations so many times. Nevertheless, the two possibilities had come to represent aspects of herself, herself in relation to Duncan.

The explosion which had been avoided by Duncan's leaving had instead occurred for her, albeit in a less dramatic way than had been promised by Duncan's behaviour. The tension of her conflicts finally erupted during a conversation with her mother over the washing up.

'Duncan takes his research very seriously, doesn't he?' said her mother, rinsing her cut-glass fruit bowl under the cold-water tap to make it sparkle.

'Of course,' said Roz, already nettled. 'You have to at that level.'

'Yes, he's done very well,' agreed her mother. 'But Roz, tell me truthfully darling, is it worth it?'

'What do you mean?'

'Duncan's a dear boy, Rosamund, and a clever one too. We

all acknowledge that. But, well darling, isn't he just a little bit in danger of becoming the eternal student? The other day you said he might be going on to do even more research after this. What did you call it?'

'Post-doctoral.'

'What is it leading to? When will it end? What will *you* get out of all this research?'

'That's what the academic life is, Mother. You build your position on research.'

'But what position, Rosamund? That's what I'm getting at. When is he going to get a proper job? At his stage in life, a man should be steadily improving his circumstances and providing for his family. Daddy certainly did and I was proud of him for it.'

'Different people have different ways of living.'

'Maybe, but some of them look rather like a shirking of responsibility, especially when you get beyond a certain age.'

'I'll say it again – he's an academic, and research is important in the academic world. It may not seem worthwhile to you, but it does to the people involved, to people who actually know something about it.'

'Now Rosamund, I expect you think I'm an ignorant old lady and I don't understand clever things like Duncan does. But I do know about life, about the things which really matter when all's said and done. Rosamund, are you happy? Are you really?'

'Yes thank you.'

'I'm not trying to interfere, but we can't help seeing your circumstances and we do worry about you sometimes, Daddy and I.'

'There's no need to worry. I'm fine.'

'You're a loyal wife, Rosamund. I hope Duncan respects you for it.'

'But I am fine. In fact, I'm doing quite well myself. I've been asked to apply for a deputy headship.'

Her mother clucked impatiently. 'That's not what we're talking about. A deputy headship! Oh, it's very well, but you're not getting any younger. Nor are we. I'll spell it out Rosamund, because like it or not, it's the truth of the situation and it has to be faced. You and Duncan are at the time of life when as professional people you would normally expect to have a nice house of your own and a growing family. A proper home. Duncan hasn't had a job in years and, let's face it, he'll be lucky to get one the way things are at present. You're talking about headships. He's the one who ought to be talking about headships, Rosamund. He should be bringing home the bacon. You should be talking about children, your children. I'm not going to beat about the bush any longer. A woman doesn't have the choice for ever.'

'You're taking it for granted that I'm able to have children,' said Roz viciously.

'Darling!' Her mother whirled round, red-rubber hands spattered with foam. 'Is that what it is? Oh darling. I am sorry. Why did you never say so? Now are you sure? Have you been to a doctor about it, a specialist? They can perform miracles, you know. Have you?'

'No,' said Roz. 'I've had no reason to yet.'

Her mother stared at her. 'What do you mean? Can you or can't you?'

'How do I know?'

'You know when you keep trying and nothing happens.'

'Exactly.'

'What are you saying, Roz?'

'I'm saying, Mother,' her voice tight with the struggle to restrain her anger and tears, 'I'm saying that it's none of your business.'

Her mother turned back to the sink. 'But it is, to a certain extent. We're your parents. We want you to be happy. We're also getting on in years. You're our only child, Roz, and we want to be grandparents. You can't deny us that.'

'So that's how babies arrive is it? Gift-wrapped for grandparents?'

'Don't be coarse, Rosamund.'

'Coarse! You stand there presuming to discuss someone else's private circumstances, not to mention biological capacities, and you call me coarse!' She lowered her voice with effort. 'Thank you for your concern, Mother, but it is none of your business.'

Her mother's back stiffened. 'If that's the way you want it,' she said. 'I was only trying to help. And all I can say now is that you've made it perfectly obvious by your behaviour what you really feel about your situation. You can't pull the wool over my eyes, Rosamund. I've seen too much of life. But don't worry. I shan't mention it again. Not to be spoken to like that by my own daughter.'

It had been difficult for either of them to recover from such a set-to. A considerable silence had been followed by very polite exchanges; then, when her father came in, by the attempt to behave naturally.

Roz had returned to London feeling in need of a holiday to recover from the holiday. It was unlike her to get worked up and quarrelsome as she had with her mother. The explanation was the same as that for her reaction to visiting Duncan's family: a resentment of other people's labelling of her lifestyle, of the lack of status afforded to it, tugging at the fact that nevertheless she did for different reasons want in her life with Duncan some of those elements which the family were deriding them for not having. Her sensibilities had been roughly handled.

Ultimately, however, the experience had crystallized her. The anger and hurt pride she felt as her career was dimissed first as 'having to go out to work' then as 'very well but . . . ' sharpened the edges of a new image of herself which had been growing without her realizing it. She was not quite the timid shadowy person she had always visualized. She was a capable, professional woman. She was qualified, trained, experienced. She was good at her job, good enough to be recognized as such by senior colleagues. The parts of herself that had fragmented and jarred throughout the holiday coalesced to form a new confidence. She was not going to withdraw her application. She was potentially a deputy head. She must act in accordance with the person she now was. The baby? She could manage a baby as well. She was one of the competent people, although she had never realized it before. With extra money from promotion she could afford a child-minder, even if not a house. Nevertheless she might buy a small flat and at least get their feet on the property ladder. If Duncan changed his mind about the baby again, as he might well, especially after the oafishness of his nephew and nieces, then she would need the compensation of a satisfying career. And if it became too late to have children of her own but subsequently they had more money and room, she could adopt one or two older children. Everything was possible. She was even quite glad that she had quarrelled with her mother. It was something she had rarely done before and marked a turning-point.

So although as usual school drowned out the intervening holidays, Roz approached each working day with this different view of herself. Her present job was one out of several she might have, a way-station from which she might soon be promoted. She told Duncan that she was not going to withdraw her application for the deputy headship, which he accepted without comment. He did not raise the baby issue again, so neither did she. She'd leave that for later, after the job was sorted out. Duncan had been rather peculiar since Christmas. Sometimes he came in looking self-satisfied in a way she did not recognize from before; occasionally she caught him grinning secretly to himself. At other times he was more strained than she'd ever known him. When she said teasingly that she was sure he had fabricated his research idea as an excuse for getting back to London, he denied it vehemently, repeated his denial several times and then brought the topic up himself again in order to deny it further. Each time he looked apprehensively at her, as if he were expecting more. She couldn't think what it could be. Perhaps she was imagining it. Or perhaps it was the effect of the new angle of research. He was rather vague when she asked him about it, but it had certainly given him another impetus. He was away in libraries more frequently than before and sometimes stayed till quite late in the evening. Maybe it was overwork that was making him edgy.

The spring term was slipping by. Pearl continued her visits to the school and it became the norm to go back to Pearl's afterwards for tea, Clovis often joining them when he had no meeting or extra tutorial. It had been Pearl's day at school today and Roz was on her way home, not expecting Duncan to be in yet. If he wasn't back reasonably early, she wouldn't bother cooking. She'd zip through her marking, eat an egg in front of the television and be lazy. How pleasant the teatimes were with Pearl and Clovis, despite their seeming such an unlikely combination. Roz always felt at ease with herself afterwards, as if whatever qualities she possessed were sufficient.

Duncan was sitting at the kitchen table reading the evening newspaper.

'Hello,' said Roz. 'I wasn't expecting you to be here.'

'Why shouldn't I be here?' he said defensively.

'Only because you said you'd probably go up to Senate House. You often stay later nowadays.'

Duncan went slightly pink. 'I decided to work at home,' he said shortly.

Prickly again. 'Did it go well?'

'Yeah, yeah.' His tone changed. 'The kettle's boiled, Roz.'

'Right,' said Roz. She made some coffee and sat down opposite Duncan to read her mail. She would refuse to let herself be ruffled by his moods. She would keep herself separate from them and carry on smoothly.

'We regret to inform you . . . Thank you for your application.'

Her stomach reacted to the letter before her brain could register its meaning. She was not on the short list. She'd been rejected. She wasn't good enough. She was no longer Roz Drummond, the stuff that deputy heads are made of. She was Roz Drummond, ordinary class teacher. How could she ever have thought otherwise? What a fool she'd been. She, Roz, the nonentity, the product of unexceptional events, the one who had to struggle to be even satisfactory. How could she have imagined herself to have changed? To be that purposeful achiever, skilfully balancing career and domesticity, organizing a school, buying a flat, bringing up a family.

All gone. All of it.

Duncan turned the page of the newspaper.

The freshness had vanished from her life. She was back to a grinding reality, the monotony of day-in, day-out school. Much the same this year as last, as next year, or even the year after. What else could she do? An uncaring, moody husband; shoestring living, bills which it was up to her to pay. What else could she do? She was trapped in the assurance of her own mediocrity.

'Roz, what's wrong?' Duncan was staring at her over the newspaper.

'Nothing.'

Yes, she was mediocre, she had no hope of ever being anything else. And she couldn't manage the things that even mediocre people seemed to get: homes, babies, comfort.

'There is something wrong. What is it?'

'Nothing. I'm all right.'

She didn't have ordinary pleasures, and she didn't have more public achievements either. She had nothing.

'You look peculiar to me.' He folded up the newspaper.

'That's about the only distinction I can achieve.'

'You sound unusual too.'

'Well I'm not. I'm extremely ordinary.'

'Why go on about it all of a sudden?'

Roz pushed the letter over to him.

Duncan read it, then put it flat on the table. 'It was a very ambitious move,' he said. 'You didn't really expect to get it, did you?'

No, of course not. Except yes.

'I said at the time you were being unrealistic.'

Pie in the sky. And now she had no pie whatsoever.

'Come on, Roz. It's silly to be disappointed about something so improbable. You should have discussed it properly with me.'

'You've been so busy recently.'

Duncan began to show concern. 'Let's sit on the sofa,' he said. 'It's like a prison visit here.'

He put his arm round her.

'I have had a lot to do,' he almost apologized.

'Yes.'

'That doesn't mean I'm not interested in you.'

'You've had other things on your mind.'

'Just work, Roz.'

'Yes.'

'You're not worried about that, are you?'

'Worried about what?'

'My having to be out so much, working.'

'It's got to be done.'

He looked relieved.

'It shouldn't be so bad now. I've broken the back of it.'

'Good.'

'Come on, Roz. Don't look so dejected. This isn't like you. How about a smile to show me you're the same old Roz?'

The same old Roz. That was just it.

Acknowledged with a capitulating smile.

21

That was a good move, Philip told himself back in his room after the day's rehearsal, to palm Anabel off on to Duncan. Anabel was a nice girl, but given the choice between her and Oonagh, there could be no hesitation. At the party he'd had that choice. He wasn't going to lose such an opportunity with Oonagh. On the other hand, he hadn't wanted to sever his links with Anabel irrevocably. She was an agreeable companion, if rather pushy, and he might be glad to have her around another time; certainly he wouldn't have said no to her during the gloom of last summer. They'd had fun together in the past and might do again some day.

Duncan could keep her temporarily occupied and out of mischief. It wouldn't last; just serve the purpose of preventing her getting more deeply entangled with anyone else. Anabel had unwittingly worked hard in line with Philip's plan, presumably thinking that she'd get back to Philip via Duncan. The four of them had gone out for a meal the evening after the party. Anabel had been cosily flirtatious with Duncan, one eye skimming Philip to note his reactions. She had been cool with Philip himself to arouse his jealousy, and pleasant to Oonagh. How easy she had made it for him. Candy from a baby.

Duncan as well. Philip could have predicted that Duncan might get out of his depth at the party, but not quite so far nor quite so thoroughly. Off upstairs with Anabel, who made sure that Philip noticed; returning her intimacies over dinner with yearning eyes and earnest admiration; going back to Anabel's afterwards; continuing to meet her on the sly even after Roz had returned.

Naughty old Duncan, although it was just as well that he had got a Roz to go back to. He wasn't up to an Anabel.

Philip had come back to London after Christmas with a view to more entertainment with Pearl, possibly with *pied à terre* included, only to find her throwing a wobbler on behalf of Clovis. It was an odd thing Pearl had going with Clovis. Perhaps it was some sort of compensation for her own deprived past, as if to take a share of what she had never had, if only by proxy.

It was unfortunate that she'd intervened. Clovis was such a weed, and Philip had been well on the way to having one of his other rooms. To have a free and permanent foothold in London would have been ideal: always to know you had somewhere to return to after working out in the sticks, not having to start looking for bed-sits and flats each time or crashing at friends'. It might be worth another try at a later date.

In the short run, it had mattered little, for suddenly Philip's London was full of friends and acquaintances again. There were parties and visits. He'd had a delicious *entr'acte* with Oonagh and no sooner had she gone off to her season at the Abbey than Melanie had made a flying trip, much chastened. The social press had died down now but rehearsals had started. He was working again. Admittedly Magus was hardly your name in lights, and it meant touring with all its drawbacks – rent-a-bath-plug time. But it was work and there would be other possibilities among the company.

So since Christmas Philip had given up his night class. Eyes-teeth training with Zora was over, at least he hoped it was, although he could already look back with nostalgia at those coffee breaks taken with Duncan and Duncan's research. Found a new area for investigation now, hadn't he? Perhaps Philip would give him a ring and see how he was getting on. He'd nothing planned for that evening. They might have a drink and Philip could hear how things were progressing with Anabel. He ought to renew contact with her before he went on tour, just in case.

Roz answered the telephone. Yes thanks, she was very well. Yes, she'd enjoyed Christmas. It seemed a long time ago now.

Yes, everything was as usual at school. Her voice cracked. No, she was all right. Yes, really. Well, she was just feeling a bit low. No, Duncan was out. She didn't really know what time he'd be back. No, no Philip. She was fine. Really. She was just being silly. No, really.

Philip arrived by minicab with a bottle of wine. Well, why not? While Duncan was out servicing Anabel, why shouldn't Philip comfort his old lady? He had nothing particular to do and Roz was a sweetie.

She opened the door looking embarrassed, led him up to the flat, took his coat, sat him down, offered him coffee. Very housewife-hostess.

'The wine's for you,' he said. 'Brought along with tender loving care. You sounded in need of it.'

Roz blushed and disclaimed.

'Bring us the corkscrew and glasses, will you darling?'

She did. Eager to please. She looked newly combed and changed for him too.

Philip pulled out the cork with a long slow movement and poured the wine. 'So,' he said. 'What ails fair Rosalind?'

Roz blushed again. 'Actually, it's Rosamund,' she said. 'It's kind of you to come. I feel very bad about dragging you all the way over here for nothing.'

It trotted out as if she had been rehearsing it.

'It's not for *nothing*,' emphasized Philip. 'I get to spend an evening with you, even if you don't trust me with your troubles.'

'It's not a case of not trusting,' said Roz hastily. 'I was just being silly. I was a bit low, and then knowing Duncan was going to be out till late – that's all. I was feeling sorry for myself when you rang. It sounded worse than it was.'

Did she suspect Duncan? Was that the real cause?

'How is Duncan? How's his research?'

'He's been working particularly hard recently. He came back from my parents' early at Christmas because he'd some new ideas he wanted to follow up, and he's been at it ever since, in libraries, testing subjects, visiting people who are working in the same area. I never know when to expect him.'

'You're on your own every night?'

'No. I'm giving you the wrong impression. He's just out

more than before, though it's not been as bad recently, and I don't always know when it's going to be. I suppose it depends on how well his work's going.'

Obviously she didn't suspect Duncan. The innocent. Philip replenished their glasses.

'What is this enthralling new line?'

'I'm not really sure. I have asked but I couldn't quite follow. You ask him, Philip. You won't try his patience as much. He'd prefer to tell you.'

'I would, my love, but I don't see him any more, you know. That's partly why I rang, to keep in touch.'

Roz didn't seem to know what he was talking about.

'I don't go to Lixbury any more. I'm working. Didn't Duncan tell you?'

He hadn't, Philip could tell.

Roz tried, though. 'Yes, of course. I'm sorry. I hadn't realized you'd stopped going to your classes. That's what confused me.'

Presumably she couldn't go on because she didn't know anything about it.

Philip gave her a few clues. 'No time for classes now, Roz. They were only to fill in until the right offer came along. It's important to concentrate now.'

'It must be a good offer?'

'Very exciting. I'm with Magus. Does that mean anything to you?'

Obviously not.

'I'd have been surprised if it had. It doesn't aim at the usual theatre audience. It's more – how shall I put it? You've heard of an actors' actor and a writers' writer, meaning someone who is fully appreciated only by professionals within the same field; only a specialist can truly understand the skill and innovation?'

'Yes.'

'I would describe this as an actors' and directors' company, in the same sense. They revive little-known gems from the past; they reinterpret classics of the theatre; they experiment using sound, light, visual images to synthesize trans-media modes of expression. They are exponents of living, evolving theatre arts.'

'Where will it be on?' asked Roz.

'Venues all over Britain, my love. We tour. At the moment we're in rehearsal; next week we're on the road.'

'Do a lot of people go to see it? Are there enough specialists around Britain to make it worthwhile?'

'That's another exciting aspect. Accessibility. Magus also establishes immediate rapport at grass-roots level. We play to factory workers too.'

'You sound very happy about it.'

Said rather flatly, wasn't it?

'I am, I am, my love. "Tinderbox" was fine, but nothing compares with that dynamic interaction between stage and live audience. And it's so very exciting to be working with such an innovatory company. To start out with nothing but the raw materials – ourselves. Bodies, words, experiences. And to know that in a few weeks' time there will be something where before there was nothing; something produced out of those raw materials. Creation will have occurred.'

He shivered with the mystery and exhilaration of the creative process. She was going rosy again. What had he said?

'I am aware,' he said seriously, 'of how lucky I am to be doing just what I want to do in my life. I'm very privileged.'

Over the top maybe but she – Sweet Jesus, she was crying. Without a sound, pressing her lips together, she was crying.

'Roz, Roz.' He leaned forward to her. 'What is it?'

Her shoulders jerked and she drew air in sharply.

Philip knelt in front of her chair and took a hand. 'Roz. Tell me, tell me. Please.'

'It's silly.'

'How can it be if it makes you like this? Tell me Roz. Trust me. Please.'

She'd applied for a deputy headship. She hadn't even been short-listed. She'd put her heart into it. Now she felt she was nothing –

She looked very vulnerable sitting there, her eyes dark with tears, her skin glowing with the heat of emotion. Still holding her hand, he got up and put his arm around her. She didn't relax against him.

Flats, babies, Duncan's research –

With his forefinger he delicately traced a tear as it rolled down her cheek. 'One failure doesn't make you *into* a failure,

Roz,' said Philip. 'You'll succeed another time.'

'It was an illusion. I'm not good enough.'

'You underestimate yourself, my love.'

He laid his face by the side of hers, pushing his hand up through her hair with open fingers, and mouthed into her ear:

'From the east to Western Ind
No jewel is like Rosalind.'

'Rosamund,' came a small voice.

'Rose of the world.'

There was no response. Was this passive resistance or passive acceptance? They remained frozen cheek to cheek for a while. Confusion probably; make the most of it. His hand slid round and stroked her neck.

'Don't.'

Aha.

'Why?' He didn't stop.

'I don't want you to.'

'Don't you?' He nosed her ear and slid his other hand up her arm to grip her shoulder.

'Don't.'

'Roz, Roz,' he crooned enticingly. 'Rosamunda.'

Roz moved slightly away. She reached for a box of tissues and blew her nose. 'Would you like some coffee?' she said.

'What I'd like is you.'

Roz sat up straight and sniffed. 'I'm not available, Philip. I'm married.'

'Need that mater?'

'Yes it does. Anyway, what about Pearl?'

'What about Pearl?'

'I thought you two were together.'

'Roz, the relationship between Pearl and me doesn't imprison us. It's flexible, respectful, joyous. Isn't your marriage?'

He knew the answer to that one. So did she by the look of her.

However, 'It may be acceptable for people like you, Philip. People like us don't.'

People like us! What a superior tone. What a little prig.

'Don't they really? Your wide and varied experience of life must have taught you so.'

'Very well then. Duncan and I don't. That's all there is to it. I'm going to make some coffee.'

She stood up to go round to the kitchen, straightening her dress, plumping up the cushions. End of conversation.

Duncan and I, my husband and I, my fiancé and I. These complacent suburban couplings. Give them a shake.

Philip sat on the sofa and draped his arm along its back. 'Duncan and you don't. Is that so? I wonder if Anabel would agree with you.'

'Who's Anabel?'

'You'd better ask Duncan.' Nonchalant. That would get her.

Roz walked towards him. 'Who's Anabel?'

'A lady.'

'So?'

She stood in front of him.

'So –' He leaned forward and took her hand. 'So.' He kissed her open palm.

Roz drew back. 'Who's Anabel?' she demanded again.

'Duncan knows.'

'Are you trying to make trouble?'

'Oh come on Roz. We're allowed to have some fun in life.'

'Are we? I hadn't noticed.'

'Now's your chance to find out, isn't it?' He looked at her from under his eyelashes, provocatively.

She looked away. She was about to give in.

'Please leave, Philip.'

'Come on Roz. There's no need for the amateur dramatics. Why not make that coffee you keep talking about.'

'Go away.'

Fiery. She was attractive again. Strange little creature. Frumpy and yet not.

'Go easy on yourself Roz.'

She handed him his coat. As he took it, he brushed her lips.

'You ought to try being a woman, Roz, before you turn into a dry old lady.'

He blew her a kiss at the door and ran lightly down the stairs, whistling. That should spice up their relationship. He almost regretted that he wouldn't be around to see what happened. At the weekend Magus began its tour. Who could tell what new intimacies lay ahead to be developed in a succession of provincial theatres and lodgings?

22

'The sitting tenant got it.'

That's what Mr Hill told Roz in the staff room. Apparently someone had been Acting Deputy Head during the previous term and had now been permanently appointed.

'One of those put-up affairs, was it?' said Martin. 'I disagree with them myself. I agree that a sitting tenant should have priority – better the devil you know. But the other applicants ought to be made aware that there's an obviously strong candidate so that they can make a reasonable assessment of their chances.'

'You will try again, won't you Roz?' said Tod.

'I don't know. I doubt it.'

'You mustn't let this put you off. Particularly not when someone was earmarked for the job.'

'It wouldn't have made any difference. I didn't get as far as the short list.'

'You will another time.'

'I don't think I'm in the running.'

'You won't be if you never apply.'

'Tod,' said Caroline Harris curiously. 'What about you? Surely you'd be in the running for higher things?'

'Perhaps,' Tod gave his habitual ambivalent reply. 'If something came up nearer home.'

'I want to be nearer home,' agreed Martin. 'Especially now, with the baby. There aren't many jobs being advertised though.'

The new teacher smirked. He had taken the place of Paula, who was now living with her parents and did not intend to teach anymore. 'I'd rather have a journey to work,' he said. 'Then you've always got a good excuse for coming home late.'

New jobs, babies, excuses for being home late.

'No need to look so worried, Roz,' said Mr Hill. 'You'll get a promotion if you keep applying. The competition's stiff nowadays so it may take some time. But you'll get there.'

So her colleagues still thought well of her capabilities. Far from dismissing her aspirations, they were at pains to encourage her further.

Similiar support came from Pearl and Clovis.

'It's their loss,' said Pearl. 'More fool them for not even bothering to find out what they'd be missing.' And Clovis spoke so kindly that the tears almost came again.

'You're really upset about that job aren't you?' said Pearl after Clovis had gone back downstairs to do some work.

'I was at first,' said Roz. 'I'd set my hopes too high. I'm readjusted now.'

'You are?'

'Yes, yes. I am. Really.'

'You don't look it. You look very tense. You're such a good teacher that you're bound to be successful another time.'

Roz smiled faintly.

'You'll apply again, won't you?'

'I expect so. Everybody's been so supportive.'

'Well then.'

'It's not that, Pearl.'

'So what is it? I mean, if you want to tell me.'

Much as she wanted, how could she tell Pearl? 'It's to do with Duncan,' she might start. Duncan. 'Mr Drummond', Pearl's lecturer. She couldn't confide in Pearl. It would be disloyal, unethical, unfair. Both to Duncan and Pearl herself. Yet whom could she tell? At school most of them thought Duncan was leaning on her anyway. She couldn't play into their prejudice. Pearl had become a friend. She wasn't just Duncan's student. It would be such a relief to state the uncertainty, send the words out into the air beyond her head instead of having them circling and clanging within.

'Do you know someone called Anabel?' she asked.

Pearl thought. 'No. Not Anabel. I know someone called Annette. She's the class librarian in Psychology.'

'He said Anabel.'

Pearl looked querying.

'I think Duncan might know someone called Anabel.'

'You mean, know her very well? Like too well?'

'Yes.'

'What makes you think that?'

'I just have a feeling.'

'You can't just have a feeling. Something must have given you the feeling. Has he been talking a lot about her?'

'No. He says he doesn't know an Anabel.'

'Don't you believe him?'

'I don't know.'

'What gave you the idea in the first place? Has someone been dropping hints?'

'Yes.'

'Who? Someone reliable?'

More ramifications. Now she had to implicate another of Pearl's relationships.

'Philip told me.'

'Ah, Philip.' Pearl's voice changed. 'Why did he do that?'

Roz answered a different question. 'I thought you might know an Anabel, or what it could be about. Since you're a friend of Philip's.'

'I used to be. I don't see him any more.'

'Don't you? I didn't know.'

Pearl had never mentioned it, but then she'd never talked about Philip anyway.

'It was me that broke it up. Some time ago now. Over Christmas.'

So Philip had already lost Pearl when he'd spent that evening with Roz. He'd given another impression.

Pearl was explaining her position. 'Philip's very charming. But – ' She spoke carefully, 'he's too good at telling other people what they should be doing in their lives. Nicely, you know. In a concerned sort of way. But I came to the conclusion that he's always on the look-out for his own advantage, to get something useful to him out of the situation. I know we all do but he goes further with it. Too far, I think. And I don't like that. I don't know what the circumstances were, Roz, and you don't have to tell me if you don't want to. But I think there would be a reason for himself in saying that to you. Duncan doesn't strike me as being a ladies' man.'

Pearl was right. Duncan wasn't. That had been part of the shock. A faithless Duncan had been like a contradiction in terms. Now she could see again how implausible it was. Roz returned to the flat reassured, and there found pleasure in the mundane orderliness of tidying, putting washing in the laundry basket and sorting out clothes for dry cleaning. Duncan was not yet home. In her new calm she felt great affection for him and a need to compensate for her unjust doubts. She took his jacket from the wardrobe almost tenderly, loath to exchange its Duncan smell for that of tetrachloride.

It was interesting what Pearl had gone on to say about Philip and herself. About how she'd always had misgivings about him, but he'd been fun and flattering and she'd had no experience of anyone like him before so it had been hard for her to judge accurately. And he was attractive, they'd agreed, giggling. Just, Roz supposed, rather shallow.

She pulled a handkerchief out of the jacket pocket and threw it on the washing pile. Biros, as always, clipped inside. Fluff. Pieces of paper.

Anabel, it said.

A telephone number.

'Roz!'

He was back. Back from where? From an Anabel he said he didn't know?

'Roz! Where are you?'

'I'm here.' She pressed the paper up her sleeve and folded the jacket, hating it.

Duncan came in, looking pleased. 'I've brought some fish and chips,' he said.

Roz continued folding. 'Have you? So that I can waste my time again cooking a meal unnecessarily?'

'I didn't think you'd have cooked yet.'

'Why should I bother cooking? Since I never know when you'll be back.' She stood up and shoved the wardrobe door.

'I'm not later than usual.'

'Goody, goody. Excuse me.' She pushed out of the door, carrying the dry cleaning to the kitchen. The jacket lay on top. Deceitful, manipulative garment. Drawing forth her tenderness only to jeer the louder with its revelations.

She stuffed the clothes in a plastic carrier and went back to collect the washing. Duncan followed, back and forth, getting in her way. He was not normally doglike.

'Have you had a bad day?'

Why should he care? 'A wonderful day.' She crammed the washing into another plastic bag.

'Shall I put the fish out?'

'If you want to.'

'Are you ready to eat now?'

'I'm not eating.' Roz put on her coat.

'Where are you going?'

Why should he care? 'To the launderette.'

'Now?'

'Now.'

'Shall I come and help?'

'No thanks.'

Roz sat in the dismal launderette watching their clothes go round and round in the washing-machine and in the dry-cleaning machine. Duncan's clothes and hers, mingling and twining together. She wanted to wrest them apart – don't touch; keep away.

Duncan had lied to her. He had denied knowing an Anabel when there she was in his pocket. All those evenings Roz had spent on her own, then soothed and sympathized over Duncan's long hours of work, all those evenings Duncan had been consorting with Anabel. While Roz had defended Duncan's way of life and compromised her own, while she praised his intellect and waded through her boring marking, he was deceiving her. While she fended off Philip and refused to believe his insinuations, Duncan was out fornicating.

How long had it been going on? Months? Perhaps the night class was a pretence too, another excuse to be out with Anabel. No no. Be sensible. Get a grip. Pearl went to the night classes. Pearl was taught by Duncan. The night classes really existed. She was getting carried away.

Perhaps she was overreacting to everything. Pearl had

thought there would be nothing. Perhaps there was an innocent explanation. Perhaps it was a mistake. She wanted it to be a mistake.

Duncan's clothes and hers mingled and twined together. She transferred them from washing-machine to dryer. She folded them from the dryer. She took out the cleaning-fluid. She cried.

At home, Duncan was treading warily. Roz softened, then raged inwardly again. Well he might be. She lay rigid in bed, sleepless, recoiling from the slightest contact with Duncan until she was balanced on the edge of the mattress.

She left early for school. Once there she explained away her state as a result of the latest circulating stomach bug. Her reactions fluctuated. Since Philip had first introduced Anabel's name, Roz had not wanted to believe the implications. To do so would jolt the pattern of her life into a radically different configuration, snatching away her orientation points and the structure she had taken for granted. She wanted to be able to accept Duncan's denial unequivocally, and Pearl's judgement added justification to her need to disregard Philip.

Finding Anabel's name and number tossed her back. She wanted it to be untrue. She glimpsed at her realigned life, if it were true, and could not face it. Her life as she had thought it was had been prised away from her life as it really was if Philip was right. Two distinct entities had been formed. She wanted to push them back together, close up the separation, make her life one again. This she could not manage to do now that the paper with Anabel's name and number existed. Unlike the previous wisps of implication, the paper was tangible, concrete, less easily discounted. At best Duncan had lied to her about knowing Anabel. Any other explanation (he'd lent out the jacket; someone had mistaken his pocket – she tried them all) was too fantastic. Why should he lie unless there were something to hide?

Had he also kept Roz a secret from Anabel? That seemed unlikely. So what had he said about her? Had they discussed her? How dare they. Laughed at her behind her back? Had fun while she marked and cooked and defended Duncan from criticism?

Her image of her own self was dragged apart into two along

with her world. Was she a patsy, the stooge, the ignorant innocent blithely unaware, the object of jeers? Or was she still the self who was part of a solid life, not one with a deceitful veneer. Even that second self had been afflicted by change recently: the competent professional versus mediocre worker. The question of maternity.

She had been pushed from one viewing-point to another, until her sense of place had vanished. How could she cope? What should she do?

'Go home, Roz,' said Mr Hill at lunchtime. 'You aren't well.'

'I'll be all right,' said Roz.

She must find out the truth: which was her real world, thus which was her real self, and thus what she should do next.

How could she find out? Duncan had already lied. Philip was on tour and anyway was not disinterested. Pearl knew nothing.

Roz went back to her classroom to set out the equipment for the afternoon's painting-lesson. Newspapers, drawing-paper, water pots, brushes, paints. She worked quickly, chanting the items inwardly to impose some order in her mind. The class paint monitors arrived to do their job and were dismayed to find it already completed.

She must ring that telephone number.

But what could she say? she wondered as she sat in the bus going home after school with staff advice about bed and a supper of rice and yoghurt. 'Excuse me, are you having an affair with my husband?' How awful if there turned out to be an innocuous explanation. What could she say to discover the truth without making her suspicions obvious?

If Duncan were to be at home, she thought, climbing the stairs to the flat, she wouldn't be able to do it. Yet if Duncan were at home, she wouldn't know how to behave towards him.

He wasn't. But she needn't ring now. She could do it another day and give herself time to plan the conversation more carefully.

And prolong the agony? She'd better get it over with. It was rather early, though; there wasn't likely to be anyone in. Then she could try again later. But what if Duncan was actually there, with Anabel, when Roz rang? She caught her breath at the thought. Well, then he'd be cornered, wouldn't he? Everyone would know that everyone else knew. The uncertainty at least would be over.

She rang the number.

'Hello.' Anabel?

'Could I speak to Anabel.'

'I'm afraid she's not back yet. Who's calling?'

'It doesn't matter. I'll try again later.'

'OK. She shouldn't be long.'

How long was long? Roz waited an hour; then an extra fifteen minutes. What if Duncan came home while she was talking to Anabel? It didn't matter. Whatever the situation, he had lied to her, and soon he'd know that she knew. She had to get it straight. She had to.

She rang again.

'Hello.' The same female voice.

'Is Anabel in?'

'Yes, she is. I'll get her. Was it you who rang earlier?'

'No,' lied Roz.

'Oh. OK. Hang on.'

Calling – 'Anabel – for you.'

An unintelligible shout back. Then the first voice.

'Hello. Who's calling?'

'It's a message from Duncan,' said Roz.

'Ah.' It had seemed to mean something. 'Right. Just a minute.'

There was a pause, then a sound of feet coming down stairs, then: 'Hello Duncan.' A breathless but not noticeably eager voice.

Roz didn't know what to say.

'Duncan? Are you there?'

'I'm not Duncan,' said Roz.

'Who are you? Why did you say you were Duncan?'

'I didn't. I said I had a message about Duncan.'

'Who are you?'

'I'm Roz.'

'Roz. The wife. Well, what can I do for you, Roz?'

Whatever Roz had expected, it wasn't such a tone.

'I thought I ought to talk to you,' she attempted.

'Did you? What about? Warning me off your old man?'

'I thought we ought to talk about it.'

'It's over, didn't you know? There's nothing to say. A pretty boring experience actually.'

There was laughter in the background. Roz felt a paradoxical surge of anger on behalf of Duncan.

'So why get involved with him in the first place?' she demanded.

'Filled a gap, as they say. And now, if you'll excuse me, I'm about to have a bath as preparation for a much more rewarding experience this evening.' More laughter. 'Goodbye Roz. Thank you for ringing.'

Click.

Roz had been managed. Anabel was infinitely more skilled than she at handling the situation. Doubtless it came from practice.

It was clear there had been an affair. It was clear that it was finished. Or was it? Maybe Anabel was skilled at subterfuge too, though it was needless now. Duncan had been unfaithful. She had been living in naïve trust. He had cheated her, lied and exploited her. How dared he order her to become some sort of earth mother while he was out snuggling down with another woman! For years she had financed him, praised him, skivvied for him and compromised her own wishes. He had lived off her in every way. 'A pretty boring experience actually.' Too true, Anabel. You said it.

Feet were on the stairs outside. The flat door rattled; feet along the corridor, into the kitchen. Duncan came round the corner, carrying his briefcase.

'Hello,' he said carefully.

Roz nodded slightly, sitting forward with her elbows on her knees.

Duncan took off his coat. 'All right?'

'Yes.'

'Coffee?'

'If you like.'

Roz did not get up.

Duncan made coffee. 'I did quite a lot today,' he said conversationally, trying.

'So did I.'

'That's good.' He held out the coffee. Roz gestured for him

to put it on the small table. He sat opposite with a conscious grunt.

'Duncan,' said Roz quietly, 'who's Anabel?'

Duncan wriggled with annoyance. 'Not again, Roz. We've been through all that.'

'We have, haven't we?'

'Well then.'

'Well then, who is she?'

'I've already told you. I don't know anyone called Anabel.'

'Strange,' said Roz. She felt quite detached, as if she were setting out pieces of cutlery.

Duncan didn't reply immediately. He reached for the evening paper in his briefcase. 'I'm not going through it again, Roz.' He crossed his legs and opened the newspaper.

'Look.'

Duncan looked.

'Strange to carry around the telephone number of someone you don't know.'

Duncan still looked.

'In your jacket pocket,' she explained helpfully.

Duncan gave a short laugh. 'Oh, *that* Anabel. Is that what's been worrying you? She's one of Philip's friends.'

'So how do you come to have her name and telephone number on a piece of paper in your jacket pocket?'

'I don't know, Roz. People do give others their numbers. It's quite normal. I met a whole crowd of Philip's friends at Christmas while you were with your mother. There are probably several people's numbers if you look.'

'No. Just this one.'

Duncan shrugged.

'Why did you say you didn't know anyone called Anabel?'

'I've told you – I don't. She's a friend of Philip's.'

'Not of yours?'

'I've told you Roz, I'm not going on with this. It's ridiculous.'

'It is. Because she certainly thinks she's been a friend of yours.'

'What do you mean?'

'She told me so.'

'How did she tell you? When?'

'Just now. On the telephone.'

'You rang her up?'

'Yes.'

Duncan stopped, then blustered. 'You know what theatricals are like. Any friend of yours is a friend of mine.'

'She's no friend of mine, Duncan. You're the one she claims intimacy with.'

Duncan's face stiffened.

Roz sat back in her chair. 'So, Duncan, who is Anabel?'

She had almost enjoyed playing with him.

23

Anabel. It was hardly worth talking about. There had been something after Christmas but it no longer existed. It had died away of its own accord some time ago and now seemed merely an alien occcurrence, sealed off from normal life. Duncan found it an effort to describe such an irrelevant business. How could he explain? After years of painstaking study, researching in a rut, his night class no longer a novelty, the Christmas holiday a taxing bore – against this the Anabel affair had burned vividly for a short time. She was confident, sharp, careless. She lived socially, eating out, visiting people and places, constantly in flamboyant groups. She was seductive, passionate, teasing. For a time he was dazed. Then it became a strain. There was no respite from the gaiety, unless someone stormed or mourned with similar intensity, and as well as that, the deceit was so stressful. Roz must really know, mustn't she? How could he be doing this without her knowing? Didn't her ostensibly innocent remarks betray her knowledge? The time involved in the affair, the energy required for coping with its various demands began to take their toll. His research wasn't so bad after all, and he resented the intrusion. He would have broken it off, except that this hadn't proved necessary: it was fizzling out anyway. Anabel no longer fixed their next rendezvous immediately each time they met, or demanded telephone calls at prescribed times and places. She became busy when he tried to arrange a meeting, and vague about when she would be available. Neither pressed the other and the relationship became desultory, leaving Duncan with little more than a sense of release and a residual guilt about Roz.

Anabel was an aberration. It couldn't have lasted: Philip must have realized that. Why then had he told Roz? It must have been deliberate. Philip knew Roz so slightly it could hardly have slipped out accidentally in casual conversation. Had he visited the flat that evening purposely to tell her? Duncan ought to challenge him about it, but where was Philip to be challenged? Duncan's anger was more conventional than actual, for must not Philip have been motivated by envy? How else could the betrayal be explained? Philip had frequently extolled domestic values. Feeling like that anyway, and then on the point of trailing around the provinces with no fixed abode, Philip must have been overcome by the recognition of what he lacked. Attempting to ruin for others what he coveted for himself was a destructive but nevertheless implicitly flattering act.

Neither was it an act which had succeeded. Far more than Philip's recent behaviour and past comments, the Anabel affair had made Duncan appreciate the value of what he had with Roz, and Roz's own conduct now, in the aftermath, confirmed her stalwart qualities. She accepted his weak explanation without comment and had not referred to the matter again. Sensible Roz. He was thankful to forget the episode and return to life as it had been before, except with a modified perspective. His life was with Roz. That was what felt comfortable and his mind was freer than it ever had been during his involvement with Anabel. Anabel had seemed exciting but since then he had seen different aspects of Roz's personality, ones he had no idea she possessed: her rebuffing fury the previous night; her audacity in telephoning Anabel; her calm but unremitting questioning of him; the dexterous revealing of her own evidence. Finally her dismissing the affair to its insignificant place in the past. She had developed these abilities without his realizing it, changing while remaining the same in other aspects. This was exciting too, exciting and secure simultaneously. He wanted more of Roz. He wanted to extend his security and comfort to their children, parts of them both. If Roz wanted a career as well, that was up to her. She could manage. And if she'd changed her mind about headships or even about teaching, well, he was a qualified teacher too, he could always fall back on that, and the prospect held more appeal than previously, for his night class had become satisfying again. The students sat their exam early, soon after Easter, and Duncan could see that some of them were beginning to consolidate their knowledge. It was surprisingly rewarding to observe how much the few months of the course had affected some people. Miss Thomas, for example, increasingly competent essay by essay and now diligently practising exam skills. She was well justifying the optimistic reference he'd supplied for her polytechnic applications. And Mr Pontiff, the class providing some assuaging of his loneliness.

Duncan could get a full-time teaching post after his PhD *and* continue to do research. There was nothing impossible about combining the two. He could have a salary as well as continued intellectual stimulation. What he needed to do first was to get that PhD out of the way. He should be more mundane about it and treat it as a job to be cleared off. He had his next appointment with Professor Reece arranged already and was approaching it in a different frame of mind from those before. It was a mere formality and he would acknowledge it only as such. He would not expect praise or encouragement. He didn't need it. He'd forge on by himself. He always had.

Treated this way, the appointment with Professor Reece passed smoothly, as if Duncan himself had decided that it would be brief because superfluous. Afterwards he went round the departmental students' common rooms recruiting subjects for his next round of experiments. They would constitute the usual unrepresentative sample on which most psychological research is based. Duncan thought about this as he swung in the home-bound tube train. Perhaps even in his new-found economy of purpose, he'd go one better and try for replication on samples from other populations. It shouldn't be too difficult to set up. It might be interesting to see if the individual differences appeared in children. Perhaps Roz would like to co-operate on that aspect. She could provide children from her school, do any unspecialized testing or organization and assist him with gathering the trial data. A husband-and-wife team. Quite impressive.

It had been an afternoon of small but keen pleasures. The lengthening day had been mild, the sky blue, and the restlessness of spring had permeated even the inner city. Duncan felt cheerful as he entered the flat. Happy changes lay ahead.

'Duncan,' read the note on the kitchen table. 'You don't seem very bothered about what's happened or what it might mean to me. I'm bothered and I haven't made up my mind yet what to do. I've gone away to think for a while. Roz.'

How unnecessary. There he'd been mentally praising her sensible attitude and she promptly belied his evaluation by going off in a huff.

The best way to deal with petulance was to ignore it. He opened a tin of beans and turned on the television. When she hadn't returned by bedtime he grew more annoyed. What an inconsiderate way to behave. Indignation prevented him from sleeping well. In the morning he was still on his own.

He'd ring her at school and find out what she was playing at. Miss Elyce would probably answer the telephone. He'd ask to speak to Roz urgently, leaving Roz herself to think of an excuse afterwards. Practising in his mind what he would say, he waited till mid-morning breaktime and dialled.

He recognized the Headmistress's voice.

'Good morning, Miss Elyce. How are you? Duncan Drummond here.'

'Duncan,' came back, 'how nice of you to call. How is Roz now?'

'I'm not sure,' said Duncan cautiously.

'Oh dear,' sympathized Miss Elyce. 'I do hope it's nothing serious. We thought she must be feeling very poorly when she went home early yesterday. She usually works on regardless. Then when she rang this morning, she sounded very weak and husky, and I said quite right not to come in. You don't know what it is, you say?'

'No,' said Duncan.

'Have you called the doctor? It's as well to be on the safe side. I can't remember the last time Roz was absent.'

'It's very unusual for her.'

'At least she's got you to look after her. Give her our love, will you Duncan, and tell her not to come back till she's fully recovered.'

'Yes. Thank you.'

'And thank you for taking the trouble to ring. Goodbye, Duncan. Nice to hear from you again.'

Not at school. Inventing excuses to cover herself. What a drama for a minor deviation. She must see that herself soon. Then she'd come back of her own accord. When she did, he wouldn't make an issue out of her over-reaction. He'd let it pass; the entire tangle would pass, and then everything could go on as before. It was Saturday next day. She'd probably return that same afternoon or evening.

She didn't.

Where was she? Was she genuinely ill somewhere? No. That was an obvious excuse. Could she have gone to her parents? He could easily ring them, but in case she wasn't there he had better phrase himself in such a way as not to give them the slightest hint of her not being with him either. It was going to be difficult to keep suspicion at bay, especially since he himself never telephoned them. It was always Roz who did that.

'Hello Duncan. This is a surprise. Is everything all right?' Mrs Latimer sounded uneasy.

'Yes, yes. Fine. How are you?'

'We're keeping quite well thank you. We can't complain. What about you busy people? Still researching away?'

'Yes, I – '

'All work and no play, you know, Duncan.' She was irritating him already.

'Yes, well – '

The conversation ground to a halt. Duncan had to get it going in the way he needed. 'I was wondering,' he ventured, 'if Roz had said anything.'

'Said anything? When?'

That didn't sound as if Roz was there.

'It doesn't matter. I just wondered. Obviously she hasn't.'

'Duncan,' severely, 'am I drawing the right conclusion?'

Anabel. Mrs Latimer knew he'd been unfaithful to Roz.

'You have heard from her then?'

'Oh Duncan. I can't tell you how delighted I am. I said to

her daddy when she phoned last week, Rosamund sounds very tired, I said, very pulled down. I hope she's not sickening for something. But even then I suspected. Woman's intuition, Duncan.'

'You haven't heard from her?'

'Not since then, no. But I don't feel slighted Duncan, don't think I do, even though I am her own mother. It takes some girls strangely. You'll have to be very understanding, especially in the early stages. She'll be feeling tired and nauseous now, so make her rest as much as you can. I must see if I can come down and do my bit for you. I'll have a word with her daddy about it. He'll be as delighted as I am. Frankly, we'd almost given up hope.'

'But you haven't heard from her since her telephone call last week?'

'Don't worry, Duncan. I'm a woman too. We understand these things better than a man can – though I must say I think it's very good of you to convey the news. I do appreciate it, and so will her daddy. He's going to be so happy when he hears. Now, what can we plan for? When did she fall?'

'Has she fallen?' leapt in Duncan anxiously. 'I didn't know. Who told you?'

'Silly boy,' said Mrs Latimer indulgently. 'It's an expression, that's all. New fathers find more to worry about than the mothers themselves. I'll begin again – when is the baby due?'

Oh no. Now what had he got into? Mrs Latimer starting on the bootees and he no longer even had Roz. Without warning, he choked. He'd have given anything for his telephone call really to have been according to Mrs Latimer's interpretation.

'Duncan! Are you all right, Duncan? Are you still there?'

'Yes.'

'Take it calmly Duncan. It's a natural, normal event, although I realize it's a very new experience for you. It'll be the making of you, you wait and see. Now, when is the baby due?'

'I don't know.'

'You don't know! Duncan, do I gather that Roz is acting a little strangely?'

'You could say that.'

'Am I also correct in inferring that you're by yourself at the moment?'

'You are.'

'And you're worried that I might tell Roz that we know although she hasn't told us herself.'

'Something like that.'

'Now, Duncan. Listen to an older friend, wise in these ways. It's early in the pregnancy. A girl had a great deal of adjusting to do, mentally and physically, and she's at the mercy of her hormones. I understand the situation and I won't breathe a word about it until she does herself. Then I'll pretend it's news. Does that make you feel better?'

'I think so.'

'And Duncan, thank you for ringing. I can't tell you what it's meant to me.'

He felt a heel. There was Mrs Latimer revelling in her secret. How was she going to be disillusioned? It would make him too look so stupid. And Miss Elyce burbling on about Roz's illness. What was going to happen on Monday? What if Roz hadn't returned by then? She was getting him into mess after mess, all through giving in to a tantrum. He'd thought more of her.

The anger sustained him into the night, then left suddenly, dropping him flat into misery. The dark bedroom stretched up and out with no bounds. There was nothing to contain him, nothing to give him definition. The sounds were only of himself.

Dawn broke with merciless unconcern. The room was cold and grey. What could Roz think he'd be doing now? Didn't she care? He entered the day alone, without support, stiffening to each creak from the building, any noise from within or without the house. He ate the last cornflakes, hadn't enough cash to pay the milkman – Roz dealt with that. Where could she be? He picked up a book, sat on the sofa. It was like Christmas. He had sat like this while Roz was still at her parents', missing her. Then he'd gone to the party with Philip and met Anabel. Roz being away had led him into the Anabel business. The Anabel business had now driven Roz away. At Christmas there had been a known time limit to her being away. Now . . .

Where could she be? Not at her parents'. A hotel? Friends? Which friends? There had been those people from the badminton club, but Roz didn't attend anymore. Could she be off with one of the other schoolteachers? What were their names? He couldn't remember the new ones. If anywhere, their details were in Roz's address book, in Roz's bag, with Roz. She didn't talk a great deal about the people she knew. What about Miss Thomas? She visited the school, didn't she? Didn't Roz go back to her flat afterwards sometimes? Might she know? Her address was in his register. She might.

No. He couldn't. What could he say, asking his own student if she knew the whereabouts of his wife? The professional and the personal shouldn't collide like that. And if she didn't know already that Roz had left him, she would know as a result of his questions. It would be too humiliating.

If Miss Thomas did already know, though, he was already humiliated. Perhaps he could phrase the question less revealingly, to protect himself if she didn't know. He could pretend that Roz had said she'd drop in on her after shopping. He could be dropping in on them too. He'd see how she reacted. Would that do?

Not really. She could easily conceal knowledge of Roz's whereabouts from such an indirect ploy.

Yet it would be something. He could but try.

He fetched the register. Up by the Common – he'd known that, hadn't he? Out of the flat, on to his bike. It felt better to be moving. He cycled down the residential roads, past the tube station and shops, up the hill by Lixbury Institute, past the library and up again to the Common.

The air was fresh by the open space. His brain felt cleansed. He looked for the number. Nice place for a flat. Which one would it be? There had only been the house number in the register. Perhaps there would be nameplates by the bells. No – only a door knocker and one, old-fashioned bell. How inconvenient. He knocked and rang.

A man opened the door. Duncan raised his chin and adopted his professional tone.

'I'm looking for a Miss Pearl Thomas,' he said. 'Can you tell me where she lives?'

'She lives here,' said the man. 'I'm afraid she's out.'

'Out,' repeated Duncan stupidly. In all his preparations he had not considered this possibility.

'At work. She'll be back later.'

'Oh.' Duncan's sense of purpose collapsed.

'Shall I tell her you called? Would you like to leave a message?'

'No,' said Duncan. 'No message. Thank you.'

He picked up his bike from where it was propped against the house wall and pushed it back out on to the road.

24

Roz was standing by the balcony window when Clovis went back into the first-floor room.

'Was that Duncan?' he asked.

'Yes.'

She stared out at the drive. 'I didn't tell him I was here,' she said dully.

'He asked for Pearl.'

'Pearl wouldn't have told him I was here.'

'I don't think he knows. I expect he's trying to trace you any way he can.'

'Did you tell him I was here?'

'No.'

She pulled her gaze away from the window. 'What did he say?'

'He asked if I knew where Pearl lived.'

'Why should he ask that? He was already here.'

'Perhaps he assumed the house was divided into flats.'

'What did you say?'

'I told him Pearl was at work.'

'What did he say?'

'He didn't say anything. He wouldn't leave any message, and he left – as you saw.'

Roz's face turned to the window.

'He may telephone later on,' said Clovis. 'Perhaps you should prepare Pearl for that possibility when she comes in.'

Roz walked round to the other chairs. 'Did you give him the

number?'

'I didn't. But he knows it. He rang before about the Psychology class.'

'He did?'

'Some time ago. In the autumn. I believe you were ill and he thought he might have to cancel the class.'

'I can't remember that. I can't remember being ill.' She gripped the back of the chair. 'Don't say he was at it even then.'

'At what?'

'Making excuses to be out with someone else. Lying to me.' Her face knotted. 'He's still lying to me. He said it was only after Christmas with Anabel. I've always thought he was teaching on Tuesday nights. Always. Without missing a single one. And he was at it all that time too.'

Clovis stroked his face. 'That wasn't the impression I got,' he said. 'I hadn't met you then so it didn't have any significance for me, but I seem to remember Pearl and Philip discussing it.'

'Philip! Philip could well have been in on any deceit.'

'Not Pearl.'

'Pearl didn't realize anything had been going on anyway.'

'No, but the point is that he *didn't* cancel the evening class. It's some time ago, but I'm sure Pearl commented on it. We can ask her.'

'He couldn't have been after Pearl too, could he?'

'Roz!' deprecatingly.

'It's possible. Who knows what he's capable of? I'd never had thought he was capable of doing what I know he has done.'

'There's no suggestion of anything with Pearl.'

Roz sat down. 'You're right. I'm being stupid again. And unfair to Pearl. He'd have her address and telephone number in his extramural file.'

Clovis sat down too.

Roz said, 'When you discover how gullible you've been, it's difficult not to become over-suspicious.'

'Naturally.'

'He's very conscientious about his teaching.'

'So I gather.'

'He wouldn't have liked to miss a class.'

'No.'

'He was going to, if I was ill.'

'Yes.'

'I can't remember being ill.'

Clovis stroked his throat silently. She had ricocheted between suspicious resentment, grief and lethargy since she had turned up there. He had been in the kitchen at the back of the house, making tea after a day at the Academy. He'd gone to open the door and found her, pale and tense, clutching a bag. She'd come to see Pearl but, as today, Pearl was at the hospital. Roz followed him down the passage and sat at the kitchen table drinking tea and replying mechanically to his conversation. She looked out at him as if she were at the back of a cave filled with murky water. Something was very wrong.

Roz struggled, then told him. And Duncan behaved as if it were so trivial, she sobbed bitterly. For years she'd put him first, bent her life around his. She hadn't minded really. His drive and certainty had given some structure to her life. She'd enjoyed his successes. Until recently she hadn't felt particularly belittled by his single-minded pursuit of a priority which wasn't her. But there had been certain assumptions in her acceptance of her role. She hadn't consciously realized it before, but they were there: that his single-mindedness excluded any double life; that she at least deserved his loyalty. He had shattered those assumptions and didn't even notice that it mattered. She herself had connived at her own exploitation. He'd deceived her and she'd made it so easy with her betrayable trust. He didn't want children, then he did; she had been expected to switch accordingly, and now because he had decided his infidelity was unimportant, then it was taken for granted that so would she. From childhood she had been brought up to be polite, to be tidy, to be unobtrusive, to be reliable, to be second-rate. To be walked over.

Clovis made more tea and they carried it up the stairs. Clear spring light lay liquid in his room. The trees on the Common braced themselves for the resurgence that would soon occur within and around them.

She'd had to get away. She'd had to leave the grip of his assumptions. She had to think from outside them. But she didn't know where to go. She came home from school early, knowing that Duncan had gone to see his supervisor. She rang Pearl but there was no reply. She did not want to wait around in the flat in case Duncan came back so she packed a few essentials and left. She walked the streets and tried to ring Pearl again but the telephone had been vandalized. So she'd just arrived.

This was told to Clovis and to Pearl when she came in. She had been doing overtime to cover for Sadie who was off sick. Could she stay with Pearl? asked Roz tremulously. Just for a short time while she sorted herself out? She hated to ask, but she'd nowhere else to go.

Clovis had offered one of his rooms. It was an offer which he dearly wanted her to accept, for over the months he had come to care for Roz. He looked forward to those times when Pearl visited the school and Roz came back afterwards. As the day's events were discussed, Clovis recognized the unvaunted practical abilities which underlay her diffidence. Such were generally too subtle to be noticable qualities but Clovis knew how obvious their absence became once they were gone from your life. Roz reminded him of Catherine: both unassuming, apparently compromising yet with an occasional blast of fighting spirit. Moreover, he could see himself in what he heard of Duncan. The self-absorption, the unquestioned acceptance that everything should be subordinated to his own career. These had been characteristics of Clovis in his own marriage.

The afternoon with Roz was pleasant for him despite her turmoil. They sat in the room together, Clovis finishing a review, Roz almost reading, talking spasmodically, not of Duncan. Clovis left it for her to choose whether to say more. When he looked up from his desk, he could see her gazing away from the book, her hand riffling its pages, her face troubled.

A tap on the door meant that Pearl was back from work. As she came into the room, Clovis raised a hand in greeting, then gestured to a chair.

'Duncan's been,' said Roz.

'Here?' Pearl stopped halfway to sitting down. 'How did he know?'

'He didn't. He came to see you.'

'Me?' Pearl looked at Clovis, who shook his head gently, then back to Roz. 'What for? What did he say?'

'I didn't talk to him. Clovis did.'

Pearl turned to Clovis again. 'What did he want me for?'

Clovis told her what had happened.

'So he doesn't know that Roz is here?'

'No.'

'What are you going to do?' she asked Roz.

Clovis also wanted to know the answer to that question, which he had not been asking all afternoon.

'I don't know,' said Roz. 'I can't – I *have* been thinking about it. I'm going to have to see him sometime. But it's too soon. I'm not ready for him yet.'

'When you left, when you walked out, what did you see yourself doing? What was in your mind then?'

'Not much. I wanted to get away. That's all I knew. I needed to find out what mattered to me, and why it mattered. As long as I stayed there I was locked into Duncan so I had to get away before he came back. That was all.' She paused. 'I will see him. I will. But if I see him now, there will have been no point in leaving.'

'We'd better pretend that we aren't here if he calls again,' said Pearl.

'Why don't we eat out together this evening?' said Clovis.

He took them to his favourite restaurant, where he usually ate alone. Now he rather enjoyed the owner's deliberately discreet incuriosity over his female companions. Clovis concealed the true direction of his own interest by feigned absorption in the wine list while Roz and Pearl studied the menu, consulting together, flushed and self-conscious. It occurred to Clovis that this was an uncommon event for both of them. They chose their food, and Clovis ordered wine and mineral water.

'This is the best meal I've had since the one you cooked,' said Pearl to Roz after the initial silences of eating. Straight away she pulled her head back and bit her lip, round-eyed, as if in rapid recognition of a gaffe.

Roz stiffened slightly at the allusion but just said, 'I'm not up to this standard. I wish I were.' Then, 'It seems long ago, now.'

Clovis wondered what had happened at that meal. Pearl mutely acknowledged Roz's last remark and the conversation was about to sag when Roz, apparently sensing the need for an explanation, described to Clovis the circumstances in which she and Pearl first met.

'You must have been very uncomfortable,' she finished, to Pearl.

'That was Philip's fault. He didn't tell me it was my teacher we were going to visit, and he obviously hadn't told Mr Drummond that he was going to bring me. I felt like an intruder, there under false pretences. You did everything you could to put me at my ease.'

Clovis imagined Roz buffering the awkwardness of the situation. With effort, he switched off the tender glow this produced and followed the continuing conversation.

'It's going to be awkward again, Pearl, isn't it? I mean, at your night class with Duncan.'

'Oh, I don't know,' said Pearl evenly. 'He never behaved any differently after you and I became friends. There's never been anything personal towards me. I've always been just one of the students in his class, so that'll probably be the same.'

'You will still go, won't you?'

'To be honest,' said Pearl, 'while I'm in the class, what I'm bothered about is the course itself. As far as I'm concerned in class, he's Mr Drummond who teaches me what I need to know for the exam. Anything else belongs outside.'

'I wouldn't want you to be affected.'

'I won't. Actually, I've got a good reason to keep going now,' said Pearl. 'Guess what?' She gave the answer without pausing, a smile spurting out as she spoke. 'I've been accepted for college. Trent Polytechnic, Applied Social Studies. Provided I pass the Psychology exam. So you don't have to worry that anything's going to put me off now.'

'Oh Pearl, that's marvellous!' Roz was becoming brighter, happier, less preoccupied. Clovis tried not to look at her too much.

'Did you hear today?' he asked Pearl.

'Yesterday.'

'I must have stopped you telling us,' said Roz.

'It's all right. I'd got the place. That's what mattered.'

'And without an interview!'

'They said my reference was good . . . ' Pearl trailed off.

'Duncan.'

'Yes.'

Roz nodded as if that was only what one might expect and did not seem particularly upset by the mention of his name.

Clovis raised his glass. 'Congratulations,' he said to Pearl.

'I wouldn't even have tried this year if you hadn't suggested it.'

'They'll be so pleased for you at school,' said Roz. 'And at your night class,' she added. 'Have you told them at the hospital yet?'

'Not properly. The one who'd really understand is off at the moment – Sadie. I'll miss her, and the patients too. It's hard to realize that I'm going to have such a complete change. Have you always taught, Roz?'

'Yes.'

'Have you, Clovis? Something Philip said once made me think you used to perform too.'

'What was that?' Clovis was sure that he had never discussed his past with Philip.

'It was just before he went on tour, when he wanted a room. He said he'd been talking to you about it and you understood the problems of touring because it was a similar situation for a musician. Something like that. Something that sounded as if you used to tour.'

'He must have meant in general terms. I don't remember any specific discussions.'

Fortunately Pearl took that as a reply in the negative and did not question further. Clovis was loath to bring up the topic of his previous career, to be obliged to give details or prevaricate. Particularly now, with Roz sitting quietly near, her future and therefore his, undecided. Clovis turned the conversation down a different alley, and his attention back to Pearl.

'Have you heard from Philip recently?' he asked.

'Yes, a postcard. Very enthusiastic. You know what he's like – "Greetings, darling, from Darlington."' Her tone was cynical.

'So he's keeping in touch with you,' said Roz, with a shade, Clovis thought, of apprehension.

'I expect he's still after a room, not being successful on his first attempt.'

'Did you definitely tell him no then?' asked Clovis. 'I assumed you had since I heard no more about it.'

'I didn't want him interfering in my life,' said Pearl. 'I was worried that I might never make it if he was around all the time. It's ironic that his card arrived in the same post as my college acceptance.'

'He managed to interfere in my life,' said Roz wryly. 'And he told me what an open and tolerant relationship you two had. Actually, you'd already ditched him, but he omitted that piece of information.'

'Philip interfered in your life?' Clovis could not leave this unexplored. Roz had said nothing about it before.

'Yes. I didn't want to go into all the details when I told you about Duncan, but it began at a party he went to with Philip. Not that that was Philip's fault,' she added. 'But it was Philip who dropped hints to me about something going on. And – ' She broke off and glanced at Pearl.

'Don't worry about me,' said Pearl. 'I know what I think of him.'

Roz looked down. 'Well, he wasn't telling me out of kindness. It was because he wanted to do the same with me.'

'I thought that was it,' declared Pearl.

'But I didn't.'

Clovis felt anger, protectiveness, relief.

'And now he sends a postcard to you,' he said to Pearl, controlling the tone of his voice with difficulty.

'It won't do him any good. He used me before – in fact he's tried to use all of us. I'm not falling for that again.'

His companions' expressions confirmed their opinion of Philip. Clovis felt a sense of great unity. This comfortable atmosphere continued for the rest of the meal as the conversation moved on to other topics, and was with them as they got into the car, Roz in front for the return journey. To Clovis it seemed so natural, warm and relaxed. Driving through the dark with the woman he loved, except this time fully aware of it. He arrived home, yearning to submerge himself in his feelings.

The knock came when they had just settled in the kitchen, with Clovis making coffee. He returned to the hall and opened the front door.

'I want to see my wife,' said Duncan. 'I know she's here.'

'Of course.' Clovis showed him into the drawing-room, pulling a dust cover off a chair as he had for Pearl that past autumn evening.

Clovis went back to the kitchen, to the smell of the coffee, to the women waiting for news, to Roz's beloved and apprehensive face.

'It's Duncan, isn't it?'

'Yes.'

'I'll see him,' said Pearl putting her cup down. 'He'll only ask me if I know where you are. Shall I put him off?'

'He knows,' said Clovis. 'This time he asked for Roz.'

Roz was standing immobile.

'I can go,' said Pearl to her. 'Tell me what you want me to say and I'll say it.'

Roz rallied. 'No,' she said. 'Thank you but I can't do that. I'll have to see him. I'll have to now. Where is he?'

Clovis and Pearl sat at the kitchen table drinking coffee as the door closed on the drawing-room.

25

Clovis and Pearl sat at the kitchen table. It was a good two hours since Roz had gone down the corridor to talk to Duncan, and the house was silent. An increasing sense of ridiculousness about their waiting on for Roz fought with Clovis's wish to be at hand if he were to be needed. There was also the fact that Pearl, who was his guest, was with him.

Pearl made the first move. 'I'll have to go,' she said. 'I'm sorry but I'm really tired. I'll have to go to bed. We can't do anything anyway. When it comes down to it, she's got to sort it out for herself.'

'I suppose so.'

'You're tired as well,' she continued. 'Why don't you leave them to it? You can't hold yourself responsible for them, even though this is your house.'

'I won't wait much longer.'

'Anyway, she might be embarrassed if she came out and saw we'd been waiting here all this time as if we were minding her. It's been too long.'

Clovis conceded the point and they both gave up the vigil, at least outwardly. Yet Clovis's thoughts lingered on Roz, on Duncan, on himself and Catherine.

Once Clovis's career too had been so important that he had put it before everything. When they married, Catherine came to live in the house. His mother had not considered this to be a good idea. 'A woman needs a home of her own,' she'd said. He had thought she was referring only to Catherine. 'She's always shared flats before,' said Clovis. 'There's more space here than that. You'll keep each other company when I'm away.' Catherine hadn't been overjoyed either. 'It's the obvious thing to do,' argued Clovis. 'I can't be thinking of moving house with all that entails at the moment. I'm too busy. We can later. This is merely a temporary arrangement.'

He was right, though not in the way he had intended. His mother had died soon after, and they stayed in their inherited house. Clovis played in concerts around Britain, then around Europe. He was becoming known. He was almost there. He must work and work, he must seize every opportunity to display himself. Catherine understood. She gave up her job to travel with him.

The Avignon festival had been a success. Elated, he had begun the drive back. That was when it happened. A freak thunderstorm outside Orange, the road greasy, a heavy lorry in front. He was scarcely injured and Catherine was dead. Nobody was at fault, the report said. A tragic accident. Appalling driving conditions.

It all suddenly goes.

He needn't have been driving that road then. They could have stayed longer in Avignon; Catherine would have liked that. But he had accepted a booking in Canterbury the following day. He couldn't afford to turn it down, not at this stage. He hadn't achieved such a position yet. Besides, he was unable to rest immediately after a performance: he was too wound up. He might as well travel on his adrenalin. Catherine doubted it. To prove his point, he insisted on driving.

A long journey up from the south. A storm, a greasy road, a lorry. Clovis now tired. The lorry was well in front, then less so – he slowed down, then right in front – he braked, skidded. Nobody was to blame, said the report. A freak storm, appalling conditions. Nobody was to blame but an uncompromising driver.

He had killed her. His ambition had killed her.

Friends argued against him: he was being melodramatic; it could have happened to anyone; it was nothing to do with ambition.

Wasn't it? Wasn't it the same force which insistently drove his career, which had insisted on the extra booking, which had insisted even on driving the car? A less intransigent will would have behaved differently. His took heed of little except its own demands.

'You have absorbed me into your life,' Catherine had said once. It was an accusation, but after her death Clovis had found another meaning. She was so part of his life, so inextricably intertwined, that when she was ripped away his existence fell apart. He gave no more performances and drifted in misery. Catherine and his career had been his life. Without them, what life had he?

He was caught before he succumbed. He was offered a post teaching music in an American college and because he did not care, he accepted it.

Five years in America, an ambitious, competitive land. Five years surrounded by the values he had learned to distrust. Yet when the worst that could happen has happened, what else can matter? He was no longer involved in life. Misery became resignation.

He might have stayed as he was had not the tenants left the London house and at the same time a vacancy occurred at the Academy. He came home, to the house, to the Academy, to writing the occasional review. He met Pearl; through Pearl, Philip, Roz, Duncan; and he lay awake now, wondering what was being resolved within the silence of his house.

It was still silent next morning and Roz was still on his mind. Clovis went downstairs, hesitating by the drawing-room, the door closed as it had been the previous night when he passed. Could they be in there yet? Preparing himself to apologize and retreat, he turned the handle. Inside the room, the curtains which he had drawn for Duncan were still closed. Morning sunshine sparked through a chink at the top. In the beige light, the furniture stood as before, covers replaced. No one was there. Clovis pulled back the curtains. There was no hint of what might have happened.

In the kitchen, the empty coffee cups made the thoughts of the night continue into the morning. Once, for a time, he had stepped aside from life. He had fulfilled the role of his paid occupation but had otherwise watched the world happen without personal investment in its proceedings. Events occurred near him and he did what seemed appropriate. They were discrete events, without context or coherent patterning. One evening he drove his car to scatter a gang of thugs who were taunting a young woman. She came to live in the empty house along with her past, her plans, her conflicts. She was immersed in life and so were her friends, each in their own way. It touched him too. Almost imperceptibly, he was drawn in, detachment giving way to involvement, stoicism opening to the risks of love.

What he had learnt, from Catherine's death, about worth! If only he were to be allowed Roz; if only she were to be free for him. Through Roz he could restore some balance to the scales of rights and dues. Last time he had exacted too much, returned too little.

'Do you know what came of last night?' said Pearl, coming into the kitchen.

'No. What happened?' He'd said it too quickly, too intensely.

Pearl shrugged. 'I haven't seen anybody since then,' she said. 'I wondered if you knew.'

'Not yet.'

'In that case, I'd better go back to my essay.'

'Have some coffee first.'

They were at the kitchen table again. The house was silent again. A knock at the door. Duncan again?

'Do you remember warning me that it might be boring living here?' said Pearl

It was Roz at the door this time, dark-eyed but unagitated.

Clovis looked at her and knew. 'We thought you must be asleep,' he said.

'I went for a walk to think things over. It's a lovely day,' she added, following his indication to the kitchen.

'All right?' asked Pearl.

'I've decided to go back.'

'You have?'

Roz nodded and sat down. Clovis listened to his hopes crumbling.

'This Anabel business,' said Roz. 'I don't think it's likely to happen again. It was connected with that party of Philip's and he was sort of taken over. When I spoke to her on the telephone she certainly controlled me. She didn't sound as if she cared in the least about Duncan. It was as if he had just been convenient for her. Duncan sounds almost surprised when he talks about it now. I'm not trying to make excuses for him. He shouldn't have done it. But it's not like him. You didn't believe it at first, did you Pearl? You said he didn't strike you as being a ladies' man. I can remember you saying it. And it's true. He isn't.'

'No, he isn't.'

'It would be stupid to break up over a single incident. It happens quite a lot doesn't it? Other marriages survive. If they really want to.'

'I thought it wasn't so much to do with Anabel. I thought there were more basic things. Babies, houses, work.'

'Well, yes. But we'd almost solved that, you know, before Anabel cropped up.'

'Didn't he keep changing his mind?'

'He did, and he did assume that I'd change too to fit in. But then I usually *did* change to suit him, so I made his assumption correct. I was in the habit of considering that what I wanted wasn't as important, so I didn't push. I know it sounds like making excuses for him again, but he's not very observant about everyday things so he wouldn't notice my reactions much unless I really thrust them at him. And I never have until now. It's been an enormous shock to him to find that what he'd taken for granted all these years had gone. It had never crossed his mind for a moment that I might not always be around.'

'So he's going to be more considerate when you go back?'

'He doesn't know yet that I am going back.'

'Doesn't he? Where is he?'

'At home. When he left last night, I hadn't said what I was going to do.'

'Did you yourself know?'

'More or less. But I wanted to think about it again without him there. He does care. It's just that it's not always very obvious. We've gone along in the same old way week after week, month after month, and I've felt that I hardly impinge on what he does, and yet occasionally something happens that makes me think I do. He was going to cancel that night class last autumn because I was ill, wasn't he? It doesn't sound much except that he hates to be inconsistent in work, and I couldn't have been very ill because I can't even remember it. And last night he was waiting outside for several hours to ask you about me. He didn't know what to make of it when he saw the three of us together.'

Clovis smiled faintly.

'So it's return to normal, is it?' said Pearl.

'I expect so. Thank you both for putting up with me. It must seem a fuss over nothing now that I'm going back so soon, but it made such a difference to me.'

She stood up.

'I'll go and get my things and then leave you in peace.'

'I'll drive you home,' said Clovis.

Roz demurred then accepted and went upstairs to collect her belongings.

'I knew she wouldn't leave him,' said Pearl as soon as Roz was out of earshot.

'You did?'

'Didn't you?'

'Perhaps.'

Perhaps he had known. Perhaps it had been a delusion to imagine otherwise. His hope no longer outran reality.

'Could you drop me off at the reference library on the way?' asked Pearl. 'Do you mind?'

'Of course not.'

Pearl went upstairs too for her notes. Clovis heard her call to Roz in explanation. They came down together, smiling at him, and they all went out to the car.

'Are you coming to school as usual this week, Pearl?' asked Roz as they drove beside the green Common.

Pearl said she would.

'Shall we do something for Easter? A play or concert?'

The trees flaunted emerging leaves as if exulting in their vitality. He had been too reserved. He had curbed his own feelings to such an extent that he had placed himself outside the range of solutions for Roz. She had never been aware of his feelings for her. He had lost Catherine by inflexible pursuit of his career; he had lost any chance with Roz by inflexible self-restraint.

After they had dropped Pearl at the reference library, Roz

gave him directions to the flat but was otherwise quiet until they arrived.

She turned to him. 'Thank you, Clovis,' she said, 'for letting me stay.'

Stay. If only she had stayed.

'Soon,' she said, 'will you come to us for a meal and meet Duncan properly, in better circumstances?'

'I should like that very much.'

'I'll see you in any case, won't I, when I come back with Pearl after school?'

'Oh yes, of course.'

'As Pearl said – it all goes back to normal now.'

Clovis smiled.

Roz thought for a moment, then said, 'Maybe not quite as before.'

'No, not quite.'

She walked up the path to the flat, paused to wave at the door, and went inside.

Was she happy to be going back or was she putting a brave face on compromise? How could he tell? He sat again in the long window of his room. He should have spoken to her. She might not want him anyway, but at least he would have made himself known.

No. Had she of her own volition already decided against Duncan, then he could have offered himself, but he could not do so unless she had made that choice. It was right to let go and keep silence, this time.

Not quite as before. No, not quite. He rose to walk on the revitalized Common.